A Lowcountry Bride

Also by Preslaysa Williams

Healing Hannah's Heart
Touched by Fate (short story)

A Lowcountry Bride

A Novel

Preslaysa Williams

AVON

An Imprint of HarperCollinsPublishers

A LOWCOUNTRY BRIDE. Copyright © 2021 by Preslaysa Cielita Williams. All rights reserved. Printed in the United States of America. No part of this book may be used or reproduced in any manner whatsoever without written permission except in the case of brief quotations embodied in critical articles and reviews. For information, address HarperCollins Publishers, 195 Broadway, New York, NY 10007.

HarperCollins books may be purchased for educational, business, or sales promotional use. For information, please email the Special Markets Department at SPsales@harpercollins.com.

FIRST EDITION

Designed by Diahann Sturge

Cowrie shell art © *Sabelskaya / Shutterstock, Inc.*
Zig zag pattern © *rudvi / Shutterstock, Inc.*

Library of Congress Cataloging-in-Publication Data has been applied for.

ISBN 978-0-06-304029-8

21 22 23 24 25 LSC 10 9 8 7 6 5 4 3 2 1

This book is dedicated to my husband and real-life hero, Daren Williams. We did it!

In loving memory of the Emanuel Nine, who died in a mass shooting on June 17, 2015, and the twelve victims of the Virginia Beach, Virginia, mass shooting, who died on May 31, 2019. May your souls always be blessed.

A Lowcountry Bride

Chapter One

I need to get this dress right. More than right. I need to get this dress perfect.

Maya Jackson dug into the plastic bin set atop her ironing board/dress design table in her tiny living room. Yeah, an ironing board doubled as her workspace. Once she made enough money from her wedding dress design job, she'd buy a real worktable, but this would do for now.

A wave of dizziness overcame her, and she wiped a sheen of sweat from her forehead. "Not now," she whispered. "I have to finish this dress."

But sickle cell anemia flare-ups didn't wait for bridal gown designers.

Ten to fifteen years. That was what the doctor had said. She had ten to fifteen years left on planet Earth. Maya had to make the most of it.

She sat on the wooden stool and took a few breaths. After a few moments, the dizziness relented. It was gone, for now.

Back to work.

This latest dress project wasn't coming together. It looked like every other dress in every other wedding boutique across America. "Every other" wouldn't cut it if she wanted to secure her promotion to head dress designer for Laura Whitcomb Inc., the nation's top bridal gown designer.

Maya stood and circled the dress form. The dress would have to stand out. Maya ran her hand across the dress's bodice, her fingers catching on the swirly, pearlescent beads. Waves of tulle cascaded into a long, seamless train. It needed something more, but what?

She bit her lower lip and stepped over the bolts of satin and tulle. Scissors, pins, and thread spools rolled around underfoot, cluttering her scratched, wooden floor. She hadn't done anything to tidy up this place in forever. Working sixty hours a week for Laura could mess up a housekeeping schedule pretty quickly.

Fine. Maybe Maya had never had an actual cleaning schedule, but still. Once she secured her promotion, she'd hire a maid.

Today, she worked.

She grabbed her portfolio, which lived on the lumpy love seat, and flipped through it for some ideas. Should she go fancy-schmancy à la English royalty? Nah.

Simple and elegant à la the late Carolyn Bessette? Nah.

The dress needed something different. It needed her personal touch.

Always put yourself into your work, Maya. You'll never go wrong by staying true to yourself. Mama's advice never failed her.

She surveyed the bright white gown. A sense of overwhelm pressed on her chest. This wasn't the way she wanted the gown to look. Color. The bodice needed color, not monotone white with shades of ivory. This dress would determine her fate. The thought nearly made her sick, but Maya could zip around her tiny New York City apartment fueled on nothing but willpower (and caffeine, of course) if it meant she'd be promoted. She'd prepared for this for years. This was her chance. If she could only fix this dress in time.

She had to.

She had to.

She had to.

Maya didn't have much time left.

Her cell phone blasted a Beyoncé song. Maya glanced up and dropped the pins she'd been holding between her teeth. That was Pops calling from Charleston. She reached for her phone and pressed Talk. "Hey, what's up?"

"My daughter finally has time to answer her phone."

Maya shifted her weight from side to side. He always joked with her. "What's that supposed to mean?"

"It means I've been trying to get in touch with you since yesterday. Have you checked your messages?"

No. "Um."

"That means no. I understand."

Her neck tensed. Guilt set in. Her father understood too,

too well. He understood that Maya worked around the clock. He understood that Maya was hustling up here in New York City. Workaholism had grabbed Maya by the throat and wouldn't let her go.

"I was working late at the design studio. When I got home, I crashed, and I just now started redesigning my latest dress project. How are things with you?"

"Not good. I broke my hip yesterday."

Worry stabbed her in the side and twisted and twisted. "What?! What were you doing?"

"Puttering around in the garage, trying to fix the car."

"Pops, you can't fix cars. You're seventy-two years old. That's what mechanics do." She tossed the portfolio aside and plopped onto the love seat. The last thing she needed was for her father to be injured further.

"I know. I know. I was watching a YouTube video on how to install new brake pads, and I figured I'd—"

"Please don't figure out anything anymore. Please." Maya's voice took on a thin note. She cleared her throat and shook off all that vulnerability. "If you need a mechanic, I can look that up for you and give you a list, okay?"

Silence.

"Where are you now?" Maya asked.

"Settled into a room at Roper Hospital. Ginger was home when I was fixing my car, and she called 911 right away."

Ginger was her father's "friend." That's what Pops called her, but Maya knew Ginger was a romantic interest. "I'm glad she was there."

"Oh, she's a godsend. She's a wonderful lady."

There was a bounciness in his voice. Her father hadn't sounded this content in a while. Ginger must be a special woman to have such a good effect on him—despite his broken hip. Maya would have to meet her to know for certain, though.

"The doctor said it'll take me a few months to be mobile again," he added.

Not good. "A few months?"

"I'll adjust, though, don't you worry."

She worried. She worried a lot.

"No, Pops. You'll need a lot of help while you recover. I'll try to see if I can come down to help for a bit." Maya picked up her dinner plate from the dented coffee table and walked into her cramped kitchen. Maya needed to eat. Pops breaking his hip was way too stressful. She lifted the lid from the stainless steel stockpot and inhaled the scent of chicken adobo. Her favorite. Even if Maya didn't have time to clean her house, she did have time to cook. Maya piled up her plate.

"Maya?"

"Uh-huh." She stabbed her fork into the chicken and took a bite. *Delicious.*

"Don't come down to Charleston."

She was going down to Charleston. That wasn't a question. This was her father.

This would also put her chances of a promotion at risk, a chance she'd wanted since forever. Perhaps Laura would understand her family situation. Yet there was no telling whether she'd give Maya another shot.

"I know this is a great time for your career. So stay in New York. I was just calling to let you know."

The thought of possibly losing that promotion unsettled her, but she cared about her dad more. Maya spread a paper napkin onto the kitchen counter and tucked it into her collar to make a bib. Yeah, a bib. This was how worried she was. "I can only hope Laura will give me some grace and not let this emergency affect whether I get promoted."

"It shouldn't," he said.

"But it could, knowing Laura. You matter more to me though."

Pops was silent for a few seconds. "Don't take that chance. I know how much you want that promotion. It's a chance of a lifetime."

Lifetimes were reserved for brides. Not bridal gown designers.

"You also have a lifetime to eat," he added.

Maya set down her fork. "How'd you know I was eating?"

"Because your chewing is loud." He chuckled. "You stress eat."

"So what?" Maya grabbed a bottle of Tabasco and drizzled it on her chicken.

"No 'so what?' Just making an observation. You do you,

Maya. I'm pretty sure your food is seasoned enough. No need to add all that hot sauce."

Maya held the cell phone away from her ear and scanned the ceiling, shook. *Did he install a hidden camera in my apartment or something?* She didn't see one. She raised the phone again. "How'd you know about the hot sauce?"

"A father knows his daughter."

He knew Maya, all right. "The hot sauce adds some kick." She half smiled. "You know there's been interest in my gowns from brides here in the city, but I prefer to focus on my work with Laura. One day, she'll like my style." *I hope.*

"Don't worry about me. Build your dream, Maya."

Dress design was all she ever wanted to do. Being head designer was the dream of dreams. That was the only thing Maya focused on attaining, given the time she had left. Both of her parents had the sickle cell trait, so they knew chances were pretty high that Maya would get sickle cell anemia—25 percent. That 25 percent went looking for Maya. She was diagnosed with the illness at birth, but her parents said she didn't show symptoms until she was four months old.

Living with it had become second nature—monthly blood transfusions and medications all kept her symptoms mostly under control. So Maya went after her career full force. Now that her father broke his hip, she definitely planned to put her career on the back burner for a few months. It was going to be so tough to leave New York now, but her father needed her.

Yes, Ginger was there, but she could change her mind and leave Pops hanging. Then her father would be alone.

Maya would have to ask for a leave of absence. No way was she going to let her father recover down in Charleston without any family. "I'm going to Charleston. I have a few weeks of vacation on the books." She chewed in silence as the ceiling fan hummed a steady rhythm. "I just have to figure out what to do with all the gowns I have here that Laura rejected. I don't want them to get damaged by too much moisture or heat while I'm gone. Maybe I can buy some good storage material."

"One day, you'll be wearing one of those gowns again," her father said.

I'm ignoring that comment. Ain't no way I'll ever get engaged again. "What do you mean? To demonstrate to a potential customer?" she asked, shifting the topic.

"One bad experience doesn't mean you should write off marriage forever."

Maya glanced at the hall closet next to the kitchen. Behind its shut door, her own wedding gown, the one she wore to her wedding, lay hidden along with mothballs and an old pair of roller skates. She wasn't writing off marriage forever. She was just . . .

"I'm focused on work now." She filled her plate with a second helping of chicken adobo.

He didn't respond. That meant he didn't agree with Maya,

but whatever. It was Maya's non-love life to live, not his.

"I'll be there very soon," Maya said, quickly changing the subject. "I'll let you know my flight details soon. I'll just have to work out the details with Laura."

Laura wasn't gonna like this, but her father came first.

"You are so stubborn. I'll reimburse your plane ticket. You work so hard, and this is an unexpected expense."

Maya smiled. He understood. "Thank you, Pops."

After hanging up, Maya's brain went splat. She'd have to be extra savvy while discussing her family situation. She'd talk with her in person, of course. Face-to-face was always better.

That plain white bridal gown lay abandoned on the dress form, begging to be evaluated for Maya's promotion, evaluated and fixed. Maya teemed with ideas for improving it. She had made a few stunning dresses that reflected her true design aesthetic before. Too bad Maya's ideas and her creations had to pass through Laura Whitcomb's Twenty-Point Design Essentials™. Most of the time, Maya's ideas didn't make it past Point Two, and so Maya ended up compromising her originality for the sake of Laura's brand.

It was all good, because Laura Whitcomb was Laura Whitcomb, and Maya was just . . .

Maya, a junior designer with a dream.

A junior designer who desperately needed to make her mark in the industry before her time ran out.

Laura Whitcomb Inc. would help Maya do that . . . somehow.

THE NEXT DAY, Maya sat in Laura's office, nervously awaiting her arrival. The massive space outside of her office was busy for a weekday morning. Every cubicle, design table, and dressing area buzzed with employees. The place reminded her of rush hour, where everyone was packed in like sardines.

She loved the chatter and the noise at work. This was where Maya's career dreams unfolded. Coming to work every day gave Maya a daily dose of her aspirations. She inhaled the ambition in the air.

Maya had been practicing what she'd say to Laura over and over and over. She had to state her case in a convincing way. She scrolled through the Notes app on her phone, worried that she would mess up her prepared statement.

Moments later, Laura walked through the front door. She was all New York chic with her black leggings, black turtleneck, and leopard-print ballet flats. The tortoiseshell eyeglasses, which sat atop her long blond hair, added another level of sophistication.

Their eyes met, and Maya stood, an unconscious movement. Maya always stood whenever Laura walked into a room. She had immense respect for the lady.

Laura gave one curt nod and sat behind her massive desk. "How's that dress you've been working on?"

"Excellent. Almost finished with it," Maya said.

Not really.

"It'll be ready very soon," Maya added.

I hope.

"Good. I'm glad you requested to meet with me today. I wanted to chat with you about something, but you go first." Laura fanned herself. "Phew. It is muggy outside today. My hair has been flat as a pancake with all this humidity. No volume at all."

Maya smiled. She had the opposite problem, being a Blasian woman and all. The humidity made her flat-ironed, straight hair revert to its naturally curly state. With some hair product and a head wrap at night, it was mostly under control.

After her first day on the job at Laura Whitcomb Inc., Maya straightened her hair. Laura hadn't said anything overtly, but the look in her eyes when she saw Maya's big, curly hair said it all: *Tone down the bird's nest.*

"You don't have my hair problems. It's a White-girl thing." Laura laughed.

Maya cringed inside, not knowing how to take her comments, but she joined in Laura's laughter anyway. Always had to follow the boss's lead. Laura's jokes were Maya's jokes. Laura's not jokes were Maya's not jokes as well.

Seconds later, Laura's phone buzzed.

"Julian Rodriguez is on line three," Laura's assistant announced on the intercom.

Interruptions were not good. Maya was ready to say what

she had to say now. Waiting would be torturous. She scrolled through her Notes app, still concerned it wouldn't come out right.

"Tell him I'm in a meeting and I'll call him back," Laura said to the intercom, and clicked the Off button. "Julian is a worrisome gnat. Now what brings you here today?"

"My father recently broke his hip. He requires assistance while he recovers. I need to take some vacation time to go down south for a while."

Laura paused. "That's fine, as long as you have the vacation time on the books."

Unease enveloped Maya like a blanket. "So that's the issue. I only have—"

"There's an upscale boutique based in Charleston that wants to carry some of our gowns. Huge, huge order," Laura said. "They're looking to expand there. Maybe you could meet with the store's buyer and show them our latest collection. Bring some dresses and our catalog with you too. It'll be a working vacation."

Of course Laura would task Maya with work while she was on a family emergency "vacation," but if it meant helping Pops and keeping her job . . . "I could—"

"It's a gorgeous shop." Laura fiddled with her ring. "Very chic. You know there's another bridal boutique down there too. You may want to check that one out as well, but it looked kind of dingy and small when I saw it online. The location was just horrible, right next to some Black history museum on Chalmers Street. They talk about slavery or something. Depressing. What bride would want to go dress shopping next to that? Not me."

Laura's disdain for the museum made Maya feel some type of way. Maya's ancestors probably arrived through Gadsden's Wharf as enslaved people, and they were bought and sold in the same area. If it wasn't for their perseverance, if it wasn't for their story, Maya wouldn't be here today. "Charleston has a rich history. I went to the museum before. I learned a lot."

"I don't think it should even be there. It's bad for their tourism business," Laura said. "I was researching the area because I was trying to figure out if it would be a good idea to even approach that other boutique. I heard that people were petitioning to get rid of the museum. I hope they do. If that happens, I may consider selling some of our designs there. Who knows if they'll succeed in getting rid of the place? Especially with the politically correct crowd opposing them. They're nothing but a bunch of troublemakers, if you ask me. Just bothersome."

"The museum and the efforts to save it don't seem bothersome to me."

For a few seconds, Laura's face froze, as if she registered what she'd just said aloud. "Oh. I didn't say it *bothered* me. I was just . . . you know . . . thinking of the tourists who visit Charleston to relax and enjoy the rest of the beautiful town. That museum is an eyesore and it needs to go. I wouldn't want to go on vacation there. I mean . . . the topic is just so . . . you know."

Laura was clearly uncomfortable talking about Black history. Typical. If Maya pushed back on this conversation, her career could be compromised. Still, Maya couldn't let this slide. "I don't know. What is wrong with the topic?"

"Nothing's wrong with it. I just think . . ." Laura's cheeks turned red. "It shouldn't be the focus in Charleston's tourism scene."

"You think Charleston's history of enslavement should be erased?" Maya asked, feeling bolder now.

Laura's eyes widened. She was sinking fast, and Maya wasn't going to help her up. "No. No. No. I was referring to that smaller boutique next to it. The one I saw online."

Why would she want the boutique to go when she just said she was considering selling her dresses there? Just trying to cover her tracks. "Oh, okay," Maya said. "Because that area holds a rich history. It's an important piece of Charleston's history."

Laura was silent. Guess they weren't talking about that anymore.

Laura reached for a pen and *tap, tap, tapped* it on her desk. "So, what was I saying? Oh—there's a new opportunity I wanted to tell you about. I'm also looking to fill a special assignment with one junior designer. It's not as high profile as the head designer job, but it's pretty important."

Maya's heart catapulted. There was only one other junior designer on staff—Kelly. They'd gone to design school together and got along well at work. Competing against her would be awkward, but it wouldn't be much different from applying for the same job: only one of them would get it.

"You'll have to make a brand-new dress, something never seen before. Kelly will do the same, and I'll choose the best out of the two. That dress will be featured on the cover of *Bridal Magazine*. Ashley Tate will wear it on the cover."

Maya's jaw dropped. Ashley Tate, the hottest movie star in town. If Ashley wore the dress, that would catapult her career. She'd be fashion's It girl. "Really?"

"Really, darling."

Laura set her pen down and folded her hands on the table, twiddling her thumbs. A diamond-studded pendant bearing her initials jangled from her smooth décolletage. The sunlight from the bay window shone on her diamond tennis bracelet. Laura's expression grew serious, restrained. "There is one caveat, however. The style of the dress must reflect Laura Whitcomb Inc.'s fashion sense since it'll be a dress under our brand name. Because of this, I'll offer feedback to you and Kelly during your design process, so that when one of you is chosen, we'll have full confidence that it reflects our style."

Maya straightened in her seat. Following the Laura Whitcomb style guidelines had always been a struggle for Maya. Where Laura wanted clean, simple lines, Maya tended toward flourish. Where Laura wanted monotonous designs, Maya tended toward the nontraditional. She especially enjoyed using the *bunga-sama* stitching technique her mother had taught her. It was a pattern of large-sized hexagons and rhombuses. Other times Maya used the *palipattang* pattern, which was inspired by the colors of a rainbow. They were techniques that had been passed down from her grandmother in the Philippines, and these techniques always had a way of making the dress fit the bride, rather than the other way around.

Laura pulled off her eyeglasses and set them next to her cell phone. "Your designs are very innovative. I already know it'll be a tough call between you and Kelly because you're both extremely talented. I don't hire just anyone to work for me."

That was exactly why Maya loved working for Laura. Being a part of Laura Whitcomb's team meant Maya was the best of the best, and that validation meant everything to her.

"So, what do you say? Are you interested in applying for the special assignment?"

If Maya landed this assignment, she'd be one step closer to becoming head designer. "Yes. Definitely. Yes."

"Excellent. Kelly agreed too. If you can whip up a pencil or computer draft of what you'd like to create before you go on vacation, that'd be great too. I'll offer my feedback on it, and we can chat when you return in two weeks."

"Yeah, so . . ." Maya bit her lower lip. "I will need more than two weeks down in Charleston. My father will take a few months to recover."

The smile fell off Laura's face. "A few months? How long do you plan on being there?"

"I'd say until the end of June at the earliest. Until my father becomes more mobile."

Laura drummed her fingers on the table. "Well, well. That poses a problem. You know you'll have to take leave without pay."

Maya clenched her fist.

"This would mean you'll be working toward both opportunities without getting paid."

Maya's skin tightened. For all the money this company made, Laura was stingy. "Why not?"

"Because I have bills to pay here too. If you get the position, of course, you'll receive a generous salary, but while you're down south, you won't get a paycheck after your vacation time runs out. Of course, you'll still be on staff."

"So you're saying I have to show your dresses to department stores in Charleston without getting paid?" Maya asked, her voice incredulous.

"I'm sorry. This is the reality of the business."

"I have to take care of my living expenses."

Laura paused. "The location scouting will only take an hour or two. No big deal."

Maya wanted to bang her head against a wall. It was a huge deal. There wasn't a subway system in South Carolina. Maya couldn't just zip around Charleston to scout locations. She'd been scrimping to make ends meet on her junior designer salary, and now she wouldn't get paid a dime—but somehow she'd have to scout for Laura *and* do the work required for these two opportunities *and* figure out how to pay her rent before her vacation time ran out. Why was this so hard?

Trust, her conscience said.

Yet the word meant nothing. Trust what?

She shifted in her seat. A heaviness pulled and pulled and pulled. "Fine then," Maya said. "I'll scout for you . . . for no pay."

Maya hated saying that.

They made small talk, but Maya's sense of overwhelm stuffed cotton balls in her ears. Everything sounded like gibberish. When they finished, Maya gathered her things and stood. "Thanks for being flexible with me," she said, tamping down her unease.

"Don't worry. You'll still have your job when you return." Laura smiled. "You're doing good work here."

Now it's unpaid work. A well of resentment bubbled within her, but she pushed it aside. Maya said goodbye and left. Heartache rushed at her in waves, drowning her in disappointment and despair. She headed to the balcony to clear her head and think.

Another missed chance.

"How will I make ends meet?" Maya muttered.

Another wave crashed in.

You won't make ends meet.

And another.

You don't have what it takes.

The feeling didn't leave. She gripped the balcony's railing and let her uneasiness settle. She'd have to make some money down in South Carolina. Maya would bring her portfolio of the personal designs she'd created, along with the dresses Laura had rejected, in the hopes of earning money from them in Charleston. Maya made a mental note to get Laura's okay to sell her dresses in Charleston. She had to say yes, since Maya wasn't going to be paid.

Would Maya be able to earn extra cash down there? Would she be able to get over this hump? Not sure. Perhaps she should listen to Pops and stay up here.

No. No. No. She was going to be present for her father.

Maya pushed aside her insecurities. The breeze rustled through her pin-straight hair, and a steely determination rose up in Maya. "I'll figure something out," she said.

The warm sunlight kissed her face. The New York City skyline exuded a peculiar peace that afternoon. A peace that Maya failed to grasp. She would have to trust.

Hopefully trust would be enough.

Chapter Two

Captain Derek T. Sullivan stood prepared for battle against another Lowcountry bridezilla ready to attack.

Bridezilla planted both fists on rounded hips. With her head cocked to one side, she aimed to fire. "What do you mean you're out of size eights?"

Could he speak any more clearly? "We're out of stock. You're wearing the last size eight, ma'am." Derek added the "ma'am" for good measure, always the gentleman.

He hung another seventy-pound wedding gown on the dress rack. Bridezilla had tried on an endless number of dresses over the last seven hours. Though mental fatigue had set in, he remained alert, ready to help this woman make up her mind. During his navy days, he'd spent many nights on watch. He was used to working long hours.

The shop had had a steady stream of customers over the past few days. Derek was certain this special sale would help him turn a profit this time. It was this or foreclosure.

The bank had sent its notice this morning. He had two months to pay the past due mortgage. If he didn't, Always a Bride would be done, done, done.

So he'd deal with picky customers whether he liked it or not.

Today, he'd have to like it. He'd have to garner every possible sale.

A gaggle of women stormed inside the downtown Charleston shop. Many of them waved red sales flyers, a thunderous sea of female buyer frenzy. It would be another long evening, but he remained optimistic. With Ginger, the longtime manager, at his side, they would triumph. This would be the day that the store made a financial turnaround.

Derek squared his shoulders, ready to take command of the boutique just as he had taken command of numerous aircraft carriers over his twenty-year military career.

Bridezilla stepped outside of the dressing room and twirled in front of a gilded mirror. "Doesn't feel like a size eight."

The sound of ripping fabric pierced the air. Panic flashed across her features. "Was that me?"

Derek winced and quickly averted his eyes. A response clogged his throat.

"Double-check the tag for me." She pointed to Derek as if he were a misbehaving child. "This is not a size eight."

Blood rushed to Derek's head. He needed to call in reinforcements. This was too much to handle. "Ginger."

"Are you trying to avoid me, mister?" Bridezilla stood

close, too close for Derek to breathe.

He took a step backward. "No, ma'am. Ginger, our manager, can help you. She's an expert at dress sizes."

Bridezilla bent over to pick at the hem of the floor-length gown. The rip deepened.

Derek took a deep breath. He couldn't afford damaged inventory, not with all the debts the store had incurred since his mother, the founder of the boutique, passed away from cancer a year ago. His mother had had a policy of never charging customers for dresses they tried on in the store, even if those dresses incurred rips and tears along the way. Derek tried his best to keep with his mother's tradition, even if it cost him.

"Are you sure this is a Leilani original?"

"Yes, it's——"

"Did ya call, hon?" Ginger freed Derek from Bridezilla's spur-of-the-moment cross-examination. As a child, Derek had avoided Ginger, especially when she nagged him about tucking his shirt in or not slouching when he sat. Now, the woman with the golden-brown skin, the auburn hair, and the 1950s-style eyeglasses was a welcome reprieve.

"Ginger, this lady needs your assistance. She doesn't think this gown is a Lei——"

"Finally!" Bridezilla threw her hands in the air. "Someone who can help me."

Ginger gestured to the bride. "Follow me, dear."

Ginger was a great salesperson. She could close a sale despite Bridezilla's blowup. Could they close enough sales to cover three mortgage payments? He hoped.

After Ginger and the customer left, Derek clambered past a dizzying crowd of women hovering over bins and bins of garters, pantyhose, bodices, and other items he'd rather not ponder. Derek had decided to sell the merchandise clogging the back room at a deep discount by placing an ad on the local radio station to attract customers. The next morning, the women of Charleston swarmed in like locusts on a mission: shop and devour.

The crowd left him dizzied, but it also gave him assurance. Always a Bride must've made good money today. Marlon, his accountant, was getting up-to-the-minute sales reports through their server. In fact, he'd call Marlon and get a status update now.

Derek grabbed the cordless from its cradle and dialed Marlon's number. He picked up after the third ring.

"Hey, Marlon. How do the sales look?"

"It's not looking good."

Derek's fingers tightened around the phone. "Not even today? We're crowded and Ginger and I have rung up a slew of sales."

"You're barely breaking even. With the level of debts that your mother left behind, along with these poor sales numbers, things aren't looking good at all."

Derek shifted. The foreclosure notice crinkled in his back pocket. "I just got a notice from the bank today. If I don't catch up on the mortgage by the beginning of May, the bank will start the foreclosure process. I've tried most everything to make a profit here. How can I turn things around?"

No sound on the other end. Then: "You really want to know?"

"Yes."

"You might want to consider filing for bankruptcy."

"Bankruptcy?"

"Yes. You'll clear all of those debts and be done with the extra stress. The efforts you've made are commendable, but they're not enough to save the boutique."

If he filed for bankruptcy, that meant everything his mother worked for, everything he promised his mother that he'd maintain, would be lost. Derek couldn't afford to let his mother down, even from the grave. He'd let his family down one too many times before.

Derek's biggest regret was with Grace, his late wife. He'd never forgive himself for not saving Grace.

This business had to work. "I'm not entirely set on bankruptcy."

"Sometimes we have to face the truth of the situation."

That was the thing. Derek didn't want to face the truth of the situation, not like this anyway. Always a Bride was a way for him to maintain his mother's legacy, her memory, as well as Grace's memory. She used to help out at the boutique too. While he was on deployments, he'd get emails with pictures of his mother, Grace, and his daughter, Jamila, working at the boutique together. He had smiled at those pictures and imagined Jamila growing up one day and taking over the family business. Always a Bride was an intergenerational legacy. If he filed for bankruptcy, those ties would be broken for good.

"You're quiet, Derek. Do you have another idea?"

"No. But I don't want to file for bankruptcy."

"You could sell the business. That would pay off the debts and save you from the embarrassment. A woman by the name of Marjorie Wilkinson sent me an email earlier today. She's interested in buying the place."

Derek's neck muscles tightened, already not liking the sound of this. Selling the business was the same as filing for bankruptcy. He'd be throwing away a legacy. "Not interested."

"If Ms. Wilkinson's asking price is right, then I'd definitely consider it. The money from the sale would pay off all the debts. No bankruptcy hassles and red tape. You'd be free and clear to move on with your life."

Move on to what? Jamila, now twelve years old, could hardly stand him, and he'd stopped getting too close to folks after Grace's death. Why get close when people left? When people died?

"I know it's tough, man. If you don't want to sell to a stranger, how about selling to a friend? Would Ginger be interested in purchasing the place?"

"No. Ginger is retiring very soon."

"Do you have any relatives who would be interested?"

A picture of his late wife's gleaming casket flicked across his mind. Derek blinked it away. She died so horribly in that mass shooting. Three years later, and the grief was ever present, still thrumming under his skin, still causing a dull ache in his heart. "No other relatives."

"How about friends?"

"I'll need some time to think this over. I can't make a decision today."

"I wasn't expecting you to. But when the business ship is sinking, you have to move on."

Move on. Easier to dole out that advice than to actually live it. "I'll get back to you with my next steps in a week or so."

"A week?" Marlon asked. "Okay. I'm holding you to it."

Derek ended the call and placed the phone back in its cradle. He thought about how his mother had worked so hard to start and maintain the store, often spending long days and nights there. She was the first Black woman to own a bridal shop in downtown Charleston in the eighties, quite a feat given the hardships she'd faced, including his father's abandonment.

Downtown Charleston used to have a vibrant Black business district. After the slow repeal of Jim Crow laws, many Black-owned businesses eventually closed down during the sixties and seventies. Black people no longer had to travel farther downtown to shop, and White people didn't rush to patronize the Black-owned businesses. Those were the unintended consequences of integration, and so starting and keeping Always a Bride was an uphill battle.

Derek had watched his mother work to keep the business running, and even when he was a kid, he encouraged her to keep going. She had worked hard and maintained hope despite it all.

What should he do with Always a Bride? How could he save it without filing for bankruptcy or selling the business? He didn't know.

Derek stood and readied himself to face the customers once again. He'd try extra hard to make a couple more sales before the day's end. He'd also let Ginger know about the boutique's financial status. Derek hadn't told her about the threat of foreclosure. He'd been too proud to say they were struggling, but he'd swallow his pride and tell Ginger now.

Perhaps she'd have some good ideas for Always a Bride. Ginger had been here since the place opened. She was as much a partner in Always a Bride as Derek, probably even more.

MAYA HAD ARRIVED in Charleston on Saturday evening. It was too late to sit down and drill her father about his health, so instead, she worked on her gown late into the wee hours of the morning.

Now that Maya had eight hours of sleep and faced a new day, she would focus on one thing: helping Pops get better.

"Have you been taking your blood pressure medicine?"

Maya headed over to the half bath down the hallway and checked his medicine cabinet.

"Yes, I have," he called from the living room.

The pause in her father's voice told Maya to double-check. Before she moved to New York City, he was notorious for being forgetful. She took the orange pill bottles from the cabinet and inspected them. The bottles were filled to the top, as if he hadn't taken any of his medicine. "When did you get these prescriptions filled?"

Silence. "Oh, I don't know."

Maya turned the bottles over in her hands and squinted at the fine print on the white label. These prescriptions were filled months ago. He hadn't been taking his medicine. She headed to the living room, her pulse pounding.

"These bottles of medicine are full." She held out one bottle and shook it vigorously.

Her father's expression looked like that of a kid whose hand was caught in the cookie jar.

"Why haven't you been taking your medications?" She set the bottles on the coffee table.

"Just got busy, love. So many things to take care of around here. I forget."

She sighed. "I have alarms on my phone for my medication reminders. I can't afford to miss a dose. You know how it is with sickle cell anemia. I take my health seriously. Why haven't you?"

Pops leaned back in his wheelchair and gestured to Maya.

"I've been doing fine without them. It's not a big deal."

"Not a big deal? You've already fractured your hip. You don't need to compound a new problem on top of it."

"You worry too much. I'm fine. Those blood pressure medications have bad side effects anyway. I read about it online."

Now he was getting his medical advice from the internet. Wonderful. "I think your doctor knows a bit more about your health than Google."

He didn't say a word. How would he fare when she returned to New York? Maya could nag him all she wanted today, but that wouldn't change a thing if her father didn't change his habits.

"Let me get your lunch ready." She headed to the kitchen.

Her father was a widowed soul with peaceful eyes. He'd spent his days puttering around the garage before his hip fracture. Now he got around in a wheelchair. He was taking his fall and subsequent recovery period in stride, better than Maya had taken it. Was his happy outlook due to the fact that Ginger had been around? Probably so. If Ginger's presence turned her father into an optimist, that was good. Leave all the worrying to Maya.

She heated up leftover sausage and red rice and set a plate before him.

"What are your plans for the rest of the day?" he asked.

"You mean after I finish making sure you're okay?"

Pops smiled. "Yes."

"I want to get this new gown close to completed."

"The one you were working on when I fell asleep last night?"

"Yes. If I get it right, I could get the promotion. It's still within my reach. And there's another potential design gig too that I have for a celebrity."

"That's wonderful." He drummed his fingers on the armrest of his wheelchair. "Take it one step at a time. Balance is key. Don't let work consume you. How are you doing otherwise?"

"Otherwise" meant *How are you doing with your sickle cell?* It was as hard for him to mention it as it was for Maya to live with it. They both knew her time was short. "As good as I can be."

"I'm proud of you, love. You don't have to stay up so late working on projects. You'll be in Charleston for a few months." He rested his chin in his hands. "Pace yourself."

No time to pace herself. She would get her regular, monthly blood transfusion on Monday, and then she'd be focused on work. "I still have to pay the bills. I emailed Laura before I left New York and asked her if I could try to sell some of my gowns since I will be on leave without pay soon. Laura said she was fine with it. I'll see if I'm successful with that. I'll also see if I can get a personal loan to cover my rent. Laura wants me to show her line while I'm down here. Just because I'm on leave doesn't mean I can slack off with Laura's request."

Pops shook his head. "Wait. Laura isn't paying you for doing this work?"

"No. That's why I'm thinking of taking out a personal loan. I want to apply for one at the bank downtown."

He was quiet, but Maya sensed his disapproval nonetheless. She made herself a plate of leftovers and sat down. They ate in silence for a few minutes as the ceiling fan hummed a steady rhythm. She picked up the pile of unpaid bills from the kitchen table and flipped through them. More stuff to handle.

"Downtown you said?" her father asked.

"Yes."

His eyes lit up. "Ah. Did I ever tell you that Ginger works at a bridal boutique downtown?"

A bridal boutique? That was cool. "No."

"Ginger plans on retiring soon. Been working at the shop for a long time. She loves all things bridal. Kind of like you and your mother."

Was that part of the reason Pops liked Ginger? Because of her similar interests in the bridal industry? How sweet. "Maybe Ginger and I can talk shop soon. I'm glad she helped you when you fractured your hip."

"I'm glad that you're glad," Pops said.

"It's a good thing that you decided to get out of the house and attend New Life last year, or else you wouldn't have met Ginger."

"I agree. She's part of a church group that runs the food

pantry. Their ministry is limited now because part of the congregation is looking for a new building to hold services while the other part opposes a new building. On top of that, half of the congregation attends services at the temporary building while the other half attends services at the old building. Pastor Clark holds services at two different locations on Sundays. Lots of squabbles." He sighed. "Three years later, the church is still recovering from the mass shooting. That was way before my time as a church member, but it's still tough for all involved."

So tragic. So many people died at New Life Community Church that day. It made the national news. Maya wondered if the church and the community at large would ever heal from it. "I can see why it would be tough."

"Very tough. Still, the church leadership is trying to raise money for a new church building and to preserve some of the historical Black landmarks around Charleston. They're working with the Black history museum on the preservation efforts. They have a lot on their hands. Despite all that, Ginger insisted on putting me on the church's sick and ailing list, but I don't consider myself ailing." Pops smiled. "Just out of service for a while. She wanted to come over today to meet you. She made dinner for me when I was recovering too."

Pops and Ginger were definitely serious. Usually people just dropped off a dinner. They wouldn't spend time in your kitchen cooking dinner. "So how were you eating before Ginger came into your life?"

Her father shrugged. "Oh, you know. I had a microwave meal or something."

"Those TV dinners have too much sodium! That's not good for your health."

"Once I get out of this wheelchair, I'll start cooking for myself. Ginger insists."

A woman who didn't make her man dependent on her for the everyday things. Not bad at all. If her father was planning to eventually cook healthy meals for himself, that was another plus in Ginger's favor. Maya opened her mouth to ask more about New Life's building fund when the doorbell rang. Its vibration resounded through the house, a thunderous clap. She needed to get that thing fixed. Another thing to do.

Then an insistent tap on the front window.

"It's Ginger," her father said.

The mystery person had arrived. Her father rolled himself in his wheelchair to the front door and opened it. An elderly woman with auburn hair sauntered in.

"Well, lookee there," Ginger said.

Ginger was . . . a lot. Everything about her screamed RED!

"Smells great in here." Ginger stepped inside and air-kissed Maya's father.

Aww. That was cute.

"Ginger, you're just in time for lunch. Come on in."

"I don't want to intrude. I just stopped by to tell you about the church . . ." She saw Maya and did a double-take. "Is this your daughter?"

Maya gave a half-smile, cautiously optimistic about Ginger. Hopefully she was the real deal.

"My goodness. You told me you had a daughter, but you didn't tell me how beautiful she was. You look so young to have a daughter, Carl." Ginger clasped her hand over her mouth.

Amused, he tilted his head, salt-and-pepper hair shiny under the dim overhead lights. "I'm young, huh?"

"Yes, you are. Handsome."

She squeezed his arm. They melded together well.

"Hello, young lady. I'm Ginger Hunter." The woman extended her hand, and Maya shook it. Ginger's grasp was firm but friendly.

"Hi."

"I'm so glad that you came down south to care for your father. I tried to fill in while you weren't here. I'm sure the two of you will have some great father-daughter bonding time."

Ginger respected Maya's relationship with her father too. Maya appreciated that. "I'm looking forward to spending time with Pops. I heard you called 911 when he fell. Thanks so much for being here."

"I was so worried when that happened. If I weren't around . . . I don't even want to think about it." Ginger's mouth took a slight downturn.

Her response appeared sincere. Perhaps she wasn't the type to skip out on Pops. Perhaps Ginger really cared for him. "Did he tell you that he's supposed to take his blood pressure medicine twice a day?" Maya swiped up a full medicine bottle and shook it.

Ginger's eyes widened. "You haven't been taking your medicine, Carl?"

Maya smiled at how Ginger was on a casual first-name basis with Pops.

Her father's eyes shifted. "Um. No. I'll take it now, Ginger." Her father motioned for the bottle. "Can I have it please?"

Maya exhaled. At least Ginger would be here to ensure Pops took his medications. Now if only Pops were as eager about his pills as he was about eventually cooking for himself.

"Your father told me that you design bridal gowns up in New York City," Ginger said.

"Yes."

"How long have you been a designer?"

"For a while. I was my mother's apprentice."

"What a beautiful gift for a mother to pass on to her daughter. The gift of bridal gown design." Ginger's eyes twinkled. "She must've been a special woman."

Maya's heart warmed. "She was," she said, her voice unsteady.

A silence hung in the room, and a knowing look crossed

Ginger's expression. She must've been giving Maya the space to process the mention of her mother. How kind.

"I'm the buyer for Always a Bride boutique, and I'm passionate about fashion. I would love to take a look at your work sometime." She smiled. "Perhaps you can bring your dresses down to the shop."

Maya hesitated. Even though she needed to sell her dresses, something held her back from accepting Ginger's offer right away.

"You should take them down there, Maya. You brought plenty of your creations, along with your portfolio. You said you wanted to earn some extra money," Pops said. "It sounds like a great opportunity."

It was. Ginger was too generous, but what if Maya accepted Ginger's offer, sold lots of dresses, and then Ginger and Pops eventually parted ways? Would Maya look like a fool for accepting Ginger's generosity?

Relationships didn't last forever. Nothing was guaranteed. If Pops and Ginger weren't together anymore, then Ginger's good influence on Pops would wear off too. He'd revert back to his old self.

"So, what do you think?" her father asked.

Maya looked at the medicine bottles on the table. Pops needed to be more self-reliant. She couldn't trust that Ginger would be present all the time. "Do you plan on creating some type of reminder system for your medications? Something that you can take care of on your own?"

He paused. "Do you plan on taking Ginger up on her offer?"

Now she paused.

"The two of you are so funny together," Ginger said, laughing. "Like father, like daughter."

"More like her mother. She was just as headstrong. A hard worker too, just like Maya. Her mother spent hours and days and weeks making dresses. I was her cheerleader." He wheeled himself over to the kitchen and grabbed a pitcher from the refrigerator. "I made fresh squeezed lemonade yesterday. I think it may surpass your mom's recipe, Maya."

The words were said lightly, but Maya felt sadness at the mention of her mother.

Ginger winked at Maya. "You should really consider bringing one of your dresses to Always a Bride. I would love to introduce a new line to the customers."

"It's a wonderful offer," Maya said. "Can I have some time to think about it?"

"Sure. Not a problem at all." Ginger shrugged. "Take as much time as you need."

Pops shook his head. "What about that new dress you were working on last night? It's beautiful."

Ginger looked from Carl to Maya.

Why was he so insistent? "It needs some finishing touches, and I'm using it to apply for the head designer position," Maya said, not wanting to feed into his pressure.

"How about your old wedding gown? You brought that

down from New York too." He glanced at Ginger. "Maya designed her wedding dress herself."

Maya froze. Her wedding dress. Why did he keep talking about that thing? She would never give that one up. Ever.

"Oh, I would love to see it." Ginger clapped her hands. "When you're ready, of course."

"It needs work too," Maya said, gazing pointedly at her father. He knew that dress meant the world to Maya. Why mention it?

He appeared oblivious to her hint. "You should take one of them to Always a Bride."

"I think Derek, the owner, would love them," Ginger added, redirecting her attention to Maya. "You can bring the dress you feel comfortable selling. Always."

Always. Ginger made it sound like she was committed, like she wasn't going to be a temporary person in her father's life. Would their relationship really last? Maya held in the question and bit her inner lip.

"Come on, Maya," Pops said. They nodded their heads in unison.

Maya wanted to disappear into the wall. Was everyone ganging up on her today?

Her father lifted his glass of lemonade and took a gulp. "This looks like the perfect open door." He leaned toward Ginger, whispering something in her ear. Ginger giggled.

Seeing her father all in love was cute. Embarrassing, but cute. Maya drummed her fingertips on the kitchen table.

"Should I leave the two of you alone?"

"No," they said in unison, still focused on each other.

Maybe their relationship would last for the long term . . . maybe.

"That dish you're eating smells great, Carl." Ginger placed her hand on his shoulder. "You have to share your recipe."

Carl winked. "It was my dear wife's recipe. May she rest in peace."

A subtle pricking touched Maya's heart. Pops and Ginger were so at ease with each other. So carefree and relaxed. He could even talk about Mama with her. It must be nice to have that kind of love. "I'll leave you two alone. I want to get back to work."

"Don't leave, honey." The sound of her father's wheelchair followed behind her. "Don't leave. Stay and chat with us."

Maya paused. If she did that, then she'd feel like an intruder. She would also be reminded of what she didn't have for herself—love. "I'm really busy."

"She's busy," Ginger said, understanding in her tone. "All other things aside, Maya, I would love to introduce you to Derek. Your father said that you're really talented, and I love fashion design. I'd be honored to take you to the store and pitch your gowns to him. My offer will always stand. Now or in the future."

Now or in the future. Ginger must've read her thoughts or something.

"I promise," Ginger added. "I know I said take your time,

but I would really love to see all of your work. Would you want to stop by the shop tomorrow at three o'clock?"

Ginger said her offer would always stand, and Maya needed the extra cash. She had an appointment at the bank to apply for a personal loan, but selling her dresses locally was better than racking up debt. Besides, Laura wanted her to check out the local bridal boutiques anyway. "Fine," she said. "I'll accompany you to the boutique and bring my portfolio too. It'll have to be on Thursday because I need a few days to . . ."

Maya wasn't going to mention that she would spend a few days recovering from her blood transfusion. She didn't want people to treat her like a sick person.

". . . I need a few days to get my dresses and portfolio ready. I'll be there on Thursday," Maya continued.

Pops glanced at Maya with empathy in his eyes. He understood.

Ginger smiled. "Wonderful. I'll be off work on Tuesday and Wednesday anyway. I return to the boutique on Thursday. So that's perfect."

Maya smiled. So now the woman who had helped her father was helping Maya too. Ginger was like a fairy godmother, but all wishes ran out at midnight, right? How long would it be before the Ginger goodness ended?

Maya didn't know, but it was best to accept it. Her bills were calling. And so was Laura's directive.

Chapter Three

On Thursday morning, Derek arrived at Always a Bride intent on talking to Ginger about the financials. They were so busy the past weekend and on Monday that he didn't have time to mention it. Now he would sit down with her and figure out a plan to save the business before he lost it.

That would be the worst. All of his mother's hard work would be flushed down the toilet. He wanted to figure this out before Ginger retired in a week. A week! Ever since Ginger told him she planned on retiring back in January, they'd searched and searched for an adequate replacement but to no avail. Once Ginger left, he could become a bridal shop flop.

Derek sighed. What would he do without her? She was the backbone of this place.

He'd brought Jamila along today. He hoped to get her engaged in working with him too. "Hey, Jamila. You want to help me straighten up some of the displays that were rearranged yesterday?"

"No." She tossed her backpack on the register's counter.

The sight of his daughter ripped off a piece of his heart. Hunched over and sullen, she wore a black hoodie, black jeans, and black sneakers, overly dressed for this warm spring day. Her dark, curly hair was dry and lackluster around her russet face. He wouldn't allow his daughter to check out on him emotionally. She was his only family left. "Okay, hon. You let me know if you change your mind."

She headed to the break room in the rear. The door slammed shut behind her.

O-kay. So much for father-daughter bonding time.

As soon as Derek flipped on the store lights, the sound of a familiar laughter greeted him.

His fingertips numbed, tingly and cool. The sensation sped up his forearms and cloaked his shoulders. *Was that Grace?*

He headed near the sound, and he spotted a petite young woman in a coral sundress and brown sandals. She rested her elbows on the jewelry counter, gold bangles jangling on her wrists. With pin-straight black hair falling loosely around her golden-brown shoulders, the woman looked enough like Grace to make his heart stutter. Upbeat. Confident.

He blinked a couple more times, a feeble attempt to steady himself. Those few seconds erased the similarities. He was lonely. That was all. The woman before him had the same build and coloring, but Grace had a simple, laid-back style, while this woman seemed like a go-getter.

"Can I help you, ma'am?"

The air conditioner rumbled to life and blew cool air through the overhead vents. She brushed her hands over her bare arms as if to warm herself. Derek glanced at her left hand. No ring.

She must've noticed him staring, because she hid her hand underneath the wedding gown she held. Was a lack of an engagement ring a sore spot for her?

Then she stood taller, as if regaining composure, no longer relying on the jewelry counter for support.

Derek held her gaze for a moment, and a current passed between them. Goose bumps prickled on his forearms. Must be a draft from the air-conditioning.

When Derek remained silent, the woman smiled. "This shop has a lot of character," she said, brown eyes glimmering. Her lashes were dark and thick, framing her rounded eyes perfectly.

"It definitely has character." Derek pushed aside his subtle attraction. Taking care of his daughter and taking care of the store were his only concerns. "How can I help you?" he repeated.

"I'm visiting South Carolina. I'm looking to sell a few of my wedding gowns and bridesmaid dresses while I'm here."

Derek would have to replace the dress Bridezilla had ripped. The last thing he needed was damaged merchandise. He needed to bring in income, not lose it.

"Derek!" Ginger's voice called from behind. "There you

are. Good morning."

"Morning," Derek said, still wondering about this woman.

"I wanted you to meet this lovely young lady, Maya Jackson. She's a bridal gown designer and Carl's daughter. You remember Carl, right, Derek?" Ginger winked.

Derek rolled his eyes. Carl was Ginger's "friend." According to Ginger, Carl started attending New Life, and they became an item a few months ago. Derek hadn't been to New Life since Grace died in the mass shooting at the church. He wasn't stepping foot in that place ever again. "Yes, Ginger. I remember."

"No need to roll your eyes at me." Ginger swatted his shoulder as if he were a child. "Carl fractured his hip. Maya's in town temporarily to help her father get back on his feet."

Derek glanced at Maya. What was the point of this conversation? He had to talk to Ginger about the financials. "Good to know."

"I was so worried when the doctor told us the news." Ginger grabbed a scarf from the rack and folded it neatly into fourths. "Hip fractures are major. Carl is a fighter. He'll get well soon."

That was sad to hear about this lady's father, but he had his own problems to handle. "Ginger, do you have a minute? We need to discuss something very important."

"Sure. Sure." She waved him off. "But first . . . I wanted to introduce you to Maya."

O-kay. "We met already."

"Maya needs to gather some income until she returns to New York at the end of June. She has a special talent and an eye for design."

"Maya told me that she wants to sell some of her dresses," Derek said.

"We should take a look at them." Ginger showed Maya's portfolio to Derek. "See this one right here?"

He saw. It was a nice dress, but he wasn't thinking about buying dresses. He was thinking about getting out of this financial hole.

"What's the wholesale price?" Ginger asked Maya.

"Seventeen hundred dollars wholesale."

"Great. We'll take it," Ginger said.

Derek's alarms went off. Seventeen hundred dollars? That was pricey. "We can't afford that, Ginger. It's not in our inventory budget."

"It is now." She smiled at Maya. "When can you bring the dress?"

"I can bring it over tomorrow morning."

"Whoa. Whoa. Whoa," Derek said. "This is not a thing that we're doing, Ginger. This is definitely not a thing that we're doing. We really need to talk about this business."

"You don't want to purchase just one dress from Maya?" Ginger asked, her voice pleading and judging all at once. How did she manage that?

"Not even one." Derek glanced at Maya. "Sorry, ma'am. I can't take on another expense. I have to figure out how to keep us from foreclosure. I hope you understand."

"Foreclosure?!" Ginger said. "When do you go into foreclosure?"

"In two months if I can't come up with the missed mortgage payments," he said. "I didn't want to tell you because I thought I could've handled it by now. That's what I wanted to talk about, Ginger."

Maya shifted her weight from side to side, apparently uncomfortable. "I get it. I guess I'll be on my way."

"Do you have a business card?" Ginger asked. "I'd still like to keep you in mind. He doesn't know what he's missing." She scrunched her nose at Derek, and he soon felt like that little kid at Sunday school again.

"Sure thing." Maya dug in her purse and handed one over to Ginger.

"Derek's being stubborn," Ginger said to Maya. "Your talents are going to bless many a blushing bride."

"How kind of you to say." Maya smiled.

A glow from an overhead spotlight spilled over her, and Derek's pulse revved two notches. Maya was beautiful. For a stretch of time, all else faded into oblivion.

Maya stepped to the left, away from the spotlight. Derek pushed aside his attraction. He wasn't ready to be interested in someone again. He would never be ready, to be honest. "Have a nice day, Maya."

After she left, Derek redirected his attention to Ginger. "I need to speak with you about the store."

"I just can't believe we're about to be foreclosed on, Derek. You should've told me earlier."

He paused. "I know. How will I run this place? How will I get out of this financial hole? I know you're retiring, but you've been here with my mother from the beginning. You know everything about this place. If you're retiring, then my only other option is to sell."

Sadness flitted across her features. "Sell?"

"Sell," Derek said. "Marlon said my options were bankruptcy or selling."

"That's what you're gonna do?"

"I have no other choice."

"Your mother worked too hard for you to up and sell it from under her." Ginger scrunched her nose at Derek. "She would be mortified to even hear of it."

The guilt set in. His mother had invested so much into this place. It was her lifeline after his father left them, and in a way, it was his lifeline too. Coming to work here every day was his way of remaining connected to her memory, and Grace's too. "I know that. I don't want to sell. I was hoping we'd discuss a way to make this place thrive, but you're leaving. I've been in the military for twenty years of my life. Weddings and bridal gowns are not my forte. You saw me here during the sale the other day. You saw me flounder with the customers here. You've got to stay."

"I don't think you should sell this place either. This business is practically a historical landmark. It's right there with

Gadsden's Wharf and the Black history museum down the block. They're trying to shut down the museum, you know. New Life Church is trying to keep it running. If the boutique closes too, that'll be a double whammy. Your mother made history when she opened this shop in the eighties. You've got to keep it running for the culture."

"For the culture"? Derek didn't know Ginger was so woke. Even still, maintaining Mother's legacy was a costly burden to bear. Yes, he had the memories, but the place was draining his pockets daily. "Your retiring isn't gonna help."

"That's why I brought Maya over. I didn't tell her that, but it was in my thinking," Ginger said. "She would be a great replacement."

"Isn't she only in town temporarily?"

"Yes, but I think she'd be able to fill in the gap until you found a more permanent replacement. We've been trying to find an adequate replacement for a while, and my last day is soon."

Her mention of a "last day" made Derek's stomach tighten. "You've been here for thirty-four years. How will Maya learn the ropes?"

"She's not a newbie at this business. She can do it. You can do it too. I have full faith in you. Don't forget that you are your mother's son. Even though you may not have bridal shop experience and customer service skills and people skills and—"

"And all the skills and know-how that's needed to run this

place," Derek said.

"You have your mother's heart. You know how much this place meant to her. That's enough to help you fill in any gaps."

Gaps like business debt? Doubted it. "I can't do this on my own, Ginger. Even if Maya wanted to fill in temporarily, I can't run this place without you." Derek wanted to say more, but he left those words unspoken. The words about how inadequate he felt not just with the store, but with relating to Jamila. The words about how Ginger had guided him through the aftermath of his wife's death and his mother's death. Ginger was an anchor during those moments when he'd almost fallen apart.

"You'll do good, son," Ginger said, smiling. "I believe in you. I'm going to get some breakfast. You need anything?"

I need you to stay at the boutique and help me run it. "Nothing for me. But you can grab a vegetable omelet and orange juice for Jamila. She's sulking in the back."

She paused. "You'll take care of Jamila too." Ginger placed Maya's business card in his hands. "Call this lady. She will change your life. Believe me."

After Ginger left, Derek studied the business card. Call her after he just turned her down? That would come across as inconsistent on his part. It wasn't like she would agree to working here temporarily, especially if she was some fancy New York designer.

He could also find some other way, but with Ginger leaving he'd be doing most of the work himself.

What now? The most logical thing would be to sell this place, but there was history on the line. There was his mother's dream to uphold.

And there was his guilt to ease.

Jamila was very attached to this place too, even if she sulked around him. Her gloom had more to do with him than with the store. Jamila grew up in this little boutique. If he sold it, his daughter would be crushed. The last thing he needed was to let her down again. He was having enough trouble connecting with his daughter already.

Right now, he didn't have any other choice.

"Guess, I'll have to call Maya after all," he said to the mannequin next to him. "You think she would be interested in being a temporary employee for a bridal shop?"

The mannequin didn't respond. Derek didn't have an answer either, but Ginger believed in Maya. So Derek would call her and ask.

THE FOLLOWING DAY, Maya started the ignition of her father's gray sedan and drove to the bank. She still thought about her meeting with Derek. That was a wasted attempt to make a dress sale. That Derek guy didn't even want to take one look at her portfolio. Why was Ginger so insistent on getting Maya down to the store if Derek was so close-minded about everything?

If she didn't bring in any income soon, she'd be behind on

the rent for her New York studio apartment. She needed her residence, much like she needed to keep her job. This whole leave without pay stuff was tough, especially after witnessing how careless Pops was with bills. Who knew if he was behind on payments? He was so disorganized.

Hopefully her meeting with the bank loan officer would go well today. If her application for a loan was approved, Maya's finances would be more stable, family emergency or not. The loan would also help cover some of her father's uninsured medical costs too. *Some.* Health insurance was tricky these days.

Too bad Derek Sullivan didn't place an order on the spot, though. Maya preferred cash income over additional debts any day.

Derek was good-looking. Didn't appear to be the emotional type. He must harbor sadness inside. His clipped speech and steady gaze told her as much.

Besides, she could recognize loss a mile away.

Maya Jackson refused to get angsty about the losses in her life. Or sour. If it weren't for her persistence, she would turn into a ball of self-pitying mush. A jilted bride, Maya refused to put herself in a position where she'd get her heart broken again. Maya and Rex, her ex-fiancé, were together for three long years. Sigh. She'd remain focused on her career.

Thankfully, she still had faith. Faith would lead to a loan approval. Right now, she was barely making it. She needed this loan *yesterday.*

Maya jerked her car into the parking lot of Charleston Community Bank. A smattering of vehicles were parked here and there. Maya checked the digital clock on the dashboard. Five minutes until her appointment time. She whipped the steering wheel, parked her car, and booked it to the bank's entrance, hoping the loan officer wouldn't notice her rushing.

The security guard swung open the front door, and she stepped inside the air-conditioned bank. Maya whistled an upbeat melody, striding to the customer service desk. Her heels clacked on the tile, a resounding noise in the silent bank. A couple of patrons turned in her direction and frowned. Maya smiled and kept walking.

While Maya had recovered from her last blood transfusion, she'd spent a few hours preparing this loan application, creating a financial statement that proved she was credit-worthy. Everything was pitch perfect. That guaranteed the bank's approval.

Whistling, Maya waited in line. When her turn arrived, eagerness got the best of her. She bumped into a baby stroller, said a quick "Excuse me," and extended her hand to the receptionist.

Still smiling.

"You made it just in time," a twangy voice called from behind.

Maya turned and saw a sixty-something, rail-thin woman in a navy suit with a severely tight bun glaring at her. The lady didn't seem too friendly. *Please don't let this be the loan officer.* "Ma'am?" she said in her most cordial voice.

"I'm Ursula Evans. You Maya Jackson, the fashion designer?"

"That's me."

The older woman gave Maya a once-over. "I can tell by those fancy-schmancy clothes. Follow me." The woman did an about-face, and Maya hustled behind her.

Seconds later, they entered a cramped, cluttered office. The walls were littered with plaques engraved with the name "Ursula Evans": one for five years of service, another for ten, another for twenty, another for thirty, and still another for forty full years of service. The woman even had a plaque for never using a sick day for two decades. The office teemed with boxes of file folders stuffed with papers. If someone lit a match in the place, it would instantly burst into flames.

"Have a seat," the loan officer ordered.

Maya couldn't find the chair.

The woman grunted, lifted two banker's boxes from a seat, and dropped them on the floor. A flurry of dust bunnies floated up to Maya's nose, causing her to sneeze.

"You got a cold?"

"Er, no, ma'am." Maya pulled a Kleenex from her black clutch and blew her nose.

"Good. I'm sixty-five years old, and my immune system is shot. I can't afford to suffer from a contagious disease. Especially now that I'm retiring and my monthly pension will be slashed in half due to the bad economy."

Maya offered a cheeky grin. *Focus on the positive.* "Congratulations on your retirement."

"Nothing to congratulate. I was forced into it. Now, why do you want our money?"

Maya's rehearsed speech turned to mush in her brain. "Well. Yes. Um."

The loan officer pulled a blue file out of her drawer and flipped it open. "Says here you are employed and—"

"I'm employed, but I'm on unpaid leave."

Ursula rolled her eyes. "You mess up on your job or something? Because we don't hand out loans to people who have disciplinary actions against them at work."

"No. I had a family emergency." Maya shifted in her seat, uncomfortable with the prospect of talking about her father's situation. The more she talked, the more worried she felt. "My father fell and broke his hip. I was in New York when it happened. Rushed down here as soon as I heard."

Ursula clasped her hands together and leaned over the desk, her sparkly red reindeer earrings glittering in the fluorescent lights. Reindeer earrings in the spring. Interesting move. "How long are you off work?"

"Until the end of June. I hope to return sooner if I can. It depends on my father's mobility."

"That's a long time without any income. How will you repay this loan?"

Anxiety strangled Maya, a response lodged somewhere

between her larynx and her throat, unwilling to let go. "Once I get back to work, things should be good. Also, I'm working on garnering revenue by selling my gowns to private clients, boutiques, and larger department stores."

"So you're self-employed too?"

"Sort of. Not officially. I haven't created a business plan or anything. It's just a way to earn some income until I return to work. My job is my main source of income."

"It isn't right now. Anyone bought your stuff yet?" Ursula asked.

An image of Derek flashed in her mind. "No."

"Have you ever owned a business before?"

Did a lemonade stand in fifth grade count? "No."

"You should give self-employment some serious thought. Employers can be fickle. I already told you about the issues with my reduced retirement check. These days, the only person you can count on is yourself. Because of your credit rating and your current leave without pay situation, we can give you a small personal loan of five hundred dollars. Not much else."

Five hundred dollars? That was it? Her rent alone was three thousand dollars a month, and it was due in two weeks. Her vacation pay and this tiny loan only covered one month of rent and nothing else. She'd have to earn money another way to cover her rent for future months. "That's it?"

"That's it." Ursula shrugged. "Don't you have a credit card?"

"It's maxed out. My savings is almost drained too."

"Sorry to hear that. If you had a small business, you could apply for a small business loan with us to cover your start-up costs. You'd have to show us a business plan and a business license and all of that jazz. You should give it some thought."

Maya's dream had always been to work for Laura Whitcomb, and she'd gotten her dream. Now that she was there, there was no way she'd give that up for a business. Self-employment was risky anyway. She tried her best to make that dress sale at the boutique earlier today, and it'd gotten her nowhere. "I'm not ready to own a business, but thanks for the loan."

"You're welcome." Ursula stood up and shook Maya's hand. "I gotta get to my lunch break. If you go to the front teller window and give them your Social Security number, you'll get a direct deposit of the loan into your account today. Have a nice day." In seconds, Ursula disappeared, slamming the door behind her.

Maya's hopes fizzled. Splat. She fisted her hands together and took a deep breath to steady herself. *Persist. Persist. Persist.* That was what Mama would say, but right now, persistence seemed hard. *I'll have to sell a dress or two or fifty. Or figure out another way.*

Grabbing her purse, Maya strode toward the bank lobby and waited in line for the next teller. Despite the cool temperature in the building, dampness clung to her skin and soaked the small of her back. Yucky worry. It did nothing but add weight to the pressures threatening to take her under.

Maya exhaled. "What do I do now?"

She waited for a response from above.

Nothing.

She squeezed her eyes shut, careful not to let emotion get the best of her. Her cell phone trilled and an unfamiliar number flitted across the screen. Who was this? Not many unknown numbers called her. "Hello?" she answered.

"Miss Jackson?"

The deep timbre of that voice jogged her awareness. Derek. She'd met him only yesterday, but she would recognize that voice anywhere. His tone held a ring to it that accelerated all that prickling.

Prickling? Since when did she let herself get all prickly? *Note to self: Stop it.* "Derek?"

"Yes, it's me. I'm calling because an interesting opportunity just came up. I know you're looking to earn some extra cash. Ginger recommended I get in touch with you again about selling dresses at the store. After I spoke to her more, I realized she was right."

Of course Ginger's right. "Oh."

"I wanted to know if you could return to the shop. Perhaps bring your portfolio and one or two dress samples. I'd like to look them over. Please?"

Maya twisted her mouth. This guy already had refused her offer. If she had any ounce of self-

respect, she'd say no.

She tugged on the hem of her sundress and inched forward in the line. Maya could also figure out another way to earn extra cash. She had to check out that other boutique in town that Laura had mentioned anyway.

"Do you think you could stop by again today?"

Oh, this dude just wants me to drop everything, huh? "I have other plans today."

"Oh really? What plans?"

He was nosy too? Sheesh. "Why do you need to know?"

"Just asking. No reason." His volume lowered and the sound of customers in the background filtered through the phone line. "I'd really like you to stop by the store again, whenever it's most convenient for you. What do you think?"

He was willing to be flexible and meet on her terms. That was hopeful.

"Miss Jackson?"

Maya floated out of her private reverie. "Yes?"

"Would you be willing to stop by again?"

Maya thought of the portfolio shoved in her attaché. All was not lost. She still had a chance to pitch her designs to Derek and hopefully make enough money to cover what she didn't get in her loan. "Yes."

His voice deepened. "When will you stop by?"

The idea of seeing Derek again sent a flurry of anticipation through the pit of her belly. She squelched it. "Does Monday work?"

"I'll be here Monday—waiting."

After saying goodbye, she went to the teller's window and arranged for the electronic transfer of her loan. When she thought of Derek's smile, Maya's steps stuttered in time with her skipped heartbeat.

Note to self: Stop it, again.

No matter what, she had to ignore Derek's beautiful smile. No matter what, she had to ignore Derek's kind ways. No matter what, she had to help brides realize their own happily ever afters, never her own.

For Maya, love was simply fodder for fairy tales.

Chapter Four

Today was Maya's chance to get extra money. She awakened early and worked for a few hours on her design concept for Ashley Tate's gown and took pictures of her gown for the head designer position. Both were as good as she was going to get them, so Maya emailed the design concept and images to Laura. Hopefully, Laura would like at least one of them. Maya also wrote a quick note about her plans to scout bridal shops later this week.

Afterward, Maya quickly got dressed and headed to her car with two gowns and her portfolio in hand. She left the rest of her gowns at home. Her heart beat triple time as she considered her impending meeting with Derek at the boutique. He sounded hunky on the phone when he called her at the bank, but she wasn't thinking about all of that. Correction: She shouldn't be thinking that. This was business.

If she could convince him to purchase at least three of her dresses, that would not only cover her rent for future

months, but it would also cover some of her father's medical
expenses.

That would be a huge blessing.

Minutes after paying the parking meter, she headed down
Queen Street. A sting of pain seized her calf muscles. She
stopped in the middle of the sidewalk. "Please, not another
episode," she whispered to herself.

Maya leaned against the window of Gus's Diner. Why'd
her life have to be so complicated? Why'd she have to fight
through this illness?

The doctor had warned her against overdosing on her
medications, but she really wanted to do so now. A thousand
tiny needles pricked up her thighs and around her back. *No.
No. No. I'll get through this. This morning's dosage was enough.*

Once she got the chance, she'd make an appointment with
a local doctor ASAP.

She quickly dug in her purse for her bottle of hydroxy-
urea. She took it like clockwork every single day, and she
hadn't missed this morning's dose. Should she take extra to
ease the pain? There was no way she could pitch her dresses
to Derek like this.

Maya was used to sucking it up and downplaying her illness
in front of others. Once her parents had alerted the school
nurse of her symptoms, it seemed like everyone started treating her like she was helpless. Maya hated it. So she learned to
push past her illness and show that she was just as capable as
her sickle cell anemia—free classmates.

Yet as Maya grew older, the symptoms became more and more burdensome. Eventually, sickle cell anemia would win.

The notion gnawed at her. It was the one thing driving her to do something with her life before she died.

"Push through this, Maya," she said. She stood away from the diner's window and shook out her legs. Moments later, the pain subsided. "Thank you, God. Back to normal."

Maya kept walking down the sidewalk and inhaled the crisp spring air. It flooded her lungs and soothed the aches she'd just experienced. This weather was a welcome reprieve from the humidity, which had been typical for the past few days in Charleston. The palmettos provided areas of shade from the sunlight. That was one thing she missed about the Lowcountry—the soothing weather, the friendly smiles, and the easygoing nature of the community.

Yet there were few opportunities to get high-profile clients and make a name for herself in South Carolina, which was another reason she moved to New York.

Maya hooked a right onto State Street and adjusted the strap of her purse on her shoulder. Tucked inside of her purse, alongside her medicine, was her portfolio. She hadn't had a chance to show it to Derek on her first visit to the boutique. She'd do so today.

The white oval sign, which read ALWAYS A BRIDE EST. 1984, came into view. It swung on its rusted hinges, keeping time with the lazy breeze. Salty dots of sweat formed on her upper lip. She was used to selling Laura Whitcomb's gowns. Selling her own designs was nerve-racking, but she put on her self-assured face anyway. "Here goes nothing, Maya," she whispered, and mustered up her confidence. "Time to sell."

She opened the door. No one was in sight. Derek must be in the back office or something. He'd probably come out soon, now that he heard the bell.

Maya set her purse on the counter and took out her portfolio. On her first visit to the shop, she hadn't had much time to take in the space. Now that all was quiet, she did.

The paint was 1980s bland, with its mustard tinge. The carpet beneath her feet was an old, dull blue. This place needed a makeover.

"Hey, Maya," Derek called from behind.

Maya turned, and her heart fluttered at the sight of him. He wore a crisp collared shirt, a pair of dark brown khakis with matching loafers that shined. Business casual and handsome.

Did she just think of Derek as handsome again? Maya sighed. Guess it wasn't a problem to notice someone's looks, but she sure wasn't going to get entangled by it.

"I hope I'm not too early," she replied, pushing aside any thoughts of his attractiveness.

"Not early at all." He gestured to the portfolio lying on the countertop. "What did you bring?"

"Have a look." She gestured to her designs and smiled.

Derek stepped closer, and Maya caught a whiff of his light cologne. She needed to stop noticing these little things about him. She was here to sell dresses, not to flirt.

"Nice work." He flipped through the designs. "Although, as a relatively new owner of the store, I only have a cursory knowledge of what sells and what doesn't around here. And with Ginger retiring soon, I don't know how I'll manage. I've been searching for help."

"You'll get the hang of it," she said, surprised by her confidence. "Remember that it's not so much about the dresses, it's about making the brides feel like royalty."

"Royalty, huh?"

"Yes."

Derek didn't respond. Instead he kept studying her work. "Last time I looked at this, I was taken aback by the wholesale prices. Those prices may work in New York, but not down here."

"They're worth every dollar—or thousand," she said, smiling. "You know that, or else you wouldn't have called me back."

A note of hesitation danced across his features. "Yes, about that. I was thinking of a consignment arrangement for your gowns. You can pay the store twenty dollars per dress, non-refundable, for showing the dresses. I was thinking we can have six or seven dresses on consignment."

Consignment? That wasn't good. A dress sale wouldn't be guaranteed.

"If they sell, we take a ten percent fee from the retail price," he continued. "You can keep the rest. This will help me keep the costs down while you get a place to show off your work. I think that's a fair enough deal. I'm offering you low enough costs."

She twisted her mouth. Selling on consignment wasn't the same as selling her dresses to him outright and on whole-sale. Would consignment be worth it? What if she didn't sell them? Then her efforts would've been wasted.

"You don't have to give me an answer today, if you're still wavering," Derek added with a smile.

Maya would give an answer today. "Selling clothes on consignment would be nice, but I have bills to pay too. I'd like to have some steady income to cover the costs of my future months of rent. While it's a nice offer, I can't accept it."

Derek drummed his fingers on the counter. "Understood. We all have to take care of our responsibilities. I have a responsibility to this store. To make sure it's fiscally sound."

A faint wash of disappointment welled up within her, and then the disappointment grew stronger and stronger. It was bad enough that Laura wasn't paying her, but now she wouldn't even be able to cover her rent while she was down here in South Carolina. What would she do if she fell behind and got evicted? Her current place in New York was the best deal she could find, and it was pricey.

This was getting worse and worse.

"I have an idea," Derek said, pulling her out of her thoughts. "I'm looking for a new buyer and store manager, and you're looking for some steady income while you're in

Charleston. How about I hire you to work here temporarily?"

Maya bit her lower lip. "You want me to work here?"

"Yes. Until you move back to New York, of course. I really need the assistance. It'll also give me some time to gather my bearings until I find a permanent employee."

"Would I still sell my clothes on consignment?" she asked.

"You sure can. You definitely can."

"I still have to take my father to his physical therapy appointments."

"Oh. That's right. You have to care for your father. You're more than welcome to take your father to his physical therapy during business hours. I wouldn't be able to pay you for that time, of course, but you'll have that flexibility." A flit of sadness crossed his features. "Family is important to me."

This could work. This would be perfect, actually. While she awaited Laura's decision on the promotion and the Ashley Tate gig, she'd work here. "You have a deal. I'll work here temporarily, and I'll bring seven gowns for consignment tomorrow."

They shook hands, and Maya smiled. This wasn't exactly what she was looking for when she walked into the boutique today, but it was a great way to make sure her finances would stay on track.

Derek was turning out to be a handsome blessing in disguise.

Two DAYS HAD passed since she'd accepted Derek's offer, and Maya had grown more accustomed to the idea of working at the boutique. It would be perfect. Not only would Maya earn extra cash and potentially sell some of her dresses, but she might even teach him a few things about the bridal gown trade during her time.

Her father was thrilled that she got the job, if only for the fact that Maya wouldn't be around all day to bug him. Maya had a plan for that too. She intended to call him during her breaks and lunch, just to check in on him. Of course, she'd also take him to all of his doctor's appointments.

From the looks of the boutique, the store was in desperate need of a makeover. Ginger's last day of work was today, and Ginger probably hadn't had the energy to devote to sprucing the place up. Perhaps Maya would help Derek in the aesthetics department as well.

Never mind that he also happened to be incredibly good-looking. He was her boss now. When she arrived at work today, she'd try to convince him to do a makeover of the store.

She might even take before and after pictures and show Laura that her skills extended beyond the outfits. She could also try to convince Laura on having her high-end merchandise featured in this store. Yes, Laura said that she was wary of having her gowns merchandised in such a "distasteful setting," but Maya had to do something to make sure she didn't fall off her radar. Maybe that would be it.

As Maya walked toward the boutique, she reached in her

purse to get her prescription medicine. It was time for another dose, but then she saw that the bottle was empty.

Darn it. Why'd she leave the refill at home? It was too late to return home and get her medication. If Maya did, she'd be late for her first day at work.

Maya swung her oversized purse over her shoulder and kept walking. This downtown area really was a charming little place for a shop like Derek's. The palmettos lining the cobblestone street, the benches situated around, and the friendly faces made this a welcome venue for tourists.

In the distance stood the Black history museum, the place that Laura had expressed disdain about. To Maya, the museum added depth to the Lowcountry. It was also a reminder of how far Black Americans like Maya had come.

Maya shielded her eyes from the sun and took another look at the museum. Ever since moving to New York City, she hadn't come back to South Carolina often, but her mother's fashion design influence served as a constant reminder to remember the past.

Maya arrived at Always a Bride and saw Derek talking to a man with a tablet in the crook of his arm.

Derek glanced her way and waved. "Morning, Maya."

Maya waved in return.

"Marlon, this is Maya, our new employee. She's taking Ginger's place temporarily."

"You didn't tell me you were hiring additional staff." Marlon's tone was clipped. "You can't afford to pay employees."

Her body tightened. So her first day of work looked like it was going to become her last day of work too.

"Maya is needed here. I cannot go at this alone. She brings a wealth of experience. Besides, it's not an additional salary. It's a replacement salary. No harm to the budget."

The corners of Marlon's mouth ticked into a frown.

"Marlon is the accountant for the boutique," Derek said to Maya. "He's been helping me keep things on track."

"Oh."

Marlon gestured to his tablet. An intricate spreadsheet was on the screen. "If you intend to keep her on the payroll, guess I'll crunch the numbers to be one hundred percent certain that it'll work."

"It will work." Derek smiled at Maya, and a sense of gratitude flowed through her.

"You'll have to give me the HR information for your new employee," Marlon said, and focused his attention to Maya. "Welcome to Always a Bride."

"Thank . . ." Maya's cheeks heated by fifty degrees. She stepped to the right and a wave of dizziness overcame her. Oh no. The medicine. She didn't have her medicine.

Maya feigned calm and leaned on a dress rack for support. The rack turned on its wheels, and she stumbled backward. She righted herself to quickly play it off.

Embarrassing. She glanced over at Derek and Marlon. Had they spotted her millisecond of clumsiness? They seemed unperturbed and in conversation about the store's finances.

Could mean they didn't notice. The last thing she needed was to show sickle cell symptoms at work.

Derek glanced at her. "You okay?"

Oh geez. She couldn't let on about her health issues. "I'm fine. Perfectly fine."

Derek didn't seem convinced.

Her heart beat quicker, and she could feel a sheen of sweat on her upper lip. *Oh God, please help me through this. Please. Please. Please.* Maya wrapped her palm around the cool metal dress rack, careful not to lean against it and embarrass herself again.

"Guess I better get moving to my next appointment." Marlon powered off his tablet and checked the time on his smartphone. "Nice meeting you, Maya." His voice carried a note of restraint.

She nodded in response, not wanting to say something and end up in a coughing fit.

After Marlon left, Maya breathed deeply. The pain then subsided. Thank goodness.

"Don't mind Marlon. He's just . . . Marlon."

"I understand."

"Ginger should be here later this afternoon. I can't believe today's her last day."

"You'll manage," Maya said.

"We hope." Derek scratched the back of his neck as if he wanted to say more.

Instead, they looked at each other. And looked. And

looked. A current passed between them, an invisible electricity that made her uncomfortable. She surveyed the store, a poor attempt to shake off the sensation. "What do you need me to do?"

"You can sort the dresses and shoes. They got mixed up after the big sale."

A sorting project. Easy peasy. Maya took a few more deep breaths to get her bearings and negotiate around her symptoms. They were gone now, but who knew what could happen?

Why didn't she put the refill in her purse? Just the other week, she was chiding her father for his forgetfulness. Ever since she came down south, she was getting forgetful too. Like this place made her not so regimented or something. Or perhaps the worry surrounding her father was getting to her.

She headed over to the pile of dresses and sorted them according to size and color. Mindless busywork, but a great distraction from what she'd just felt. Maya hung two lightweight gowns over her forearms and inspected the tags on the dresses. They were both from well-known designers and competitors of Laura Whitcomb Inc. "What are your most popular dress lines?"

He shrugged. "Leilanis. Versaces. Vera Wangs. The usual big-name designers are always popular."

"Only big names, huh?"

"They're the safest bet."

"True, and I'm grateful that you're giving my dresses a chance." She grabbed an empty hanger and shoved her hair out of her face. "Seeing some of my dresses on sale here is encouraging."

"All those designers were once ordinary people looking for a break," Derek said in that confident way she'd been noticing.

"Of course." Maya hung a gown on the hanger. "I'm hoping to make that break at my New York job. I'm applying to be head designer, and I hope to get the gig when I return. It would be a dream come true . . ." Her voice trailed off. The desire she had for the position had overwhelmed her. "The competition is tight in New York."

"You shouldn't worry about that. I don't know much about these dress styles, but"—he gestured to two of her dresses now hanging on the clothing racks—"I know yours are unique, different."

"You're too kind." She smiled.

"Not kind. Just telling the truth."

"I want to make my mark in the bridal gown industry. I want to make something so good that Laura will be super impressed. I've been designing for a while, and I've had a lot of hits and misses along the way. Life is so short." Sadness hit her. "I want to make the most of my talents while I'm here."

Derek put a shoe on display. "Pretty sure you have a lot of years ahead of you."

Maya didn't say a word.

He reached for a dress strewn across a footstool, his mouth curved into a wry smile. "Your career matters a lot to you, huh?"

"It does."

He put the dress on the counter and wrote something on a clipboard. "Somehow I think you'll be very successful as a designer."

A thrill rushed through her. "You do?"

"Definitely. I'm usually right about my hunches."

His store was failing financially, and the space definitely needed a makeover. His hunches may not be too spot-on.

Derek continued arranging the shoes. He studied the display for a good while, and a dimple formed on his cheek. Way too cute.

"Can you help me arrange these shoes, Maya? There are mountains of them everywhere."

"Sure." Maya bent to pick up the stray shoes. Derek knelt next to her, doing the same. She scooched around him and avoided eye contact, hand contact, elbow contact—any contact. When she moved away an inch, he moved closer by two inches. On top of that, his light cologne was intoxicating.

Flustered by this sudden man invasion, she headed toward a nearby ecru settee, but tripped over a shoebox, which toppled over. The lid flew across the store.

Then a sudden dizziness overcame her. Everything blurred and hazed in front of her face.

Oh no. Here we go again.

Maya tried to right herself but failed to judge her distance from the bench. As she sat, her bottom hit the floor. Hard. A sharp pain shot up her spine. "Aargh!"

He reached out his hand to help her up, and she grabbed it.

"Are you all right?"

Her pulse accelerated and her breath shortened. "Fine, thank you."

"You look like you're glistening."

Trying to appear calm, she focused on a spot on the wall. "I . . . I'm good. Just a little out of breath." She took one step back.

"Here." Derek pulled the settee toward her. "Sit."

She plopped down, happy to find the padding underneath her this time. A few deep breaths and her pulse slowed, steadied, then returned to something approaching normal.

"How do you feel now?"

"Great!" she squeaked. Why did she squeak?

He sat next to her. "Positive? You seem shaky."

She really needed her medications. "No problems here," she double-squeaked.

"If you're not feeling well, let me know."

"Okay." Maya forced a smile and tried to sound like the most composed, most together, most cosmopolitan woman on the planet. Yeah, right.

Maya mentally whispered a prayer-plea that her symptoms would go away, quickly. She couldn't risk a painful episode. If Derek knew she was ill—if anyone knew she was ill—she'd be treated like she was weak, and she hated when people said she was helpless.

"I can get you some water," he said.

"I'll get it myself. Thank you." She scooted to the edge of the seat, stood up, and headed to the break room. Unease rolled through her body. Once there, Maya grabbed an unopened water bottle from the fridge and guzzled it down.

Maya stood and waited a few seconds to regain her orientation. Then she returned to the sales floor and resumed rearranging the shoes, wrapping them in tissue paper, shoving them into boxes. Derek watched her from behind, but she didn't crack or crumble.

No more weakness, Maya. No more weakness. Her mother's words echoed in her heart.

Chapter Five

Derek was sure something was bothering Maya. It was more than just tripping over shoes. She was uncomfortable the entire time. *Wonder what that's about.*

The door opened, and he looked up. Ginger entered the store.

"It's my last day. I'm a free woman." She smiled. "How's it going?"

Derek shrugged. "It's going."

"You sound like you're in despair." She swatted him playfully. "You'll do great now that you have help."

"I'm going to miss you. Thank you for all you've done over the years."

"You're quite welcome." Ginger's eyes shone, and then she blinked. "Now here you go making me get all emotional. I'll be in the stockroom. Let me know if you need anything."

"I will."

She headed to the rear of the store, and Derek sighed. He'd have to figure out a way forward, somehow.

Moments later, Jamila entered the store. Derek checked his watch. "Kind of late today from school," Derek said with a forced casualness. "Where were you?"

"I was talking to friends after I got off the bus."

Friends. Derek should meet her friends. "Oh, who?"

She tilted her head to the side as if to say, *I don't have time for an interrogation.* "Just some people."

"Some people"? Was this how it was gonna be with his daughter? They'd talk to each other over this wide, invisible chasm? He'd have to connect with Jamila via another angle. "All right, then. How about you stick around till closing time? We can go out for dinner."

"Can't." Jamila pulled her smartphone out of her back pocket and stuck the buds in her ears.

"Why not?" he asked, incredulous.

"I have band practice tonight, remember?"

He should remember. A good father would remember. "Sorry, hon. I forgot."

Derek released a slow breath and leaned against the wall. This store occupied his mind too much. He needed to get this place profitable so that he could focus on his daughter. In two more years, she's be a freshman in high school, and who knew what those years held?

Jamila rolled her eyes and then fiddled around with her smartphone. The chasm between them widened.

"I really am sorry about forgetting," Derek repeated.

Jamila's eyes grew distant, distracted. "Don't matter."

But it did. "We'll leave at four o'clock for your band practice." Derek walked to the register. An orange flyer stuck out from her backpack. He squinted at it.

END-OF-YEAR PROJECT . . .

Derek picked up the flyer. "What's this?"

Jamila flushed. "Just some stupid project for school. They said an adult should help us with it, but I told them you were busy."

So Jamila expected him not to participate in her life? *Not good, Dad.* "I'm not busy. I'd love to help." He read the flyer. It was a sewing project.

Oh. Maybe not.

Jamila must've read his expression because she said, "See? I knew you wouldn't be interested."

He set the paper on the counter. "I haven't a clue about sewing, but I know someone who does."

She was silent for a moment. "Who?"

"Maya. She's the new temporary employee here." He pointed across the store to where Maya was busy arranging the jewelry and hair accessories.

Her eyes widened. "New temporary employee? A woman?"

She said the word "woman" with such disdain that Derek almost cringed. "Yes."

Jamila's eyes hardened. "So you have a girlfriend now?"

"Girlfriend? What? No way, Jamila. She works here. This is her first day. Ginger recommended her because she's retired after today. We needed a replacement."

Jamila crossed her arms and huffed. "I can't come to this store anymore if your girlfriend is here."

Derek rolled his eyes. "She is not my girlfriend. She's a temporary employee. I'm trying hard to connect with you, Jamila. You really have to help me out here. You want me to keep this boutique, right?"

Jamila nodded yes.

"Then I need assistance to do that. Maya is providing that assistance."

Jamila headed to the corner of the store where Derek had set up a small desk for Jamila to do her homework after school. Okay, she didn't want to talk.

Shortly after Grace died, he'd promised Jamila he'd fly home the next day to be with her. His commanding officer didn't approve Derek's leave until a week later. It was agonizing to read all the news headlines about the mass shooting and not be able to be with his daughter through it all. When he finally arrived home, Jamila felt betrayed. She had never said it outright, but he sensed it through her nonactions, heard it through her nonwords. How would Derek reach out to her today? He didn't know.

Across the store, Jamila pulled out a textbook and opened it.

Perfect opportunity to ignore me. Stick your nose in a book. Well,

Jamila wasn't going to blow him off this time. "What subject are you studying for?" He pointed to the textbook.

"Science," Jamila said, not looking up.

Science. A one-word response. Hey, at least it was something. "Let me know if you need help with your homework. I definitely want to check it when you finish."

She didn't say anything, so Derek returned to his work. One day she'd come around—he hoped.

Seconds later, Maya stopped rearranging the display and walked over to the desk where Jamila was seated. Maya did a double take when she saw Jamila's book. "Hey, that's not a science book. That's a fashion magazine." Maya smiled.

Jamila slammed her book shut. "What's it to you?" she asked, defensive.

Maya held her hands up. "Hey, hey, hey. It's nothing to me. I was just noticing."

Derek's neck muscles tensed. It was one thing for Jamila to be rude to him, quite another to be rude to Maya, a person Jamila just met. Should he step in? If he didn't, things could blow up. But if he intervened, an opportunity for Maya to connect with Jamila could be lost.

The connection was more important, and perhaps Maya could do or say something that would help in that arena. Derek didn't interfere.

"You know, I love fashion too," Maya continued. "I overheard you talking to your father about a sewing project. You may not be ready for any help now, but if you ever are, I'm willing to help."

Derek's ears pricked. Maya was holding out a peace offering. Interesting. Jamila didn't answer, however. She took out a notebook and pencil and started writing.

Moments passed, and Maya headed to her oversized bag behind the register and pulled out scarves and different accessories. Maya carried that stuff around with her? Guess it was part of her job.

"Want to try on some of my scarves, Jamila? I think we could find the perfect color scheme for you. I use them to help clients who don't know how to begin with their wardrobe."

"I'm not your customer," Jamila said, not looking up.

Man, why'd Jamila have to be so mean?

"I know that, Jamila," Maya said. "This is just a friendly ask."

"Not for me." Jamila rolled her eyes.

Maya's brows lifted.

Okay, that was it. This was gonna blow up. Derek opened his mouth to say something, but Maya subtly held up her hand and mouthed, *I've got this,* to Derek.

He paused. Maya sensed the tension too, so he'd respect her request.

If you say so, he mouthed in response. Derek stepped back, waiting to see how this would play out.

"You look like a fall," Maya said to Jamila.

"A what?" Jamila scrunched her nose.

"Your coloring is that of a fall. I can find just the perfect shades for you. Offer some color scheme ideas to spark your creativity."

Jamila seemed to be deep in thought. Derek bit his bottom lip, hoping Maya's kindness would work.

"You said you know how to sew?" Jamila asked.

"Yes." Maya glanced over at Derek, and her expression filled with hope. "I'm a pro at that. What do you have to create?"

"A T-shirt or a dress or something. I dunno."

"For you to wear?" Maya inquired.

"Yes."

"Then we definitely have to try on a scarf. Just to figure out the best color scheme for you. Want to try them on?"

Jamila paused a moment. "Sure."

"Sure"? Did his daughter just say "sure"? Amazing.

Derek stood back, intrigued by this conversation. The most Jamila had spoken to him was the other week when she was staring at pictures of her mother. Since then, it was back to the usual.

Yet Maya—Maya had got her talking. Maya had skills.

"Let's see how these scarves look on you in front of the mirror," Maya said, gesturing for her to stand close.

Jamila stood in front of a full-length mirror, while Maya stood behind her.

"What do you think, Jamila?" Maya asked.

Maya held a burnt-orange scarf and gracefully wrapped it

around Jamila's shoulders. "Warm colors bring out your rich skin tone. See? You're definitely a fall, not a spring."

Jamila stared at her reflection in the mirror, expressionless. "Maybe."

"Maybe? Definitely. Fall is the best season. Cool weather. Leaves are falling."

"I used to play in the leaves when I was a little kid." Jamila shrugged. "Not anymore."

Maya smiled. "Oh, you're too big to play in the leaves these days, huh?"

"No. I stopped playing when . . . never mind." A shadow fell across Jamila's face.

Maya glanced over at Derek, and his heart pinched. Jamila stopped playing after Grace died.

"I think if you have clothes in deep reds and oranges and golds, they'll really bring out your gorgeous skin tone, Jamila. A deep purple would look fabulous on you too. You'd look like royalty."

Jamila's mouth curved upward slightly. "Like a queen?"

"Yes. An African queen," Maya said, adjusting the scarf on her shoulders. "Do you have a pattern for the dress or the T-shirt? Have you decided on something for your project yet?"

"Nope."

"How about a simple sheath dress? I think it'll look great on you.

"Sheath dress?" Derek said. "Are those tight? If so, she's

too young."

"Dad, I'll be in eighth grade next year. They're not tight either."

Maya rolled her eyes. "It's very modest attire, if that's what you're worried about, Derek."

No need to push this issue. Perhaps he was being a tad overprotective of Jamila. And besides, what did he know about fashion? Nothing. Derek pursed his lips.

"I don't need help with my school project. I can do it on my own." Jamila glanced at the items on the counter. "Can I try on the gold ponytail holder?"

"Sure you can." Maya grabbed the ponytail holder and placed it in Jamila's hand. "You have such gorgeous hair. Doing a good job taking care of it, Dad."

"I don't do Jamila's hair. She does it all herself."

Maya raised her brows, impressed. "You've got skills, Jamila."

"I watched a lot of internet videos after . . ." Jamila's voice trailed off. "Lots and lots of internet videos."

His heart broke. *After Grace died.* That was what Jamila didn't say. Jamila started doing her own hair after Grace died, and Jamila never let Derek braid or comb or twist her hair or anything. He tried to do Jamila's hair once, and she nearly flipped out.

"Can I put this in your hair?" Maya asked.

Jamila twisted her mouth. "Sure."

"Sure"? This was incredible.

Maya fluffed out Jamila's curly hair, and then Maya stepped back, assumedly to take a better look.

Watching Maya brought up memories of his wife getting Jamila ready for church on Sunday mornings. She would always do Jamila's hair in four pigtails with a white ribbon tied on the end of each.

"What do you think of her scarf and hair with the ponytail holder, Derek?" Maya asked.

Derek studied Jamila's new accessories. She looked like a lovely young lady. "Beautiful." His voice held the love of a father. "Your mother would be so proud."

Jamila's face changed from soft to hard. "Mother. She should be doing my hair now. Not you, Maya." Jamila took two steps back.

Maya's shoulders slumped, and she looked away. "I'm sorry. I . . . uh . . ."

Derek's heart folded in on itself. Why'd he say something? Now he'd ruined the moment.

Jamila was right. Grace should be doing Jamila's hair. Grace should be helping Jamila with her dress project.

Yet Grace was gone, and there was nothing he could do to change that fact.

THE FOLLOWING DAY, Maya arrived at the bridal boutique fifteen minutes early and sat at the front register. She couldn't stop thinking about Jamila. The girl must hate Maya, and for good reason. Jamila felt like Maya was trying to replace

Jamila's mother, and that wasn't the case.

If only Maya could give Jamila a hug and tell her it would be okay, but who was Maya fooling? Jamila couldn't stand her.

Today Maya would try to make peace with Jamila, but how? There wasn't much that Maya could do in that department. Perhaps Maya would just be a friendly face and let Jamila know that she's only there to work, nothing more.

It's not like she was Derek's girlfriend.

She didn't want to be Derek's girlfriend. Period.

Maya would explain all this clearly to Jamila. That was a good enough plan. She checked her watch. Jamila should be arriving at the boutique in an hour or so.

A few feet away, the door to Derek's office was half open. The sound of tapping on a keyboard snapped Maya out of her thoughts. Was that Derek? Sounded like he was stressed. She headed toward the back of the store, closer to the sound of the noise.

That was Derek all right. His mouth was scrunched, and the lines around his eyes deepened. He looked kinda cute with that worried expression on his face.

"Hey," Maya said. "You okay?"

Derek shrugged. "Just trying to make these numbers balance out. This boutique is a money pit. I don't know what to do with this place anymore. I've run out of ideas. If we don't bring in more revenue, I'll have to take Marlon's advice and sell this business or go into foreclosure in six weeks."

"Sell or foreclosure?"

He blinked. "I don't know what else to do."

She shifted her weight from side to side. "If you need help bringing in more sales, I can help."

"I'm open to all ideas." Derek scrubbed his hand over his face. "The last thing I need is for Jamila to be mad at me over selling the business."

"She would be mad if the store closed? That wouldn't be your fault."

"Jamila wouldn't think so. You've already seen how hard it is for us to relate."

Maya didn't respond. No need to rub in the obvious. "When Jamila returns from school today, I was thinking I could have a talk with her. Clear up any misconceptions she may have about me."

The lines around Derek's eyes deepened. "I'm afraid you won't get to do that. Jamila refuses to come to the store while you work here. She's going home with a friend today, and I'll have to pick her up later."

So Maya's presence was driving a wedge between Derek and his daughter, and Maya had been here only one day. What could happen on the second day? "If I'm that much of a problem, perhaps I shouldn't work here."

"No. No. No. You have nothing to do with my failures as a parent. This is something between me and Jamila. I want you to stay."

This was even more out of sorts that Derek was asking her

to stay. "You sure?"

"I'm positive."

Jamila could think Derek was taking sides. "I don't want to get in between you and your daughter."

"You aren't. I need your experience, especially since Ginger is no longer working here."

"All right then. I'll stay." Maya exhaled. "If things ever get too tense with you, your daughter, and me, I can look for another way to cover my bills while I'm down here."

"I understand, and I appreciate that you're willing to do that. Hopefully things won't get to that point."

He sounded sincere, but Maya could sense his internal tug-of-war. It must be hard to try to balance pleasing his daughter with running this business. "I guess it's a good thing I'll be here for a few short months. You can always tell that to Jamila. She can return here as soon as I leave."

Derek was silent, and he twiddled his thumbs, apparently taking in Maya's words. After a few seconds, he said, "What did you have in mind for this place? You said you were willing to help."

"Trunk shows."

"What's that?" he asked.

"They're events that would showcase high-end designer clothing at discounted prices. We could have a theme for the trunk show. They're a wonderful way to get brides to try new designs, and, of course, purchase those designs."

"How is that different from the sale I had a few weeks

ago?"

Maya immediately went into sales pitch mode. She had put on many a trunk show during her time up in New York. "The trunk show's appeal is its exclusivity. It's held for a limited time and the invited guests would get to preview dresses that aren't open to the public. They'd get discounted prices too. Whenever I put on a trunk show, I also like to add in a personal touch and make it feel like a party with close friends instead of a sales event."

"Oh, so you're saying the sale I held was a little low budget? That I targeted it to bargain hunters versus women with 'high-end retail experience'?" Derek joked.

"Perhaps."

"I'll take that jab. Like I said, I need all the help I can get. What would we need to do?"

Maya hesitated. How would she bring this up? "I think a rebrand is in order for this business."

"A rebrand?" he asked.

"Yes. When was the last time this place was remodeled?"

Derek paused. "I couldn't even tell you. It was definitely before I took over. Way, way, way before I took over."

"I think with a good rebranding—some new carpet, some fresh paint, and a new logo—you could draw new attention to this place. Even changing the floor layout will do wonders for this store and attract clientele. It'll exude a high-end yet homegrown feel."

Derek rested his chin in his hands, his eyes filled with

admiration. "You see all of that for this little old boutique?"

"Yes, I do." Her voice wavered. Lordy. Why'd she have to sound like that? This was a professional conversation, but the intense way he looked at Maya made her shook.

He didn't take his eyes away from her. This was both unwieldy and comforting. Unwieldy in the sense that she wasn't checking for a guy, especially someone like Derek. His daughter basically couldn't stand her. Yet it was also comforting. There was an ease about Derek that made her feel like she could slow down, take a breath, and not be all about the hustle.

Derek smiled. She smiled in return. If only life were as easy as this little moment in time.

It wasn't. These kinds of moments never lasted.

"You've probably deduced that I don't have the funds to hire folks to paint a store, put in a new carpet, and all that. So while I appreciate the idea of a trunk show, I can't contract folks to do that labor. I can't spend all that money on the supplies."

"So you're not going to remodel this place?"

"It definitely needs a remodel, but I need a cost-effective solution. I can do the work myself, but I'm already doing a lot."

Maya didn't want to take time away from caring for her father to help at the store. He was the reason she came down in the first place. If she spent more time at this place for renovations, then it'd take away from father-daughter time.

Besides, this job was only a means to cover her bills. It wasn't the be-all and end-all of her career. Getting that promotion, on the other hand, *was* the be-all and end-all of her career. Laura hadn't responded yet to Maya's dress design sketches, but she would soon. Maya's stomach flipped at the thought.

"Could you help with some of the remodeling work too?" Derek asked, interrogating her thoughts. "It could cut down on costs."

Maya's suggestion meant that she also volunteered herself. "You want me to work extra hours?"

"I would pay you for those hours, of course. I wouldn't want you to do anything physically strenuous. I can put in the new carpeting myself. It'll take longer since I'm DIY-ing it, but it can be done."

"Hmm." Maya tapped her finger on her chin, thinking.

"No pressure or anything. You can still take your father to his appointments. I know you have other obligations that are more important. However, if you're interested, perhaps we could brainstorm some of your ideas today after the shop closes. Then we could head out to the hardware store on Sunday morning. Let me know."

If she worked extra hours here, that would also mean that Ginger could possibly spend extra time caring for her father. That would be great. Ginger was retired, so she had even more time to bond with Pops. Maya didn't want to return to New York knowing that his relationship with Ginger was a superficial one. He didn't have any family in Charleston.

The thought of her father and Ginger ever breaking up tugged at Maya. Her father would be heartbroken and alone again.

"You look deep in thought," he said, laughing. "Hey, it was an idea, but we don't have to go through with it if that's not your thing. I understand."

He really didn't understand. Not in the least.

"I have to pick up Jamila from her friend's house shortly," he added. "I'm pretty sure that she's having the time of her life with her friend and all, but I'd like to spend as much quality time with her as I can."

That's when it hit her again. Quality time with Pops. That opportunity would be gone once she returned to New York. Could Maya trust that her father and Ginger would still be solid—even after she left?

Even if it didn't work out between them, Maya would have to trust that Pops would be okay in the end. Working on this extra project with Derek would also require that Maya let go of her expectations of what Pops's happiness looked like. Well, not fully let go, but at least a little bit. Ginger could check in on her father on the days that Maya worked late. It would definitely help Maya to earn some overtime cash. That would be a good thing.

"Let me call my father and let him know that I'll be working a little late today," Maya said.

Derek's eyes lit up. "So you're willing to help out with the renovation?"

"As long as you're willing to pay me and I can figure out the logistics with my father." She smiled.

"Cool."

Maya left and headed over to the store's landline and dialed her home number. Her father picked up on the second ring.

"Hey, honey," Maya's father said. "I saw the store's number on the caller ID. You're checking in on me again. I told you everything was fine."

She cracked two knuckles. Now that she was actually on the phone and had to say something, had to actually show some trust, she was all nervous.

"Maya? You still there?"

"I'm still here. I was just calling because, well, um . . ." *Say it, Maya. Just say it.* "I wanted to let you know that I'll probably be working late tonight . . . and for a couple of nights after that. There's a big project going on here at the bridal shop, and Derek needs the extra help. I'm still taking you to physical therapy. That hasn't changed."

"I'm glad you're spending more time at the boutique. That's great."

That's it? That's all he had to say? No *Oh, darling, I wanted to spend more time with you while you were here?* None of that. "I was also thinking that perhaps Ginger could make you dinner tonight or something. I don't know. It was just an idea." Maya's voice turned all warbly. This letting go stuff was hard.

There was silence on the other end, which made Maya's heart ramp up a couple of beats.

"Sounds like a plan. I'll call Ginger . . . And, Maya?"

"Yes?"

"I'll be okay. You know this, right?"

He would be okay. No matter what. "I know." Maya said a quick goodbye and hung up the phone. She actually did it. Now all she had to do was focus on this store stuff.

Derek waved at her and called out. "Everything good?"

"It is. I'll stay here late today."

"Excellent. Operation Save Always a Bride shall begin," he said.

And Operation Save Maya would begin too, because the way Derek winked at her just now made her skin feel a tad too tingly.

Chapter Six

The following Sunday morning, Derek arrived at the hardware store fifteen minutes before it opened. Maya's sedan wasn't in the parking lot yet. The thought of her arrival made him jittery. Or perhaps it was the three cups of black coffee that he'd downed getting ready for this day.

He hoped this remodel and trunk show would help him bring in enough profit to catch up on the late mortgage payments. He had a little more than a month to pay the bank, which refused to work out an alternative payment arrangement. Derek already started marketing and advertising for the trunk show in anticipation of the event. Hopefully, this plan would work.

Derek turned off his ignition and drummed his fingers on the steering wheel. He decided against bringing Jamila along today. No need for more drama. She went to New Life with Ginger this morning. Maybe one day, he'd make Sunday morning services a norm again.

Another part of him didn't see the point in returning to church or doing anything spiritual. For what? Why try to talk to God when God obviously didn't have his best interests in mind? Two deaths in the span of a few years was more than he could bear. Nope, not even going there.

He bit his inner lip. Then again, Jamila was so excited about the youth group's cookout, which New Life was hosting next week. Her excitement was refreshing, and he really wanted to be a part of it—that is, he wanted to spend time with his daughter at the cookout. The fact that the cookout was to raise money for a new building and to donate to the Black history museum and the church's Black History Society was a good thing too. Perhaps he would go. It wasn't like attending a place of worship since it would be at a park. It was a way to move forward after the tragedy three years ago, move forward in his own way.

Would Jamila want him around for an entire day? Probably not. Someone else would have to be present to smooth things over. Someone neutral and not involved.

Seconds later, Maya's sedan pulled into view, and something in him flipped. The feeling reminded him of the first time he had gone on a date with Grace. He was so nervous. Derek even spilled spaghetti sauce on his shirt at the Italian restaurant they'd visited. That was when he knew Grace was someone special. Derek never lost his cool.

He hopped out of his truck and headed her way. She was exiting her car too. As she did, the sunlight hit her hair at the perfect angle, and it reflected the gold and amber in her dark curls. He hadn't noticed those colors before. She'd been wearing her hair natural lately. He liked it. "Morning."

"Morning." She pressed the auto-lock button on her key fob and adjusted her purse on her shoulder. "Ready to shop?"

"Shop on a budget," he said. "I'm not made of money, remember? I gotta get current on the mortgage."

"Don't worry. I'm confident this will work." She smiled and headed toward the store entrance. Derek followed. Once inside the store, the cool air from the vents brushed against his skin, sending a chill down his arms.

"I brought the rough sketch of the new floor plan," Maya said. "I was thinking that after we figure out the paint colors and all, I would head to a garage sale."

"Garage sale? For what?"

"We'll need some set pieces that will blend in with the new color on the walls and the new carpeting. I'm pretty sure the settee you have won't work anymore."

"We'll see. I can't spend too much money," Derek said. "I can rebrand without set pieces."

Maya stopped in the aisle next to the fertilizer and gardening supplies. "Oh really? How?"

"Get the paint in the same color scheme as the settee." He gave her two thumbs up.

A smirk formed at Maya's full lips. "You actually think keeping an eighties color scheme is a good idea? First of all, they probably don't even carry those colors anymore. Not unless you want an outdated vibe."

"Ouch." Derek feigned offense. "You know you're talking about my mama when you say those things."

"I'm pretty sure your mama would agree. Her style was popular for the time, but now we need something new. Something modern and fresh."

Maya was right. If his mother were alive, she'd probably agree. When he was a kid, his mother was always so fussy about the store's appearance. She had a fashion designer's eye too, but she never did anything with it, unfortunately. Owning a bridal shop was her next best thing to being a designer.

His heart squeezed. Derek missed his mother dearly.

"Want to look at some color swatches?" Maya asked, snapping him out of his thoughts.

"That's what we're here for."

They spent the next forty-five minutes looking at ten different shades of blue, fifteen shades of pink, and thirteen shades of green. Discussing color variations was making him anxious. "Is it really this serious, Maya? I mean, we can go with whatever. I'm sure you'll be able to make it work."

She gave him a half-smile. "Different colors give off different messages. When I was in design school, I took an entire course on color psychology. It matters. With that in mind, how do you want people to feel when they step into your boutique?"

"I don't know." Derek shrugged. "Like they want to spend their money. And lots of it."

Maya's face brightened, and it was enough to send a ray of sunshine through him. This lady was special.

"I guess I'll make the decisions on the colors. We're going to need a little more nuance than 'spend money.' Most folks come to a store wanting an entire experience. That could mean feeling special or appreciated or like an insider on something exclusive. That sort of thing." Maya laid out three swatches of pale blue and positioned them next to a swatch of ivory.

"Those all look good to me. I'll let you be the judge, since you took a college-level course in this and all."

"Really? You trust me with the store that much?"

Derek paused. "Of course I do."

An uncomfortable silence stretched between them.

"Did I say something wrong, Maya?"

"No. Nothing wrong at all. I guess I'm so used to Laura Whitcomb being nitpicky that I expect the worst."

"You don't have to worry about that with me." He tapped his index finger on a paint can. "I like your way of going about things at the store. You make every customer feel at ease, while I'm a bull in a china shop."

Maya's laughter sent a smile across his face. Yeah, she was cool.

"We'll go with these." She set a pale blue and ivory swatch before him. "I think they're understated, yet classy. These colors will do well with any style of dress that you display at the store. They're timeless and elegant."

Much like you. Did he just think that? He needed to rein in his musings.

After she picked out the colors, they decided on a carpet to match, and Derek purchased everything on the business credit card. When the total amount flashed on the cash register, Derek did a double take. "That was three hundred dollars less than I was anticipating."

"Told ya I would get you a good deal without sacrificing quality." Maya tucked a stray curl behind her ear. "I know how to pinch pennies. I bet you anything that I'll find some good chairs and chaises at the garage sale too."

"I bet you can."

She checked her watch. "I may have to make a quick go of it, however. I'm supposed to check out a shop for my boss in New York and then meet my father at New Life this afternoon too."

"Oh . . . I haven't been there in years." He cleared his throat, not wanting to say why.

"The youth ministry is planning their annual cookout, and my father wants to sit in on the meetings."

"You're volunteering at their cookout?" Derek almost stuttered on his words.

"Nooo," she said carefully. "I don't have any room in my schedule to volunteer. I spend most of my early morning working on dresses before working at the boutique. My father used to volunteer with the youth ministry before he broke his hip. He still has an affinity for the young folks, and he just wanted to listen in. But me? Volunteer? No way. Not happening. I won't be able to fit that in my schedule now that I'm working extra hours at the store."

She was really committed to helping him with the boutique. The whole saving money part helped tip the scales in her favor even more. He liked her, a lot.

Well, not in a personal "a lot." More like in a professional "a lot." That made sense.

Why was he overthinking this?

She took her car keys out of her purse, and they jangled between her fingers. "Better get going. See you tomorrow morning."

He wanted to ask her to the cookout, but if he did, that could anger Jamila. The last thing he needed was to anger Jamila again. "See you tomorrow morning."

They fell into step with each other and headed to the parking lot. Once there, nervousness overcame him, and he felt like a school kid who secretly crushed on a girl in his class. This was way too overwhelming.

"How's your father doing with his recovery and all?" he asked.

"He's getting there. Physical therapy is going well. I'm so glad that Ginger's helping out when I'm working late. She's a godsend."

"Ginger's a miracle worker," he said. *And so are you.*

These thoughts about Maya were coming out of nowhere, and they were coming quicker and quicker. Perhaps if he asked her and her father to come to the cookout together, it wouldn't look so odd. It wouldn't look strange to Jamila—or Maya. They'd just happen to be there, and Derek would just happen to be there as well, even though he hadn't been at anything church related in ages. "I was thinking of attending that cookout too. Jamila seemed pretty excited about it. Hopefully, I'll get to see you and your father there."

He phrased his words carefully. It wasn't an invitation per se, just a casual mention of faint interest.

Why was this so complicated?

It was complicated because his feelings were getting complicated, and he needed to tread carefully here. One wrong move, and he could completely alienate Jamila. Also, seeing Maya outside of a work-related function would be a tiny step toward . . .

Toward what, Derek? What do you want from this?

There wasn't anything to want. She was a nice lady, talented too. Just wanted to get to know her a bit better. That was all.

"Dad really misses working with the young folks, so I'll most likely drive him to the cookout."

"You'll stay there too?" The question flew out of his mouth before he had the time to temper it.

Maya's eyebrows lifted.

Was she delighted? Or was he reading into it too much?

"They're using the proceeds from the event for some good causes. I don't mind being a part of that."

"I'll be there too, since I'm driving Jamila and all." He tipped his baseball cap to her. "I'll see you at the store tomorrow morning, Maya."

"See you tomorrow." She slid on her dark sunglasses, and they parted ways.

Happiness. That was what sprung up within him as he headed to his truck. He hadn't had much happiness of late, but for this one little moment, Derek decided to revel in it.

DID DEREK INADVERTENTLY ask her out yesterday?

Nah. He was just being friendly.

Friendly. Friendly. Friendly.

Yet the question invaded Maya's thoughts as she worked on the initial renovations of the store early the next morning at the boutique. Maya had arrived at the store two hours before it opened to get started. She laid the tarp down in the back corner of the store where the painting project would begin and covered the baseboards with painter's tape.

How did he end up pseudo-asking her out anyway? She pressed the mental Replay button, and the conversation filtered through her head. Something about saving money. Then her father. Then the cookout. Then Derek's mention of wanting to see her at the cookout.

Maya was way overthinking this one. He was just being friendly. The end.

After they parted ways at the hardware store, Maya checked out a boutique for Laura. Afterward, Maya headed to a garage sale in her neighborhood alone. She didn't find the exact chairs for the store, but she did find some cute royal-wedding-themed decor. Brides loved to feel special on their wedding day—rightly so—and having a few royal-themed pieces in the boutique would add a special touch.

She just needed to stop considering this whole Derek thing and focus on her job, which was to bring in lots of sales and make sure this place looked up to date. That was all. Anything else could jeopardize her work, even musings about "friendly invites" to church cookouts.

The first thing on Maya's agenda was painting and decorating, not thinking about Derek.

Maya popped the lid off the paint can, and the scent of the fumes wafted up her nostrils, metallic and heady. Whew. That smell was both gross and addictive. She dipped her paintbrush into the can of pale blue paint and got to work.

"This looks fabulous, Maya."

The sound of Derek's voice made her paint a crooked zig-zag along the wall.

He stopped. "Oh. Sorry, I broke your concentration."

"Not a problem," she said, though his presence most definitely distracted her. Maya glanced in the direction of the miniature castle with the horse and buggy display, which she'd positioned to the right of a mannequin. It glittered underneath the store lights. "You like my idea over there?" She pointed to the display.

"I surely do. It wasn't something I'd come up with."

Derek brushed his fingers along the chrome carriage wheel. "Where'd you get it?"

Maya told him about her garage sale finds.

"Excellent." He stepped to the right, and the shadows fell across his face just so, emphasizing the sharp planes and angles of his features. Man, he was a cutie.

Nope. Nope. Nope. Not going there. Maya dipped her paintbrush in the can and brushed over the zigzag. This man was not going to mess with her focus. Not happening.

Her phone alarm dinged, and she glanced at the screen. It was time for her to take her medication. Maya wasn't going to forget that again. She set the brush in the bowl of water and put the lid back on the paint can. "Will you excuse me for a minute? I have to do something real quick."

"Sure. No problem. The store won't open for a while anyway, and it's a weekday."

"I won't be long." She stood and quickly headed to the break room. *Better get this over with fast so that he won't notice anything.*

Maya stepped inside the break room and got her purse out of the locker. Her medicine was right there. She then grabbed her water bottle from the fridge and twisted open the pill container's cap. She'd have to do this about two more times during the workday.

Just then, the break room's door creaked open. Her skin tightened. *Oh God. Oh God. Oh God.*

"Maya?"

It was Derek. What in the world? Her body was facing his, and so he saw the pills, the pill bottle, and the water bottle. Shame washed over her like a soggy, cold fog. Maya couldn't even move. Her entire being froze.

He looked down at her hands, and Maya could see that he was trying to assess her state. Judging her, just like Rex, her ex-fiancé, used to do.

Early into their dating relationship, Rex had walked in on her when she was just coming out of a particularly painful episode of sickle cell. She called her doctor immediately, worried that she needed to be hospitalized. She'd lived with the illness all her life, but its effects had grown stronger. The nurse on call calmed her fears and basically said the disease worsens with age, worsens as she nears her . . . life expectancy. From here on out, the only thing Maya could do was manage it.

After she'd gotten off the phone, Rex had a million questions. Most of them centered around how this illness would affect them (meaning him). She told him that she'd understand if he couldn't be with her anymore. She told him it would be hard to be in a relationship with her, knowing she had a limited time. Even though Rex had known about her illness well before they were dating, Maya said he could back out now if he thought it was too much.

Rex said that her illness didn't matter, that he still wanted to date her. Yet after that moment, he changed. She ignored the signs and kept going along with their relationship—right up until that fateful wedding day when he ditched her.

He proved to be a selfish prick, and he broke her heart—all because Rex was too cowardly to express his true feelings about her illness.

Maya had feared that would happen, but she always hoped that it wouldn't. She always hoped that Rex would be more honest with himself and what he could deal with—before all her emotions came into play, before she wanted to spend the rest of her life with him. Didn't happen.

While Derek wasn't Maya's fiancé, she now feared losing her job if he found out. Who needed a sick girl on their payroll, even for a few months? Maya was a liability, not an asset to Derek's business.

He didn't know that yesterday, when he was boasting about her skills and budget sense, but he would know that now.

"You okay?"

The question of the century. No. She was not okay. "I'm great."

He kept looking at the pill bottle.

This was what Maya hated about having a chronic illness. Once people knew of it, or at least that something was "wrong," they started looking at her differently and treating her differently too. They could even fire her.

She didn't want to get fired, at least not on account of this. If it was because of Jamila, then fine, Maya had no problems walking, but if she lost this job because of sickle cell, it would prove what she'd always feared—she wasn't enough.

Maya tossed the pill bottle back in her purse. If she lied and Derek found out, then that wouldn't be good either. She had surmised that Derek was the type of guy who valued honesty, and so did she. Maya wouldn't want to break his trust.

But there was no use in telling him since she was only here temporarily. "I was just taking ibuprofen," she said. "I was getting a headache. That's all."

His expression held a mixture of disbelief and belief. The seeds of distrust were already being planted. Not good, but it was the best out of two bad options. Maya wasn't going to give Derek a reason to see her as fragile. She couldn't do that.

"Oh, okay then," Derek said. "A customer arrived, and she started asking some highly detailed questions about your dresses. I figured you'd be the best person to answer them."

"I'll be there," Maya said quickly.

He closed the break room door. After he left, Maya collapsed into the green hard-backed chair. He didn't believe her, and she didn't blame him.

Even though she hated the idea of hiding this secret, Maya wouldn't tell him the truth. Maya's illness was not Derek's business. Her illness was her own burden to carry.

Chapter Seven

Something wasn't right with Maya, and that bothered him. No matter how much Derek tried to shake it off, his sense of unease hadn't lifted. She said she was taking ibuprofen, but that didn't look like an ibuprofen bottle.

When he'd walked in on her in the break room, the air shifted. It tightened and stifled and suffocated. For the rest of the workweek, things had been on edge between them. They spoke in short clips, and Maya never looked him in the eye.

Would this carry on today at the cookout? Would Maya even be at the cookout? He didn't know.

He pulled his truck onto the highway and headed south to Battery Park in downtown Charleston. Jamila was in the passenger seat, quiet. When he'd told her that he was taking her to the park today, she didn't react either way, and that was a good thing. Before she would've changed her mind about going.

Should he mention the possibility of Maya being there? If

he did, and Maya ended up being a no-show, he would've been stressing out over nothing. If he didn't tell her, and then Maya ended up being there, Jamila would be angry.

"You excited about today?" he asked.

"Yes." She kicked at the volleyball lying at her feet. "We're gonna have a volley match today. I'm hoping to win it."

"You could. I'll be cheering you on regardless."

Jamila didn't say a word. Derek couldn't tell whether she was moved by his statement or not.

"You know I love you forever, right?" Derek asked. "Nothing will change that."

Jamila shifted in her seat and leaned on the armrest. "I know."

She agreed. Breakthrough! Maybe he could ease into a conversation about the possibility of Maya being present today. "I heard that Carl Jackson used to be active in the youth ministry before his injury. You know of him?"

Her eyes lit up. "He's a cool guy. Old but cool for an old guy."

Making progress. Making progress. "You know of his daughter?" That next set of words came out slowly.

She was quiet. "It's Maya. I know. He always brags about her."

"I know you don't want to be around her, and I respect that completely. However, Maya may be at the cookout today. I just wanted to give you a heads-up."

"What?" she asked, incredulous. "Is that why you're here

today? So you can see her?"

"No. No. No," he said, but Derek sensed that his "noes" meant nothing to Jamila.

"Then why'd you bring her up?"

Good question. Why did he bring her up? Was he fully, 100 percent committed to giving Jamila a heads-up, or was it something else? "I mentioned Maya since I know how you feel about her. I didn't want you to be surprised or anything."

Her silence sliced through him, harsh and deep.

"Dad, you haven't stepped foot in the church since Mom died. Even when I kept going to services with Ginger, you never came along. I'd hoped you'd do that, for my sake, but you didn't. You don't care."

"I do care about you, Jamila."

"You don't. You're only going to this cookout today for that woman, not for me. Stop lying to yourself and just admit the truth."

"Admit the truth"? "What truth, Jamila?"

"That you're interested in her." Her voice was filled with hurt.

He thought Maya was attractive, but that didn't mean he was interested. Still, Jamila just called him out on his sudden interest in church-related activities. Those actions spoke. Those actions told a different story. "Jamila, I'm trying to move forward from your mother's death. The mass shooting at the church tore me up inside. I'm not just here to see Maya. I'm here because I want to take a tiny step forward toward healing."

Jamila was silent. "Really?"

"Really."

Jamila crossed her arms. "Then promise me you won't date Maya. Ever."

"Ever"? Did Derek really want to close that door when Maya was one of the best things to step into his life since Grace died?

Whoa.

Maya was one of the best things to step into his life since Grace died. He hadn't realized it before, but now he did. Maya brought hope into his life. Hope that the boutique could be saved. Hope that he could even start going to church functions again. Hope that he could move on.

The idea of shutting out the possibility of being something more with Maya hurt. Derek's life had become one big sacrifice, and Maya had helped him see beyond that, even if she didn't intend to do so.

He gave his all to his family all the time. The only reason he'd joined the military was because it provided the best benefits for Grace and Jamila. Doing so had been the right decision. Derek didn't want to become a deadbeat dad like his father had been to him.

"Promise," Jamila repeated.

The hurt in her voice hadn't left, and he sensed it carried with it a ton of memories that he wouldn't be able to erase or heal or mend. No matter his feelings toward Maya, he had a duty to Jamila first. That was what he'd learned in the military, right? Duty first. He shoved his feelings about Maya in a closet, never to return again.

Things were broken between Jamila and him. They could be permanently broken. The notion ripped him apart. No "interest" in Maya or any person was worth that. "I promise, Jamila. I won't date her or anyone. I'm only here for you."

Jamila sniffled, and he glanced over at her quickly. Her eyes shone with tears, and his heart carried all of them. He exited the highway and made a much slower drive to the park.

They drove in silence for a long while, and the weight of his words pressed down on him even more. *No feelings toward Maya. No feelings toward Maya. No feelings toward Maya.*

That was the best way.

"Dad, do you want to play volleyball on my team at the cookout?"

Volleyball? She'd never asked him to play volleyball or anything with her. Perhaps he'd made the right decision after all. "I'd love that, Jamila." He glanced her way.

"Thanks, Dad." Jamila wiped a tear from her cheek, but another one soon followed.

How can I fix this wound between us? How can Jamila and I be a family again?

Derek didn't know.

THE COOKOUT WAS surprisingly chill, even for Maya. She'd

been so busy since she arrived in Charleston that she hadn't had time to attend New Life's services at its temporary building.

To be honest, Maya was low-key avoiding coming to the cookout. First, Maya wanted to avoid Derek outside of their work environment.

Having Derek see her with those pills the other day was extremely inopportune, and she still hadn't figured out how to just "be" around him after that event. There was always going to be the possibility that he'd ask her more questions, that he'd probe into her personal life. Questions about her medications or her dizzy spell could arise at any moment, and she didn't want to answer them.

To make things worse, New Life was like her extended family, and as with all families, it had its share of black sheep. Some folks thought she was "straying from the faith" because she suddenly moved to New York to pursue her dream. Some members of the congregation thought New York City was too wild.

No one asked her why becoming a successful bridal gown designer was so important to her. They didn't care about that.

Taking a break from fielding not-so-polite questions about why she was back in South Carolina, Maya found an empty spot at the edge of a long table and scrolled through her inbox on her phone. Her heart skipped when she saw an email from Laura Whitcomb. She was responding to the dress designs that Maya had sent. Despite her hesitation, Maya opened the message.

Dear Maya,

Thanks for checking out those other bridal shops for me. A last-minute project came up, and so I'm going to hold on partnering with a boutique for now.

Also, I looked over the designs for both the Ashley Tate gig and the head designer gig. They both don't work. The Ashley Tate design is too avant-garde for Ashley's brand, and so you won't be working on that assignment.

Your submission for the head designer position looks . . . amateurish. I don't understand why you would have those zigzag patterns on the dresses. And those shells embroidered into the hem? What are they? Doesn't make sense. Can you revise the dress design and send me a picture? I'll look it over.

—Laura

Maya expected this, and yet she'd hoped that Laura would see that the designs were innovative. The cowrie shells represented wealth in West African culture, and the "zigzag" designs, as Laura put it, were indigenous Filipino patterns. Just because Laura was plain and traditional didn't change the fact that Maya found inspiration in her own heritage or that she wanted the dresses she designed to reflect something of her in their design. It was important to Maya to use these patterns because her mother taught her them. Maya wanted to hold on to that. Maya sighed. This sucked, but she'd try again. She'd have to tone things down for Laura.

Maya replied to the email with a professional response, stating that she'd send Laura a revised dress. Then she tossed her phone in her purse, bummed about not getting the Ashley Tate gig, but Maya was still holding out for the head designer position.

How was she supposed to enjoy herself after all of that? She'd make herself enjoy the cookout. Maya was just here for her dad. She would just interact as little as possible with all the people here, especially Derek.

Maya still wasn't able to get that moment when he'd walked in on her while she was taking her medication out of her mind. She'd been halfway looking forward to seeing him in person today—if he hadn't seen her in the break room.

Maya headed over to the refreshment table, intent on stuffing her face with pretzels and cheese until the event was done.

"Maya? Is that you?"

Her skin pricked. She would recognize that voice anywhere. Louise, her former high school classmate and current frenemy. Ever since that time Louise stuck an unopened stick of deodorant in her locker during their sophomore year of high school, Maya couldn't stand her. Louise had spread this awful rumor around school that Maya had body odor. It wasn't true, but Louise was cruel like that.

Maya turned and fake smiled, trying hard to push aside that memory from her brain bank. Yet those memories died hard. "Hey, Louise." She kept her voice even and civil.

Louise had changed since high school. She looked as if she'd aged two decades. Her skin held a dull gray tone. Her eyes were scattered and tired, hair graying at the temples. Life must've taken a toll on her.

"You're back in town!" Louise said.

Maya nodded once, forcing herself to be civil.

"Weren't you a . . ." Louise's gaze shifted up and to the right as if she was trying her hardest to remember. "You did something with clothes. Were you a seamstress?"

Maya cringed inside. "Close but not quite." Her voice clipped every word. "I'm a bridal gown designer, Louise."

"I remember. You left for New York and everything. What happened with that? It didn't work out?" Louise's voice was casually cruel, friendly with a hint of snark.

"Nothing happened to it. I'm still a bridal gown designer. I'm down here temporarily for my father."

"Ahh. I'm sure it's competitive up there and all. Must be hard for you to gain a footing. Everything's so fast-paced in the big city." Her words held that same mocking tone.

Maya took two deep breaths. Did Louise not hear a word

of what Maya had said? She wasn't a struggling dress designer like Louise was implying. Perhaps Louise didn't want to hear her. Whatever. "I'm only down here for my father. Temporarily."

"Oh."

"I haven't quit my career," Maya said.

"That's too bad. Perhaps then you would've been able to make a nice home and family for yourself. Like me." Louise held up her left hand and showed off her engagement ring.

What a louse. "What's that supposed to mean?"

"Exactly what I said. If you would've laid off that career of yours, perhaps you and Rex would still be together."

This woman was throwing shade! "Whatev—"

"Now Rex and I are engaged."

Maya's eyes widened. "Engaged?"

"Yes. Engaged."

"For how long?"

"About two months now."

Two months. Good for them. Looking back on that relationship, Maya was too young, too naive, and way too hopeful when she was with Rex. She'd never settle for someone like him today. "Congratulations."

"Thank you! I'll see you around. Good luck again with that designer thing." Louise gave Maya a half-wave and then sauntered off.

"That designer thing"? Louise was so petty. Maya grabbed a handful of chips and tossed them on her plate. People like

Louise were the very reason Maya refused to get comfortable down south. Why should she with hecklers around?

Just as Maya was going to look for her father, Derek's pickup truck pulled up to the curb. A hush came over the rest of the church crowd. Hmm. What was that about?

Maya had the sudden urge to hide out from Derek. "No need to fret about it," she whispered to herself. "Act normal."

Acting normal meant being away from most of the people here. Period. Louise had given her enough conversation for the day. She scanned the crowd for her father but didn't see him. So Maya spotted a shade tree and went into Operation Introvert Mode. All she needed to do was hang out there for a few hours, and then she'd be good to go.

She brought her belongings over to the magnolia and plopped down. "Looks like it's just you and me, tree," she said, munching on a chip.

Despite good intentions, Maya couldn't keep her focus off Derek. What did he think when he saw her with the pill bottle?

"Hey, love."

Her father's voice pulled her out of her thoughts. "I was looking for you, Pops."

"Why are you hanging out by yourself?" Pops swung his wheelchair closer to her.

Because I don't want to be around people like Louise. "Just chilling over here." She smiled. "Nothing to be concerned about."

He gave her one of those *you can't fool me* looks. "I saw you talking to Louise. Didn't you two go to high school together?"

Oh Lordy. "Unfortunately, yes. She's engaged. To Rex." And that was all Maya was gonna say about that.

Pop's brows lifted. "Oh really?"

"Really." Maya rested her chin in her hands. "You know what? I'm glad Louise and Rex found each other. She didn't have to be all snippy about it, though."

Her father shook his head. "I know you're not going to let one person ruin your fun. Come on with me. We're playing spades near the grill."

Maya didn't budge.

"All righty then. I know Louise hasn't been the kindest to you, but you can't toss them all into the same basket, Maya. There are more good people here to cancel out one bad interaction." Her father gestured in the general direction of where Derek stood and watched Jamila play volleyball. "Wait a second. Is that Jamila's father? He's the one who hired you, right?"

Maya hadn't even told him about the fiasco that popped up at the store. "Correct."

"It's amazing that he's here. I heard that Derek used to attend New Life when he wasn't on deployments. That was way before I started attending. He stopped coming to services after his wife died in the shooting."

Maya's eyes widened. "She did?"

"Yes, she did."

Maya's heart crimped. "That's so awful. Derek never mentioned it. I can understand why, though."

"I would like to say hello. I never met him. He seems like a fine young man. Can you introduce me?"

Maya pursed her lips. This new piece of information about how Derek's wife died would make talking to him even more uncomfortable. If she introduced her father to Derek, then she'd have to get over her insecurities about the other day too. That would be unnerving.

If she didn't introduce them, then her father would probe, and she really didn't want to explain it all to Pops. Plus, her father could be a buffer between the awkwardness. "Sure, Dad. I'll introduce you."

She stood and wiped the blades of grass from the heels of her palms. Her father appeared to be waiting patiently. She grasped the handles of Pops's wheelchair, and they moved toward Derek. Maya was moving slower than slow. That was purposeful. It gave her time to work out what she'd say to Derek and how she'd say it. No matter what, she'd try not to be too strange.

Derek's back was to them, and Maya glanced in the direction of Jamila's volleyball game. She was on the team that wore white shirts, and her face was glistening with sweat. Jamila focused intently on volleying the ball.

Derek was watching his daughter closely, doing the dad thing.

And Maya was about to interrupt. It was bad enough that Jamila didn't like her. Maya shouldn't interrupt this moment when Derek was focusing on his daughter.

Maya's steps slowed until she stopped pushing her father's wheelchair. "Maybe I should introduce you later on. He seems busy."

"Bah!" Her father waved her off. "You're overthinking things, Maya. He's just watching the volleyball game. I wanted to watch it too. Come on. Push me or I'll roll myself."

"O-kay." She pushed him in Derek's direction. Then they stood before Derek, and Maya waved. His face was serious for about three seconds, and then he smiled. "Nice to see you, Maya." He switched his red Solo cup from his left to his right hand. "And this must be . . . ?"

"My father, Carl Jackson."

"Nice to meet you," her father said, extending his hand.

"Likewise." Derek shook her father's hand. "It's been so long since I've been around most of the congregation. I'm getting reacclimated."

"We're all glad that you're here," Pops said.

Derek glanced away, a shadow of sadness covering his eyes. Then Derek looked at Maya and her father. "I see the resemblance. Although I have to say, Mr. Jackson, that Maya is much prettier."

Heat climbed up Maya's cheeks. Good thing Blasian girls didn't blush.

"Maya gets that from her mother," Pops said. "She was a beauty."

"I'm pretty sure she was."

Self-conscious, Maya glanced at the brown sandals on her feet and the bright blue polish on her toenails.

A chorus of cheers filled Battery Park. Maya redirected all her attention on the game. Jamila's team had scored a goal.

"Your daughter is playing well," Pops said. "Jamila is a wonderful girl. You must be proud."

A wave of unease filtered through Maya, and Derek glanced in Maya's direction, as if questioning whether she had told her father about Jamila.

"She's the best." Derek crossed his arms. "I'm lucky to be her father. On our way here, she was raving about you, Mr. Jackson."

"She was?" Maya and her father asked in unison.

"She was. Jamila loves New Life, and I think a lot of it has to do with you and the youth ministry."

If Jamila loved her father so much, then there could be hope for Maya to mend things with her.

Pops smiled. "Once I get up and running again, I hope to be more involved. The physical therapist said I should be transitioning to a walker in the next few weeks or so."

"Good to hear, Mr. Jackson," Derek said.

The speakers near the DJ booth squeaked to life, and Maya closed her eardrums with her fingers.

"All right, ladies and gents. I know that y'all are enjoying this volleyball game, but no cookout is complete without some dancing." The DJ put on some dark shades and twisted his baseball cap to the side. "So let's get some folks on this grassy dance floor."

Maya turned her attention to her sandals and toenail polish again. Seemed like the best place to focus her energy.

"I'm going to find Ginger," Pops said. "I may not be able to dance right now, but I can sway from side to side with my lady."

"My lady"? This was too precious. "I love that you want to dance, but you're still recovering. You don't want to move around too much and get injured."

"I'm fine, darling. See you kids later," her father said, and then he winked.

What was that wink about? Was her father trying to send her a message or something? He left, and Maya stood next to Derek. Discomfort edged through her. "Nice to know that Jamila and my father get along," she said to Derek.

"I've been thinking about that ever since Jamila mentioned your father." Derek didn't elaborate.

Was that a good thing? Maya could only see it as a good thing. If Jamila loved Pops, then that had to be a positive step in the right direction.

Maybe coming to this cookout wasn't a bad thing after all. It was the perfect opportunity to get to know Derek outside of work and show him she wasn't physically ill (or at least pretend that she wasn't ill). She could also build on the good seeds her father had planted with Jamila. Derek and Maya could start with a dance, right?

Maybe not. Derek already lost his wife. It wouldn't be fair to get involved with him. Maya didn't want Derek to deal with her health issues too.

This was complicated, but after seeing how her father put them at ease, Maya placed her bets on hope.

"Would you like to dance?" Maya blurted the question.

Derek's face turned a shade of grim that Maya hadn't seen before. Regret bubbled within her, and a flushed heat made her cheeks tingle. Not good.

"I don't think that's a good idea." Derek's words came out slow and pained, as if he had to force himself to say them.

Embarrassment hung on her like a deadweight. "O-kay. I thought I'd ask." She motioned to the dancers. "Looked like they were having a good time out there."

"They are. And that's fine you asked. Completely fine."

Not "fine" enough since you said no. "Enjoy the rest of the cookout. Nice to see you here." Maya left and zipped right on over to the tree, to her comfortable spot. How stupid of her to assume he wanted to dance. Even more, how stupid of her to think she could have a fighting chance with Derek.

Maya glanced over at happy little Louise, and sadness poked at her. Maybe Derek turning her down was a blessing in disguise. She shouldn't be thinking about building connections when Derek had lost so much. He'd experienced a lot of grief already. No need to even try.

Chapter Eight

Maya opened the store early the following Tuesday, arriving there before Derek. She needed to get her head in the right place for today, and that meant owning up to the fact that yes, she'd made a fool of herself at the cookout. She should've never taken the liberty of asking Derek to dance.

First, he'd already mentioned his priority was Jamila—which meant his priority wasn't bridal gown designers based in New York. Second, the fact that he was returning to a church-related event after his wife died so tragically at a church, well—Maya should not get too friendly with him. Derek couldn't handle knowing about Maya's predicament after living through what he'd experienced. Third, hadn't she already told herself that work was first? Mixing up work with a man would only hurt her in the end. The sting at the cookout served as a potent reminder.

Soon as Derek arrived today, she would apologize. The last thing she needed was for there to be any tense moments between them. An apology would get rid of that right away. She was only working at the boutique to make money and take care of her father before returning to New York.

Maya flipped on the lights in the rear of the store and immediately started on painting the back walls. She'd spent the next hour painting when Derek entered the store. Their eyes met and he waved. "Morning, you're here early."

"I figured I'd get a head start on the remodel," she said.

"Head starts are good." He smiled. "I wish Jamila would've gotten a longer head start on her school project. She's still stressing about it, and I can't help her with it at all."

"The sewing one?"

"That's the one," Derek said.

Maya didn't say anything, seeing that she was on shaky ground with Jamila. No need for her to impose. She'd help if she could, but Jamila most likely didn't want her help. "I wanted to apologize to you."

His eyebrows raised. "Apologize for what?"

O-kay. Maybe he wasn't thinking about that uncomfortable moment at the cookout as much as she was. If that was the case, then this was going to be completely embarrassing. "About asking you to dance and all. I didn't mean to put you on the spot or anything."

He bit his lower lip. "When I declined, I didn't mean for that to be a slight on you. I just have a lot going on. I also wanted to focus on Jamila's game. She was pretty nervous about it and really wanted me to watch her play. That's all."

Maya nodded. She completely embarrassed herself all right. "Makes total sense. Guess we won't dwell on it then. I'll focus on painting." She returned to the work at hand, putting the finishing touches on the white trim on the baseboard. At least she'd gotten the apology out of her system; now they could return to being their normal selves—whatever that was.

The sound of Derek's footsteps made her heart skip. He was drawing near.

"I love the paint color, by the way. It looks great." He surveyed the place. "You're a godsend."

A godsend, but not cool enough to dance with. *Stop it, Maya.* "Thank you. Nice to hear a compliment every once in a while."

His eyes flashed for a quick second. "Did I do something wrong?"

"No. I wasn't referring to you. I was thinking about my boss back in New York. She's opinionated about my work. I mean, I know she thinks I'm a good designer and all since she hasn't fired me yet, but she rarely hands out a compliment. Her criticisms are harsh." Something squeezed inside of Maya. She would have to work on that redesign for Laura. Hopefully she wouldn't rip it to shreds this time.

"You like her to give compliments?" he asked.

Did she? She did. She cared about Laura's opinion way too much, and that bothered her. "I do. She's a talented woman who has made a big splash in the industry. Now that I've

worked for her, I see how she does it. How she's so successful. Laura works long hours. She's competitive and a perfec-
tionist. If that's what it takes to succeed, that's what I'll do."

"So you like the fast-paced, competitive nature of your
job?" he asked.

"Yes."

Derek clasped his hands behind his head and seemed to
consider her statement. "It was like that for me in the military, especially in the early years. I sacrificed a lot to get promoted. With each promotion came greater sacrifices. Cost
me a lot of time with my family. Time that I now can't get
back."

"I've always wanted to work for Laura Whitcomb. It's
been a dream of mine since . . ." She stopped talking. Last
thing she wanted to do was get into all her reasons for working for Laura.

"Since what?"

"Since Mama passed away nine years ago." The words
came out of her mouth slowly and deliberately. "She always
thought that Laura Whitcomb was the business. When I was
my mother's fashion design apprentice, she always hoped
that I'd work for Laura Whitcomb one day."

Derek tapped his fingers on the counter. "What are your
hopes?"

She did a double take. "What do you mean?"

"You mentioned what your mother hoped for you. What
do you hope for yourself?"

Discomfort flitted through her. What did she hope for herself? "I don't know."

Derek paused. "Laura Whitcomb is a pretty prestigious brand. The customers typically mention her dresses as ones they're considering, but I can't afford to put her merchandise in our inventory. Her wholesale prices are way too expensive. Still, she seems to be the design standard in the bridal gown world."

"That she is." The memory of Laura's last email came to life and stung.

"You don't sound too happy. What's on your mind?" Derek asked.

Maya took a deep breath. "The prestige of working for Laura Whitcomb comes at a cost, that cost being my creative freedom. I've tried to incorporate my signature Afro-Asian style into the Laura Whitcomb line. I've suggested a West African design pattern or a Filipino method of stitching. As soon as Laura saw it, she shot it down quick. Said that there wouldn't be a market for it anywhere. Sometimes working for Laura is like being tied in a straitjacket."

"Straitjacket." Maya let that word settle into her. It stabbed at something she'd never paid attention to before, something she held dear and close to her heart. It stabbed at her mother's advice.

Her mother's maxim to always stay true to herself rose in Maya's conscience, but on the other hand, her mother wanted her to work for Laura Whitcomb. Strange. The dichotomy was unnerving.

"A straitjacket? That's not good. Do you really want to work in a place where you're stifled?"

Did she really want to have this conversation right now? Gah! Why'd she say all of that aloud? Maya had never come close to this hard-hitting realization, yet standing in this tiny boutique made her do so, for some reason.

If she really let the idea stick, if she delved too deep into it, then she may find something even more unsettling underneath, something she didn't want to face. Perhaps she'd ignore the idea of her New York job being a straitjacket—yet ignoring this truth had led her to a quiet misery up north.

"Maya? Do you think working for Laura is worth compromising your creative freedom?"

She snapped out of her musings. "Yes?"

"So you really want to work in a place where you're not appreciated?"

It was best to bury the realization. Burying it was best. "I never considered it seriously until now. It's not that important really. Just some jibber-jabber. I really like my job."

Saying those last words sounded fake coming out of her mouth.

"I see . . . but maybe you should consider the limitations on your creative license. I wouldn't want to be in a place where my uniqueness was devalued." He nodded. "Working in the military, there's not much room for creativity. It's all about obeying orders and listening to your superiors. You're a designer. You should guard your creative freedom. Uniformity and following orders are a matter of life and death in the military, but it's not a matter of life and death in your industry."

Her heart revved. If only Derek knew. For Maya, dress design *was* life and death. If she was honest with herself, that was her one true hope: that she'd leave a legacy of beautiful Afro-Asian gowns behind for future brides to wear on their special day, especially since Maya would never ever become a bride herself. Not while living with sickle cell anemia.

She had to make something of the work she had created, the unique work she had created. Maya had to get it out and circulating in the world. Laura's micromanagement had stifled Maya in so many ways.

Thinking about Laura was unsettling. Better to push it aside.

"I'm very excited about this remodel." Derek walked around the store and inspected it more closely. "I've done some preliminary advertising for the trunk show. The next thing we need to do is get clear on a marketing plan. Can't have a pretty place without anyone to fill it. I have to bring in sales. The bank is waiting for their mortgage money."

"True. We need to bring in a good crowd. We can start with promoting and advertising the trunk show."

"I'd love to hear your ideas on that, Maya. Feel free to take creative liberties in how you promote the event, within budget of course. I don't think you'll go over budget. You have an eye for style and finances."

Exercising creative leeway was something she loved about working at Always a Bride. In addition to the remodel, Maya worked on new dress designs whenever the store wasn't busy. Creativity was Maya's oxygen. It gave her life. "There are a lot of ways that we can promote this event."

She tapped her chin, thinking. Cat Clyne was the biggest fashion reviewer and blogger in the industry. She ran a high-end website and started a print magazine two years ago that recently received national circulation. Maya did some emergency alterations for Cat's wedding gown last year. Cat had offered to return the favor one day. Perhaps this was that "one day."

"I know some media folks. They could possibly help out with publicity."

"Media contacts are great, especially if they're national ones."

Despite owing Maya a favor, Maya would have to make this little shop in Charleston appealing to Cat—appealing enough for Cat to travel down to cover the story. "We'll have to put a spin on the pitch. Something that'll pique the interest of readers. Something that'll grab their attention. We need a story."

"We need your story," Derek said quickly.

"Me?"

"Yes, you. Your story. I think you should not only have your dresses on consignment here, but we should feature them in the trunk show. The Afro-Asian slant on your gowns will be a definite draw, as well as the story behind it. How you apprenticed under your mother and she taught you Filipino stitching techniques." He rested his chin in his hands and studied her with admiration in his eyes. "Folks will love it."

Was she that interesting of a person? "I've only sold two of my dress designs. That hardly counts as a draw to an entire trunk show. Are you sure you want my dresses to be the main feature?"

"No one can believe in you like you do, Maya. That's the first thing."

She twisted her mouth. How did this turn into a pep talk? Did she really believe in her designs? Were they good enough to carry an entire trunk show? Maya wasn't sure. Also, doing a solo trunk show might jeopardize her career with Laura— and that would include her chances at being head designer. Even though Laura was allowing Maya to sell a few gowns since she was on leave without pay, an entire trunk show was a different story. Laura might think that Maya was trying to undermine her. "The boutique is the main attraction actually. What's the story behind the boutique? What led your mother to start this business? I recall you saying that she had a tough time with it in the beginning. What encouraged her to persevere?"

Derek was quiet for a moment. "After my grandmother died, she left a whole bunch of money to my mother. About one hundred thousand dollars of cash sitting in a savings account. We were surprised, because all Grandma did was clean houses for the White ladies living in the suburbs and sell her handwoven West African–style baskets to the tourists in downtown Charleston. She sold them pretty close to the Black history museum down the block. Grandma was Gullah Geechee to the core, and the basket weaving craft was passed down through generations. I believe even prior to the Civil War. My mother knew how to make sweetgrass baskets too."

"Does Jamila know?"

He shook his head. "Maybe. I never asked. Always been so busy on deployment."

There was a note of sadness in his voice. He probably carried so many regrets. Too many for Maya to know.

"Anyway, Grandma saved the money and Mama got it all when she died. The money came with a note. I framed it right over there." Derek gestured to a tiny frame hanging near the front door. "You can read it if you'd like."

Maya headed to the entrance. She hadn't noticed that frame before until he pointed it out. Then she read the note:

My dearest Vivian,

Our ancestors came here on ships as enslaved people. They arrived on new lands, and with new lands came new struggles. But we retained some of our ways. I sold my baskets right near

the docks where our people were enslaved and auctioned off.
This is our history. This money is the culmination of their
stories. Now it's for you. Do something good with it. Make
us proud.

Love,
Mama

Maya turned teary-eyed. "My goodness. That's beautiful."

"It is." Derek's voice hoarsened. "My mother opened this bridal shop and became the first Black business owner in downtown Charleston during the eighties. It was a big deal because so many Black-owned businesses shut down in the sixties and seventies. Hopefully she made them proud."

"I can see why you struggled with whether or not to sell this place. The story and this boutique are so meaningful to your family."

"They are. Mama had to take out a second mortgage on this place because of her cancer treatments. Still, I want to keep this place. I want to continue to do right by them."

Maya bit her lip. This was a chance for her to do something good. "If you're looking for an angle to pitch your story, then the boutique's history will be it. Heck, it could even rally folks together to want to keep this place in business. The boutique is living history."

"True. I'm trying to preserve something that is in danger

of dying," Derek said.

Dying. There was that word again. She was dying. Perhaps giving life to Always a Bride was another way that Maya could make an impact—before she died. "I will help you do that."

"So you'll feature your designs here too?" Derek asked. "It'll be an added bonus to showcasing the store's history. Are you in?"

An unsettledness overcame Maya. Was it worth putting it out there? If Maya didn't feature her gowns in the trunk show, she'd never get the chance to see if her work had merit on its own. She'd never get a chance to leave that legacy she so desperately wanted.

Laura had torn down her work before. If Maya took that risk and showed her dresses in a big event like a trunk show, it could get torn down by the public. That would be even worse than Laura's criticisms. Laura was a gatekeeper in this industry. If Laura didn't think her creativity had merit, who would?

Make us proud. Those words in the letter settled into Maya's spirit.

Maya had to try. She would try. Like Derek had said, if Maya didn't believe in herself, who would?

A seed of confidence took root in Maya. Confidence— and hope.

LATER THAT DAY, Maya pulled up the phone number for Cat

Clyne on her cell phone. Time to call in her favor.

Maya dialed the number and the phone rang and rang. The last time she'd spoken to Cat was when she did those emergency alterations for her.

"This is Cat."

OMG. "Hello, Cat, it's Maya from Laura Whitcomb's office."

"I was just editing the interview with Laura. I may have some follow-up questions for her. Could you forward them to Laura?"

"I sure can." Maya twisted a stray curl around her finger. "I wasn't calling for Laura, however. Remember when you said that if I ever needed a favor to call you?"

A pause. "Yes."

"Well, I need a favor."

A longer pause. Maya's stomach churned. Was Cat having second thoughts?

"If you don't—"

"Go ahead," Cat said.

Maya spoke about the Charleston-based trunk show and how they were holding it in a historically significant boutique that was in danger of going out of business, a boutique whose story held weight in the community, and how Maya's ethnically inspired gowns would be featured in the trunk show.

She blurted out that last part very quickly.

"Sounds interesting," Cat said. "When is Laura going

down to Charleston for the trunk show?"

O-kay. This was inconvenient. "Laura won't be here for the trunk show. She's not involved in it."

"Oh really?"

There was a note of gossipy curiosity in Cat's tone. Cat was the type to spread industry rumors. She prided herself on always having the "inside dish," as she called it.

Cat could spin this trunk show any way she wanted, just to get more followers and buzz on her blog. Lordy. Maya did not want to be part of Cat's inside dish. "Nope. Laura's not involved." Maya definitely wouldn't go into the reasons why.

The sound of rustling crackled through the other end of the line. "When's the trunk show?"

"In about three and a half weeks." Maya crossed her fingers, hoping she'd say yes and not ask any more probing questions.

More rustling on the other end. "You said these are Afro-Asian dresses?"

More probing questions. Cat said the phrase "Afro-Asian" like she was trying to pronounce a foreign word. "Yes."

"So Laura Whitcomb's looking to add some new styles to her fall line, I see."

How was Maya going to explain this one? If she told Cat the truth, that this was Maya's own thing, then Cat the Gossip could go back to Laura and hint (or even say!) that Maya was trying to break rank and branch out on her own. That could put Maya at risk of losing her job with Laura. She definitely wouldn't get the promotion then.

Bad. Bad. Bad.

Why did Maya think calling Cat was a good idea anyway? Cat's opinion on fashion was the most coveted—and the most critical—in the industry. She rarely handed out compliments. If Maya got a thumbs-down from Cat, that would be a disaster.

Yet Maya couldn't live in fear forever. Maya didn't have that much time to *live*. "Take a risk," she whispered. "Just do it."

"Excuse me? What did you say?"

"Oh, nothing. I was just . . ." Maya remembered that letter to Vivian. "Laura hasn't made any plans for these designs. This is my own thing."

There. She said it. And it felt . . . freeing. Maya was stepping out on faith.

"Oh."

That was it? Just "oh"?

"I can make a quick turnaround trip for the trunk show. Just to return the favor," Cat continued. "I'm not promising a glowing review. I'm simply promising a review and some publicity. You understand that."

Maya's nervousness amped up two notches. It could be bad publicity. Cat was a biting fashion reviewer. "Yes. I completely understand."

"I can post an article online and promote it on social media, not in our print magazine since those articles are planned a few months in advance. But consider it done."

They exchanged logistical details and then hung up.

A sense of bravery took over. Bravery and exhilaration and nervousness all at once.

Maya was getting national coverage for the store and her dresses. She didn't know what *type* of coverage she'd get. This whole effort could tank and be a complete failure—but Maya did something new.

She believed in herself.

LATER THAT EVENING, Derek and Jamila sat at the dinner table and ate in silence. His talk about the store's legacy had sparked curiosity in him, especially when it came to Jamila. He wanted her to hold that same sense of appreciation for their family history. Perhaps it would help her mend some of the pain she'd been feeling surrounding her grandmother's and mother's deaths. "I was talking today about the store's history, and a conversation came up about your great-grandmother. She'd taught your grandma basket weaving. Is that something you learned too?"

Jamila pushed her Hoppin' John with her spoon. "What of it?" Her voice carried a note of suspicion.

"That's great that you know basket weaving. The skills you learned there could help you figure out your school sewing project."

Jamila laughed. "You don't weave a dress, Dad. You weave a basket. It's not the same as sewing."

He smiled. Nice to see her happy for once. "It could be. I mean, the skills are similar. I wouldn't knock those similarities."

Jamila played around with her food, apparently deep in thought.

"You don't agree?"

"No, I don't. It'll actually be kind of hard to do that school project since I don't have much help for it. I haven't made any headway whatsoever. I think I'll just take a failing grade."

"A failing grade? No way will you fail that project. Maya's offer to help still stands."

Jamila twisted her mouth and glanced away. "You know what I think of that."

"You don't have to like Maya in order for her to help you," Derek said. "She has a lot of experience, and it could help you ace that project."

"Nah." Jamila shrugged. "I don't really want to mess with her."

Derek sighed. "If you don't want to consider her, then I think that basket weaving, in the way your grandmother taught you, may help you some."

"Not interested in that either."

"Why not?" Derek asked. "It's an honored tradition."

"Not to me. It's not that important. We could just go to the department store and buy a basket if we really wanted one."

"It wouldn't be the same, Jamila. It's been passed down through the ages. Something that should be preserved and remembered."

"Something from slavery. Who wants to remember that?" Jamila said, her voice a low mumble.

The mocking in her voice pricked at Derek. He must've really failed as a father if Jamila didn't think her history was important. Should he just let it go and leave Jamila to her opinions on her history? Or should he push the issue and say more?

Letting it go would mean that the legacy that his grandmother had written about in the letter would be lost, but pushing the issue would probably annoy Jamila. Their relationship was already tenuous. Still, he'd have to push the issue. It was too important for Derek to ignore.

"Not true, Jamila. This particular way of basket weaving came all the way from West Africa. It transcends slavery. We may not have much of our history left, but we have those traditions that have been preserved from generation to generation. Each basket was made by the hands of a person who struggled and triumphed. Each one tells a story."

Jamila shoved a spoonful of peas and rice in her mouth. Still silent.

"How about you and I go downtown to where the women sell them in the marketplace? That'll get you interested in it again."

"You want me to go to those slave auction blocks and that

Black history museum near the boutique? No thank you."

Okay. Guess that was a no-go. "Then how do you intend to complete that project?"

"Dunno." Jamila shrugged. "Like I said. It won't be the first time in my life that I flunked something."

Derek rubbed his temples, frustrated. How would he get through to her? He searched for the possibilities, but nothing good came to mind. Then an idea: "Hey, Jamila, have you ever read your grandmother's prayer journals?"

"I didn't even know she had them."

This was what he could use to connect with Jamila. Derek stood up and walked to the tiny wooden desk in the living room and opened the desk drawer. He took out his mother's journal and set it before Jamila. "Turn to the front page."

Jamila did, and as soon as she saw her own name written in the first line, she leaned forward, intent on reading more.

Derek exhaled. Hopefully, this would work.

"Grandma prayed for all of these good things for me? She wanted me to thrive and stuff?"

"Of course she did."

"She had a lot to say about me." Her eyes squinted at Grandma's ornate script, and she flipped the page and read further. "She really thought I was something special, huh?"

"She definitely did," Derek said.

Jamila bit her bottom lip, still studying the pages.

"She knew the truth," Derek added, hoping this would help. "I think she would love it if you went down to the marketplace and watched them weave baskets. We can go there right after the trunk show in a few weeks."

Jamila looked up. "So, you want me to go to the trunk show . . . that Maya will be at."

"It would make the most logistical sense for you to accompany me to the trunk show. When it's over, we can head on over to the marketplace. Like I said, it'll be your call with Maya, but you don't have to like her to get her help."

Jamila looked at the journal again and her fingertips traced the edges of the pages. "If Grandma thought all of this good stuff about me, then maybe I can try to work on the school project."

Derek's mouth lifted in a tiny smile.

"That don't mean I'm working with Maya or nothing. I'll just go with you to the trunk show and check out the basket stuff afterward."

"Sounds wonderful."

Their broken relationship was beginning to mend itself together. It wasn't a perfect mending, but it was a semblance of reconnection that made him believe in the possibility of healing.

Chapter Nine

Maya hated being late. Especially today, the day of the trunk show. Tardiness would shorten her set-up time, and Maya wanted to have all the preparation that she could get.

She sped down the interstate to the boutique. Maya had stayed up till four A.M. to finish stitching the hems of the gowns for the event, then crashed, planning to nap only an hour—or four. When Pops had tapped on her bedroom door, she'd panicked, dressed, and left the house.

Kicking herself for not managing her time better, she rehearsed her apology to Derek on the way. When she hung a right into an empty parking space in front of the tiny shop, it was closed. Did something happen to Derek?

She opened her handbag and pulled out her phone to see if he'd left a message. He'd texted her.

Maya, we're on our way.

"We're"? Did that mean Derek and Jamila? She'd soon

find out. Maya set her phone down. If Jamila came along, then perhaps this would be the perfect time to try to connect with her, to help Jamila see that Maya wasn't the bad guy.

If Jamila wasn't coming along, then Maya wouldn't sweat it. She had enough on her plate as it was with the trunk show. This was her chance to show off her work. That was a lot in itself. Nerves rattled, she took a deep breath and rested her head against the steering wheel.

Cat's media influence would help spread the word, but Maya would have to bring the talent. Four hours of sleep didn't make for being too energetic. Derek would help out too. Despite their clumsy moments, he was proving to be a godsend overall.

Derek's generosity was almost too much. Although the boutique had been financially challenging for him, he still agreed to give her designs a chance. He was open to her creative ideas too, anything to keep the store's legacy intact.

If his mother were still alive, she would be proud.

Yet his openness took her off guard at times. She had never cultivated solid friendships with people, people who could help her whenever she was in a fix and who believed in her so much. Derek's constant kindness tugged on her emotions. It made her consider another possibility for her career. It didn't help that she liked Derek. She liked him. A lot.

She groaned. Liking didn't mean anything. She liked a lot of things—five-hundred-thread-count sheets, designer handbags—but she couldn't afford any of it. Falling for him wasn't prudent. The notion of getting involved with anyone made her cheeks flare. She glanced at herself in the rearview mirror. Yup, good thing she had a brown hue. Otherwise, she'd be red right about now.

Maya decided to wait until Derek arrived. She needed to take a breather after rushing out the house this morning. She was fatigued and didn't want to risk having a pain episode during the trunk show. Maya rolled down the window, but southern humidity exacerbated the frizz in her natural hair. When she first arrived in South Carolina, she tried to fight the curl. She straight-ironed her hair every chance she got. But the more Maya grew accustomed to the Lowcountry, the more she let her hair go back to its natural state. It was freeing.

She turned on her car and blasted the air, hoping this would calm her nerves. It didn't. Maya reached in her purse and spritzed a curl refresher spray in her hair, twisting the strands so they'd be bouncy again. When in hair-doubt, tie the curls up into a loose knot.

She needed to ignore her blooming feelings for Derek and focus on this trunk show. It was all business. Nothing more.

Maya slid her seat back a few notches and stared at the car roof. From here on out, she'd make a concentrated effort to focus on her business.

Do not get distracted with Derek.

Derek's truck pulled into an empty parking space next to her. Jamila was in the front passenger seat. She'd accompanied him after all. Jamila had been on an anti-Maya campaign since they'd first met. Did she have a change of heart?

Jamila glanced out her window and gave Maya the side-eye.

Nope. Didn't have a change of heart. Guess Maya would navigate all of that today too. Operation Win Over Jamila was now in effect.

Brown shopping bags, a trunk, and some boxes filled Derek's pickup. He turned off the ignition and walked around the front of his truck to meet Maya on the sidewalk.

Maya smoothed the front of her paisley skirt. "How are you doing?"

Derek grinned. "Doing good. I brought supplies." He motioned to the back of the truck. "I figured you'd need help prepping for the show, so I brought some extra things."

Maya glanced at Jamila. Her arms were crossed over her chest and she had a permanent frown on her face. "I see."

A knowing look flitted across Derek's face. "I wanted to take Jamila with me to Gadsden's Wharf after the trunk show today. So I brought her along."

"Jamila complied?" Maya whispered.

"I wouldn't say all of that. But she's here," Derek whispered, and then he gestured to his daughter. "Come on, Jamila. We're going to need your help today."

Jamila hopped out of the truck, her mouth pursed into a thin line. Maya still wanted to figure out a way to reach out to Jamila. She hadn't lost hope of that occurring.

Derek unlocked the tailgate at the back of the truck, and Maya followed him. She reached in and lifted a black trunk from the pickup bed.

"I'll carry the heavy items," Derek said.

"I can carry them." Maya worked her arms around the trunk's gold handles and lifted it with a grunt. Did someone pack this thing with bricks?

He suppressed a grin. "Are you sure?"

"Positive," Maya said, her voice certain. She'd carried heavy things before. Why should this be different?

The trunk dropped to the cement pavement.

Embarrassed, Maya stepped back. "All right, all right. You can help."

Together, they lifted it and walked it up to the curb. A cool breeze rustled through her hair, and her ponytail holder slipped loose. She finger-combed her curls away from her cheeks, only to have them whip over to the other side of her face. Lordy.

Derek stopped and stared at her. His gaze made her zing. Should she be thrilled or embarrassed about the feeling? The more he stared, the more embarrassment took over.

"What?" Maya asked.

"Nothing." He cleared his throat. "We better get set up."

Don't put your feelings out there, Maya. Derek has enough to deal with. Plus, Jamila was staring at them. Best to stay away.

They stepped inside the boutique, setting the trunk on the floor. Jamila opened her Spotify app and connected to the speaker. A hip-hop song blasted through the store.

"For decor, we'll have an African and Asian fairy-tale theme," Maya said. "I figured that a few touches here and there would make it stand out."

"It would. I thought this may help too." Derek opened the trunk and showed Maya the gorgeous red and burnt-orange fabrics, which shimmered underneath the store lights. "I got them from Mother's storage."

Maya brushed her fingers over smooth satin. "I use these colors a lot in my bridal gown designs."

"I figured you'd like them. Those gowns don't have to fit the traditional mold. They can be anything you envision. They can be uniquely you."

Maya let those words settle in. She needed to hear them just as much as she needed to say them. *Anything you envision, Maya. Not anything Laura Whitcomb envisioned.*

"You got these fabrics from Grandma's storage, Dad?" Jamila asked.

"Yes. Is there a problem?"

Discomfort flitted through Maya. This was not good.

"There's a huge problem," Jamila said. "You can't just give her Grandma's things."

Derek exhaled. "It's for the store's benefit, Jamila. I didn't give anything to Maya. It's for Always a Bride."

Jamila didn't say anything. Instead, she surveyed the space. She was probably mentally criticizing the redesign.

"So you did all this with the store?" Jamila asked.

"A little here and there," Maya said. "Thought it would help with rebranding."

"What's rebranding?" Jamila asked.

"A company's strong visual image coupled with that company's story. Something that makes it identifiable in the marketplace. That sort of thing."

Jamila looked up, as if considering this. "Oh, I get it. Like logos and TV commercial jingles and stuff."

"Exactly," Maya said.

Jamila walked around and seemed to note the changes Maya had made. For some reason, this young girl's evaluation made Maya nervous. Maybe because she sensed that Jamila was also evaluating her.

"Grandma would never have this castle and carriage display in the center of the store," Jamila said. "She was all about showing off the dresses. She'd probably say, 'I ain't putting it in the center unless I'm selling it.'"

Oof. Maya had messed up. She was already on Jamila's bad side, but if Maya also didn't follow Vivian's vision, then Maya could just forget about connecting with Jamila on any level. Best to just suck it up, take the loss, and see if that could help her get on Jamila's good side. "That's a great suggestion, Jamila. The decoration shouldn't get in the way of the design. I'll move the carriage." Maya headed over to the display and gently pushed it to the side near the floor-to-ceiling mirror. "How's that?"

Jamila squinted her eyes. "Maybe a little off to the side.

Don't want to distract from the mirror when folks are trying on dresses."

"Excellent point." Maya shifted it a few inches.

A quiet fell between them. Maya tried to reach for more from Jamila, a sense of truce, a sense of connection, a sense of something good. Maybe Maya was overthinking this.

After they finished setting up, Jamila drifted over to one of Maya's dresses that was on display. "Is this gown yours?"

Maya paused, not knowing if she'd get criticism or kindness from Jamila. "Yes," she said cautiously.

Jamila squinted at the hem. "Is that a topstitch?"

"Yes."

"My grandmother used to do this stitch a lot." Jamila ran her fingers over the thread. "All by hand."

Okay, should Maya probe and try to connect with Jamila now? Or would doing so bring on more grief for Jamila? Maya didn't know, and she didn't want to mess this up. Maybe she'd play neutral. Yes. Neutral was good. Neutral was safe. "Good on you for recognizing the stitch."

"I can't stitch by hand," Jamila said. "Too hard."

She was slowly opening up to Maya. This was a positive sign. Maya would extend a peace offering. "It takes a while to learn, but you'll get the hang of it. In the meantime, you can use a sewing machine. I have an extra sewing machine. Do you have one?"

Jamila shoulders sagged. "Nope."

"You can borrow mine if you'd like. If that's okay with

your father." Maya glanced in Derek's direction.

"Sounds good to me," Derek said.

Jamila looked between them, her eyes filled with hesitation. "I'll borrow your sewing machine. Thank you for offering."

A pleasantness filled Maya. This was good. Real good.

Chapter Ten

Bringing Jamila here wasn't as bad as Derek figured it'd be. There weren't any blowups or major disasters. Except for Jamila's one comment about a display, she seemed cool. Perhaps he could get her on board with the new direction that the store was taking with the remodel and all. But how?

Dessert. Kids loved dessert. "Since you're here, Jamila, I figured this would be a great opportunity for you to work today. I'll take you out for ice cream as compensation."

Her eyes widened. "Really?"

"How's that sound?"

She nodded. "Sounds great. Cookies and cream is my favorite flavor."

Derek laughed. "I brought in an extra stock of accessories, but I haven't the time to put them on display yet. They're in the stockroom in a stack of three boxes. Mind setting them up for me?"

"Sure." Jamila left for the stockroom, leaving him and Maya on the sales floor.

That went easy enough. Perhaps getting Jamila on board wouldn't be so hard after all.

"This should be a good day," Maya said, smiling. "Cat Clyne texted me to say she'll be here this afternoon to take pictures and ask questions."

"Good. That'll give me time to think about what I want to say."

"There's not much to think about if you ask me." Maya gently tugged on the train of one of her gowns on display. She pulled a needle out of a red pincushion and threaded it. "The history you shared was plenty. All you have to do is tell her that."

"That's the thing. I feel hesitant to talk about that history. My mother always did, but I'm not my mother. Not everyone wants to hear about the history of this boutique."

Maya stopped tugging on the gown. She remembered Laura's reaction to the news about the museum on Chalmers Street. "You're right. Not everyone wants to hear about our history. That's doesn't mean it shouldn't be told."

Derek was still wrapping his mind around the fact that he'd even told Maya. She made it easy to talk about those things. Telling a reporter, telling the world, would be different. There was an additional pressure to represent his family well. Derek glanced at the framed letter from his grandmother.

Make us proud. The words echoed within him. Always a Bride needed to make more than a profit. It needed to be acknowledged for what it truly was, a symbol of perseverance and hope. "You're right. The boutique's story deserves to be told."

"It does." Maya walked over to him, pincushion in hand.

Electricity thrummed between them. It was a low buzz, but he sensed it nonetheless. This woman was unraveling the threads that wrapped around his old beliefs, his old notions of what was possible and what wasn't. He'd never thought that one day he'd be here sharing a long-forgotten history of his family. He'd never thought his history would be the possible key to saving the family business.

Now he held that key firmly in his hand, and Maya had made that possible. "You're my good luck charm."

Surprise flashed across her face.

Did he just say that aloud? Yes, but he wasn't taking it back because it was true. "You're my good luck charm," he repeated.

The door to the stockroom opened, and the spell between Derek and Maya broke. He shifted his attention to the sound of Jamila coming out, pushing one cardboard box. "Can you help me with this, Dad?"

"Sure, baby girl." He headed in her direction and lifted the box, carrying it over to the empty space where it would be displayed. "I'll get the rest of them too."

"Who painted these walls blue?" Jamila asked. Her nose

scrunched like she smelled something bad. "Grandma hated the color blue."

Derek stilled. "She did?"

"Yes. Grandma always said it was a bad luck color."

He searched his memory, but it came up lacking. "I never heard her say that."

"That's because you were hardly around." Her tone hardened.

Here we go again. "I'm here now, Jamila."

She stared him down, but Derek didn't relent. Jamila needed to understand this truth. She crossed her arms and walked to the rear of the store, inspecting the color on the walls. From his periphery, Maya took two steps back. Was Maya wilting under Jamila's critical eye?

"I like the color," Derek said. "The store was looking a bit outdated. The new color makes things look more modern and up to date."

Jamila ran her finger along the dried paint on the walls. "If you say so."

This wasn't working out too well. If Derek told Jamila that Maya was the one who picked out the paint, she'd be mad. Nothing Derek did was good enough for his daughter, and a part of him was getting exhausted with trying to win her allegiance. Something had to give.

"Jamila?" Maya asked.

Jamila glanced up. "What?"

"Don't be so hard on your dad." She clasped her hands

together, apparently nervous. "I picked out the color, and I'm sorry. I didn't know about her preferences for the store."

"I figured that much," Jamila said, moving toward the cardboard box.

"We were just trying to get a new look for the store," Derek added. "You haven't been around here. I didn't know that you were interested in the store's remodel."

"You. Never. Asked. Me." Jamila set a veil down on the counter next to her. "You. Never. Asked."

Jamila's words cut through Derek, and his shoulders subconsciously slumped. "You're right. I never did. You spent the most time with Grandma. You spent the most time in this store. I should have asked you."

Jamila's lower lip trembled, but she grabbed the veil again and plopped it on a mannequin's head. A tear trickled down her cheek.

"Oh, baby girl." Derek headed her way to give her a hug, and Jamila fell into his embrace. He bowed his head. "I miss them too."

Jamila's tears soaked his button-down shirt, but he didn't care. This was needed.

"If you want to change the colors on the walls to something that Grandma would've liked, we can."

Maya blinked. "I agree. We can change whatever you want to change, Jamila."

"Changing things won't bring Grandma back. She's been gone for a year, and I miss her," Jamila sobbed. "Won't bring

Mama back either."

Helpless. That was the only word that came to mind for Derek. He was helpless. No amount of repainting or hugs or conversations or cookouts would ever erase the sense of loss inside of his daughter. The magnitude of her grief overwhelmed him. He knew she was hurting, but not like this.

Should he brush it aside in order to protect her feelings? Or should he talk her through this and get the full brunt of it right now, right before the trunk show?

Pushing this aside for another time wasn't going to help. He needed to face this head-on.

"There's nothing we can do to change that, but you see this?" Derek pointed to the framed letter.

Jamila lifted her head and wiped the tears from her brown cheeks.

"That's our charge. That's why we renovated the place. We need to keep Always a Bride going, understand?"

"I understand."

A weight lifted from his shoulders. Breakthrough.

"Your mother worked at the boutique too. Is that right, Jamila?" Maya asked.

Jamila wiped another tear from her cheek. "That's correct."

"Perhaps you and I can sit down one day soon, and you can tell me about the place. There's a fashion reporter who will be here this afternoon. You could tell her too. Let her know what this store means to you—that is, if your father and you agree."

"A reporter is coming here?" Jamila glanced at her father.

"She's writing about the store," he said.

"If I talked about it, will it help save the place?"

"I don't know if it would, but it's worth a try," Derek said.

Jamila sniffled and studied the framed letter on the wall. "Then I'd like to talk about the store too."

A sense of peace washed over Derek. This wasn't his usual modus operandi but choosing to talk about it helped Jamila. She was going to talk about the store too. That was a blessing.

JAMILA AGREED TO talk to Cat. Awesome. Awesome. Awesome. This was the perfect way to ensure that Jamila was involved in this business.

How could Maya have picked the wall color without consulting Jamila first? The last thing Maya wanted was for Jamila to feel as if she were getting pushed out of the picture. Maya would be here temporarily, but Jamila would be here permanently. Her opinions and ideas should hold more weight.

Maya would make that happen.

Derek flipped the store sign from CLOSED to OPEN, and thirty minutes later, the first customers trickled into the boutique. Nervousness flitted through Maya for a host of reasons. This was her chance not only to promote the store, but to promote her work to buyers, to see if there was a wider market for her designs. Selling a few dresses on consignment here and there was one thing. Getting word of mouth and recommendations and a slew of dress sales was quite another.

On top of that, Cat Clyne would walk into the boutique at any moment. This was Maya's time to shine. If she did, then Laura would have to promote Maya to the head designer position. Maya had to work on the revised designs regardless. She'd been so busy with the boutique that she hadn't gotten to it yet. She made a mental note to work on it this weekend.

For now, Maya would focus on the trunk show and really, really make this her time to shine.

"Here goes nothing," she said to herself. A flit of nervousness zipped through Maya. Was that Cat? Maya glanced up.

A group of women entered the store and encircled one of Maya's gowns like eagles surrounding a nest. *Please like my dresses. Please like my dresses. Please like my dresses.*

"Morning, ladies. Can I help you with anything?"

"We're looking for a wedding dress." The brunette picked at Maya's dress design. "This one is meh."

Maya's skin tightened. Meh. Not a good sign. "We have other dresses." She gestured to the racks. "What were you going for?"

"Simple and traditional. Nothing too frilly. I want pure elegance."

Pure elegance meant pure Laura Whitcomb. Maya directed her to the dresses that would fit her style. She and her friends oohed over all of them.

This was gonna be hard. Maybe Laura was right. Maybe her dresses were too outside of the norm. She should move her gown that was on display.

Just as she was about to do so, the door opened. Was that Cat?

Nope. Another young woman entered the store. She wore a black-and-white peplum dress and silver ballet flats.

"How can I help you?" Maya asked.

"I heard about your trunk show on social media, and I wanted to stop by and see it for myself. I'm looking for a gown for my wedding."

Probably not one like mine. "Is there a particular style you're looking for?"

The woman shrugged. "I'll know it when I see it. I've searched everywhere, and so far, I haven't seen it."

Maya showed her the dresses on the rack, and the woman flipped through them quickly. "Nah. This isn't it. They look like everything else that's out there."

They sure do. Maya glanced over at one of her designs. Would this lady go for something like it? "How about this gown?" Maya gestured to the gown with the burnt-orange accent color at the trim.

The woman's face lit up. "That's so different. Can you take it off the mannequin for me?"

"Sure." It took a few minutes to get it off the mannequin— the dress was heavy. Probably because of the additional appliqué and beads.

The young woman stood in front of a tall mirror and held up Maya's dress. "Lovely."

She liked it. That was refreshing after the first wave of ladies' reactions. Maya stood behind her.

"I always say it's the bride who makes the dress," Maya said. "Not the other way around. For you, this dress would only need minor alterations. Tuck it in around the waist and tighten at the arms. You'll be ready to go. Try it on and we'll see."

The woman went into the dressing room. When she returned, Maya pulled out her measuring tape, a pincushion, and got to work. The door opened, averting Maya's attention. Cat Clyne walked through the entrance.

OMG. That was Cat Clyne. That was really Cat Clyne.

Calm down. Calm down. Calm down. Should Maya go up and greet her, or should she stay focused on this minor dress alteration?

Seconds later, Derek greeted Cat. They shook hands and started chatting. Cat glanced in Maya's direction, and Maya nodded a greeting, a thread pursed between her lips.

At least Derek had things under control for now. Maya would focus on the customer. Thirty minutes later, Maya finished with the dress adjustment. "What do you think?"

"I like it." She twisted her mouth.

Maya sensed her anxiety. "But . . ."

The woman exhaled. "I need something more. Something

that is uniquely me. My wedding will be at my father's place. I wanted to have it at Hilton Head, but Mother insisted that a governor's daughter should have her wedding at home."

Maya's eyes widened. "You're Heather Gates?"

"The one and only."

"Oh, wow."

Heather held the dress up a few inches higher. "Picking my dresses is the only autonomy I have over this wedding. That's only because I insisted on paying for them myself. My parents are controlling everything else." She held out the gown and read the tag. "Maya Jackson Designs. I've never heard of this designer."

"That designer is me."

"You made this dress?"

Maya nodded, unsure of whether Heather was impressed or repulsed. Sometimes Maya got the repulsed reaction. Folks weren't used to Blasian bridal gown designers. Maya braced herself for both responses.

"This dress is beautiful. Do you have a catalog or something of your other designs?"

She liked it! "Sure. I do." Maya flipped through her mental Rolodex. Did Maya bring her portfolio today? She should've. "Be right back."

"Sure thing."

Maya slow jogged to the break room. As she did, she overheard Derek chatting to Cat about another one of her dresses. Hopefully Cat would like it.

Once inside the break room, Maya scanned the space. Ah. Her portfolio was on the desk. Yes. Yes. Yes! Seconds later, Maya returned to the sales floor and flipped it open for Heather.

Maya stood off to the side, nervous as Heather (the governor's daughter!) looked through her dresses. Cat was inspecting the inside of another one of Maya's gowns very closely, and anxiety flitted through Maya. She could only handle one thing at a time.

Snatches of Derek's conversation with Cat filtered her way.

"What do you think of this dress?" Derek held out the wedding dress with the red bandeau top and Filipino baybayin characters around the waistline. Baybayin was the indigenous language of the Filipinos, and Maya's mother had taught her how to write it before she died.

Cat scrunched her nosed. "Meh. Wedding dresses are supposed to be classic and elegant. That red is too gaudy."

Maya deflated. *Gaudy? That dress wasn't gaudy!*

"Hmm. I love these, but I think I want something more custom designed," the customer said, drawing Maya's attention away from Cat's comment. "Something that would be a one-and-only type dress? Do you custom design dresses?"

Custom design dresses? Did Maya even have the time or energy to do that, with working at the store and taking care of her dad?

Maya wasn't sure. Perhaps she should ask more questions.

"When is your wedding?"

"June."

Maya's face took a turn for the serious. "June? I'm set to return to New York in late June. What day of the month?"

"The ninth. It's a Saturday."

Maya looked up, considering her schedule. That was six weeks from now. Six weeks was plenty of time to work on Heather's dress if Maya simply had to alter an existing design. A custom-made dress would take much longer.

From the corner of her eye, she saw Derek show Cat another one of Maya's dresses. Cat just shook her head no.

Now what would Maya do? Her entire brand was based on cultural influences in her designs. "Are you sure you don't want a more traditional wedding gown? I can make that for you." *It'll also be something Cat would like.*

"Oh, no way. I need something that will reflect my full heritage."

Maya twisted her mouth, trying to figure out where this customer was going with that comment. She looked very European with her creamy skin, golden-brown hair, and green eyes.

"My mother and I have been working on our family tree. It's been a multiyear project. A few weeks ago, we discovered that my great-grandmother was Black, but she passed as White. We had no idea. I want to tell my great-grandmother's full story. She's deceased now, and there's not much I can do. I feel awful that she had to hide who she really was. Would designing a dress that was reflective of her be something that would interest you?"

Maya considered it. Maya could go with a New York traditional dress, something Cat would like, or she could take this chance with Heather Gates's request.

Why should Maya care so much about what Cat thought of Maya's style? If Cat didn't like it, then Cat didn't like it. There was little Maya could do to change her opinion.

"I'd lived my entire life thinking my great-grandmother was White. I don't want an entire piece of her identity to be erased in our family any longer," Heather continued. "If I could wear a dress that speaks to my entire ancestry, that would be beautiful. It would be a way to honor my great-grandmother."

"It sounds like she was special to you."

"Very special. She died when I was nine years old, but prior to that, I was very close to her. I didn't understand racism as a child, but I do now. She sacrificed her identity to fit into White society and not face the hardships that many Black people faced. Hardships like segregation and discrimination. We didn't know about her Black family members. We never met them. So my great-grandmother must have shunned her Black family completely." Heather shook her head. "It makes me wonder how my family would've received her if they knew that my great-grandfather married a Black woman."

"Your great-grandfather didn't know?" Maya asked.

"Not to my knowledge. He used to make all of these off-color remarks about Black people when I was a kid. So he couldn't have known that his wife was Black. Now I wonder how she felt hearing his cruel words." Heather sighed. "Just awful all around."

Maya was silent. Heather's desire to want to honor her great-grandmother was compelling.

"My great-grandmother used to tell me 'make-believe stories,' as she called them. Stories about Black teachers and pastors and sharecroppers back in Georgia. Now I wonder if those stories were her way of talking about her family without talking about her family. I wonder if those stories were her way of preserving herself." Heather shrugged. "I don't know. I won't ever know."

"Do you know if she had any family in Georgia?" Maya asked.

"No idea. We did find her birth certificate, and her mother was a Black woman. The father's name isn't listed on the certificate. I want to weave her story into my dress somehow."

Heather's desires resonated with Maya. She wanted to weave her parents' influences in her gowns too. Until now, Maya thought she was the only person in the world who felt this way. Not anymore.

"I like the way that you blend in different-colored fabrics into the wedding gowns too, Maya. I wondered if you'd be able to do that with my wedding dress, but in a way that was meaningful for my family history."

Maya's creative wheels turned in her brain. She could stop this entire conversation and focus on Cat and try to appease Cat's design sensibilities, or Maya could continue with this opportunity. "June ninth will work if you choose from my existing selection of dresses. If you do that, then I can make alterations to reflect your desires. However, if I created a dress from scratch it would take five to six months. That would be way past your wedding date."

"Have your dresses been mass-produced?"

"No. Each one is unique. I'm not at the mass production stage yet."

Heather paused, apparently thinking. "Then I'll choose one from your existing selection and we can tweak it as needed."

"Excellent," Maya said. "We can collaborate on tailoring the dress to fit your story too."

"Sounds like a plan."

"I couldn't help but overhear you two talking, Maya." Cat walked over to them. "Are you Heather Gates?"

Heather nodded.

"Your story is amazing. I would love to cover it in my fashion blog. We could do a wedding style edition with your dress."

"For real?" Maya asked.

"Yes. Of course." Cat adjusted the leopard-print glasses on her nose. "This is something that readers will like to know about. You'll get some extra publicity too, Maya."

Cat may not like Maya's style, but she liked it enough if the governor's daughter was involved. Maya would ride that publicity wave. "Sounds great."

Heather clapped. "This is gonna be so wonderful. We'll have to set up a time to chat about design ideas."

"Yes, we do."

This was good. Following her creative heart paid off. Excitement and a bit of trepidation flitted through her. She could deliver a stunning dress. Maya could definitely do it.

D erek and Jamila were riding in the truck to Maya's house. She had offered to let Jamila use the sewing machine, and now they had time in their schedule to get it. The trunk show had been a success. More than a success, it had been amazing. Cat. Heather. Everything. The event was more than he'd hoped for or even conceived. After going over the books with Marlon, Derek found they'd made enough money to get caught up on the mortgage and then some. He was going to pay the bank soon after this stop at Maya's house.

Maya was helping him make all these good things happen. This sewing machine that she was lending to Jamila was another way that Maya was building bridges.

He wanted to get to know the woman behind the designer, but doing so was risky. It would mean admitting to himself that in some ways, he was moving on from Grace, but was he really? If he did move on, would that be a betrayal to Grace?

It would also mean that he'd risk causing a deeper rift in his relationship with Jamila. He promised Jamila that he wouldn't date Maya or anyone else. Jamila seemed to be slowly warming up to Maya. Still, a promise was a promise. Derek wouldn't date anyone unless Jamila was okay with it.

"Dad?"

"Yeah, baby."

"How did you know that you were in love with Mom?"

Hoo boy. Nope. Jamila wasn't ready to know his thoughts about Maya. "I just knew. First time I laid eyes on your mother, I knew."

"When y'all were at that party, you mean?"

He laughed. "Yes, when we were at the party."

Derek had told Jamila that he met Grace at a college party. It was a freshman mixer. He took one look at Grace and knew she was The One. Grace had a way about her that was calm in the midst of a storm.

He'd brought the storm. Ever since his father had walked out, he'd been a rebellious kid. Derek had given his mother more grief than she should've gotten—he flunked classes, partied, got in trouble with the law. Meeting Grace made him want to get his life together, because for the first time, he wanted to build a life—with her.

"Was it love at first sight?" Jamila asked.

"For me, it was. I don't know about your mother." He chuckled. "She couldn't stand me at first. Thought I was just a jock. She didn't take too kindly to me flirting with her."

"I don't blame her."

Derek did a double take, then refocused on the road. "Why not?" he said, humored by her response.

"You told me that all boys are evil. Doesn't that include you?"

He'd told her that. It was his fatherly duty to tell her to stay away from crushes and romantic interests—but he didn't expect Jamila to turn his advice against him. "I'm your father."

"But to Mama, you were a boy."

Jamila was too smart for her own good. "True."

There was a silence, and then: "Dad?"

"Yes, babe."

"Did you know that Mama was your one and only?"

A sinking feeling had come over him. At the time, he thought that Grace would be his forever love, his forever one and only. Now that he was getting to know Maya, he wasn't so sure.

If he was frank with Jamila, she'd probably get angry again. If he kept quiet, then he could be denying himself the opportunity to let go.

To let go of the silent grief.

To let go of the guilt surrounding his wife's death.

To let go of the fortress he'd built around his heart.

"Did you hear me, Dad?"

Loud and clear. "I did. I was thinking about your question."

"So what's your answer?"

He paused. "When I first met your mother, I knew she was the one for me. During our entire marriage, I knew she was my one and only."

Jamila drummed her fingers on the dashboard. "You still feel the same way about Mama, right?"

Did he still feel the same? Was true love a one-time thing, or did his heart have room for a second chance at falling in love?

The more he knew Maya, the more he wanted that second chance, but then there was Jamila and this guilt he'd felt about letting his heart feel what it felt toward Maya.

Once Grace had said that if she ever passed away, she wanted Derek to find happiness again. Derek remembered that conversation now. Grace was so selfless and loving, but he hadn't paid much attention to her comment. Derek always thought they'd have a lifetime together. Who would've known that going to church one day would prove deadly?

At the time of that conversation, Derek didn't think he'd want to find happiness again in the off chance he became widowed, but now Grace's words were a gift, a rare and treasured gift. Derek would find happiness again, and perhaps he'd find it in Maya. "I'll always love your mother, Jamila. That will never change."

She didn't respond.

Did Jamila sense Derek's newfound feelings? Unease settled in him. Derek couldn't bear to have her upset with him again.

This was too complicated, but one thing Derek knew—his heart still longed for a slice of joy again. He wanted that joy by having a restored relationship with Jamila—and maybe a love relationship with Maya.

MOMENTS LATER, DEREK pulled into the driveway of Maya and her father's home. It was a ranch-style house with a driveway and a car shed. Whew. This was surreal. They were there only to pick up a sewing machine, but it felt like something more.

Did Derek want it to be something more? Did he want to go further with Maya and ask her on a date?

No.

He made his promise to Jamila. No need to push it. They'd simply pick up the sewing machine and leave. He'd even wait in the truck and send Jamila to get it.

They were fully parked in the driveway, and Derek turned off the ignition. "I'll wait here while you get the sewing machine."

"You sure?"

He wasn't. Derek really wanted to go inside and hang out for a while. "I'm positive."

"O-kay." Jamila got out of the truck. By the time she was halfway up the driveway, Maya greeted her.

Maya's smile was enough to light up the entire block.

She wore a floral sundress that skimmed her ankles, and her smooth sepia skin glowed.

At the sight of her, Derek unconsciously reached for the door handle, but then he stopped himself. *Stay here, Derek. Jamila is just going inside for a second.*

"Hey, Jamila." Maya glanced his way, and Derek gave a friendly, distant wave. "Why don't you two come inside? It's nearing ninety degrees today. I just made a fresh batch of lemonade."

Oh Lord. "I'm okay," Derek called from the car. "Don't want to be too much of a burden."

"No burden at all." Maya motioned to him. "Come on in."

Jamila turned and waved to him too. "Come on, Dad."

He was outnumbered. Derek got out of the truck, as nervous as a teenager on a first date, and headed up the narrow walkway lined with geraniums.

They stepped inside of Carl's one-story house. The air-conditioned living room was a welcome reprieve from the muggy Lowcountry weather. The space was small and cozy, like a welcoming bed-and-breakfast or a small inn. The Asian-print throw pillows and vases filled with red and white tulips had Maya's designer eye all over them. On a small worktable off to the side were a bunch of fabrics, sketches, and the sewing machine. Maya motioned for them to come to the living room, and they did. Derek sat on the comfy couch, and Jamila sat next to him.

"Where's your father?" Derek asked Maya.

"I drove him to physical therapy. This session would be a long one, so I decided to return home for a bit to meet up with you guys."

"Oh? Why so long?" Derek asked.

"They're gonna try Pops on a walker today. So hopefully when I pick him up, he won't need his wheelchair anymore."

"Sounds wonderful."

"It is. He's looking forward to being more mobile."

Derek clasped his hands together. "I counted the sales from the past few weeks. We made enough profit to get current on the mortgage. The trunk show helped too. Always a Bride will not go into foreclosure."

"Wonderful!" Maya smiled. "That's excellent. And who knows what good can come from Heather's wedding."

"You're right. It can only get better from here," Derek said.

A silence stretched between them, a silence filled with possibilities and hope. He relished in it.

"Is that your sewing machine?" Jamila asked, breaking the moment.

"Yes." Maya gestured to it as if she were a game show host. *Cute.*

"Can I see it?" Jamila asked.

"Of course you can. I'll get the lemonade, and then I'll show you how it works." Maya headed toward the kitchen.

Jamila studied the sewing machine. "Last time I used one

of these was when Mama was alive."

Her words hit him deep. The fact that Jamila was willing to accept a sewing machine from Maya said a lot. "Maybe your mother is looking down from heaven and saying it's okay to pick up a sewing machine." *Maybe she's saying it's okay for both of us to move on.*

"Maybe," Jamila said, her expression serious.

"You don't agree?" Derek asked.

Jamila shrugged. "I dunno. It's been kind of hard to take up sewing again after Mom died. That's probably why I've been stalling on this project."

"I understand that. I really do, love," Derek said.

Jamila glanced away.

The shuffling of feet signaled Maya's return. "Here's the lemonade, guys." She set it down on coasters and then grabbed a pamphlet from her worktable. "Here's the user's manual. Ready for me to show you how to use the machine?"

"I already know how," Jamila said. "I'll have to get used to this one, but I know the gist of it."

"Great. Want to practice sewing on a sample piece of cloth?"

Jamila paused and glanced at Derek, who smiled. Jamila then nodded yes. Perhaps Jamila really did value his advice.

For the next few minutes, Maya showed Jamila how to line up the cloth with the guide points on the machine. Then Jamila pressed the power button, and the machine came to life.

"Look at you." Derek clapped. "You're an old pro."

Jamila's eyes shifted, apparently embarrassed. Maya gently guided the cloth as Jamila worked through the stitch.

Derek searched his memories and came upon one that shone clear. Jamila was right. She'd used a sewing machine with Grace, though he didn't remember it right away. Jamila had a hole in her jeans, and Grace helped her patch it up.

Here was Maya today, patching up his little girl's heart. He blinked back a tear.

When they finished, Jamila held up the cloth for Derek to see, proud of her work. "That's awesome, hon. You shouldn't have any problems with your project now."

"I still have to think of a design, Dad." Jamila glanced over at Maya, uncertain. "Could you help me with designing my dress for the project?"

"Sure can." Maya opened a sketchbook. "Right before you guys arrived, I was sketching ideas for Heather Gates's gown. She handed Jamila her sketchbook. "Maybe my sketches will give you some ideas."

Jamila flipped through the pages. Seeing the two of them work together filled Derek with a sense of peace. This was what was missing in their lives—or was it?

A heavy weight pressed on him. *Be careful, Derek. Don't get too close. You've lost loved ones before.*

"I have an idea," Maya said, pulling Derek out of his thoughts. "You know how Heather wanted her great-grandmother's memory reflected in her dress somehow?"

Jamila nodded.

"How about we do the same for your project? How about we honor your mom and your grandmother in your dress? We could even name the dress after them. I'd have to brainstorm some ideas, and you should too."

Jamila stopped turning the pages. "I like that."

The weight pressing on Derek lifted. "I like that too." He stood and looked at Maya's sketchbook. She was one talented lady.

"We could talk more about it when you're at the store," Maya said. "We'll have it ready in time for the project's due date."

"It's due in four weeks." Jamila sighed. "I might have some of my mother's and grandmother's clothing that I could sew into the dress."

"Or you could also go with a variation of their favorite colors. I was thinking of that burnt-orange scarf that looked so good on you." Maya rearranged the spools of thread on her worktable.

"My mother loved that color."

"That's just one option." Maya held up her index finger. "We'll work out the details together. I'll brainstorm more ideas before then."

"Thank you, Maya," Jamila said.

"You're welcome. This is a great opportunity for us both."

Contentment washed over Derek. Seeing Jamila like this

was thrilling. This was a great opportunity, in more ways than one.

After exchanging goodbyes, they headed to the truck. Derek put the key in the ignition, and Jamila stared out the passenger window, apparently deep in thought.

"Maya's cool, Dad."

"You think?"

"She's nice. If you wanted to hang out with her more, I guess that would be fine with me."

Was his daughter a mind reader? Or were his feelings that obvious? Probably the latter. "That means a lot to me, J."

"I know." Jamila smirked.

He smiled. She was still a smart aleck.

"Do you want to date her?"

Derek stilled. He did, but he'd also be taking a risk by dating Maya.

People leave. Maya was in Charleston temporarily.

People changed. Things could go bad between them.

People died. Grace and his mother had passed.

But people also lived. "Yes. I want to date Maya."

"I knew that too." Jamila grinned.

Derek started the ignition and pulled out of Maya's driveway. He'd ask Maya out on a date. Joy filled him as the Lowcountry sun beamed onto the car dashboard. Stopping inside Maya's house today wasn't such a bad decision after all.

MAYA CLOSED HER fashion magazine and glanced up at the

digital clock on her bedside table: 12:43 A.M. The amber
light from her cobalt stained-glass lamp illuminated her tiny
room. An owl hooted outside the window. All was at rest,
except her. After her meeting with Jamila and Derek today,
she'd been thinking and thinking and thinking about the
best kind of dress to make for Jamila. Maya wanted it to be
special, and the pressure to perform and make everything
perfect settled deeper and deeper. Designing dresses for a
high-profile figure in South Carolina and a girl who was
struggling with grief, taking care of her father, working on
those revisions for Laura, and continuing to make dresses on
consignment were a snowball of responsibilities that Maya
now had to juggle.

She wanted Jamila's dress to also be reflective of her mother
and grandmother. Maya was determined to come up with an
unforgettable idea, but the options were too many. Should
Maya suggest something trendy and fashionable? Should the
dress be timeless and classic? Maya grabbed her notebook
and wrote more preliminary ideas.

What about Heather's gown? How would it reflect Heather's great-grandmother? Maya tapped her pen on her chin,
thinking. Then she did an internet search on Heather Gates.

A lot of articles popped up about Heather's genealogical
research and her Black ancestry. One article said that her
great-grandmother loved the color purple. "It is the color
of hidden treasures revealed," her great-grandmother was
quoted as saying.

Was Heather's great-grandmother referring to herself and her true, yet hidden, identity? Could be.

As Maya pondered this, her phone buzzed. It was a text from Derek.

Hey, Maya.

Her heart fluttered. Since when did her heart flutter because of texts from Derek? Since today.

Why was he texting her so late? Was something wrong?

Hey. What's up? she texted back.

Do you have a minute to chat?

Something must be up if he was texting her this late at night. Sure, she typed.

Seconds later, her phone rang, and Maya's heartbeat went into overdrive. She had to get these Derek feelings under control. Maya picked up the phone. "Hi."

"Hi."

Silence. Maya bit her bottom lip, waiting. It must be serious if he was calling her this late.

"I was calling you because . . . well, I was really impressed with how you and Jamila connected today."

"Great." Why was he calling her again?

"I spoke with Jamila, and she's really warming up to you."

"Also great." Was this cause for a phone call in the middle of the night, though? "I was brainstorming some ideas for her dress."

"She likes you a lot."

Something must be on his mind. Maya set the sketchbook

aside.

"And so do I," Derek added.

Her heartbeat triple-timed. Oh.

"Would you want to go out to dinner tomorrow? Nothing serious. Just two people enjoying each other's company. Of course, if you don't want to, I completely understand. I just figured I'd ask."

She wasn't expecting that either. "Dinner?"

"You don't have to say yes. I was just wondering in case you wanted to say yes."

He really liked her. She had to tell him about her illness, but how? Should she blurt it out or wait for another time?

"Maya?"

Sickle cell demanded her energy, her time, her life. It would also demand a lot from anyone she seriously dated. Derek didn't need to deal with all that. He was already navigating fatherhood and a business and trying to heal from his wife's tragic death. Maya wasn't going to subject Derek to her burdens.

"You still there, Maya?"

"Yeah, yeah. Sorry. I was just thinking. I don't know, Derek. I'm moving back to New York."

Maya could feel his disappointment through the phone. "I completely understand. And you're right."

The finality in his voice tugged at her. "I'm not saying no. I have a lot to consider. I need some time. Is that okay?"

"Take all the time you need. No rush."

"Thank you."

After they hung up, Maya's heartbeat slowed. She tugged at the edges of her plaid comforter and stepped out of bed. No need to fool herself into trying to fall asleep after that phone call. Her bare feet padded against the hardwood floor as she made her way to the kitchen and plugged in the coffeepot.

A faint shuffling could be heard from the hallway. Her father. She sighed, thinking of a way to respond when he asked the inevitable.

He yawned, his hair sticking out every which way. He leaned on his new walker. "What are you doing up, my favorite daughter?"

"You mean your only daughter." She turned on the tap and filled the coffeepot with water.

"You're still my favorite." He smiled. "So why are you up?"

Because I'm afraid. "No reason. Thought I'd make some coffee." She needed to figure this out. Would it be right to take this next step with Derek, knowing what it would demand of him? Knowing that he'd already lost his wife so tragically?

Her father rubbed his eyes, his walker helping him to stand. "It's one o'clock in the morning. Coffee isn't needed for another five or six hours. Unless, of course, you're a farmer."

Maya smiled, amazed at his calm and his ability to find

humor in every situation.

"How are you really feeling?" her father asked.

Her shoulders slumped. "Okay."

He grabbed a blue mug out of a kitchen cabinet. "You don't sound okay."

She relayed her conversation with Derek.

"You said yes, right?" her father asked.

"No."

"Why the hesitation?"

Maya took his mug, ignoring his question. She was too tired to answer—well, she was really too stressed. "I'll pour you a cup, Pops."

"It's because of your sickle cell, isn't it?"

Discomfort edged through her. Time to change the subject. "I thought you'd be sound asleep. You're definitely not a night person," she said.

"Okay then. We don't have to talk about it if you're not ready." Her father adjusted his brown robe around his shoulders. "And I am a night person, by the way. You've been keeping me up since your mother and I brought you home from the hospital. Besides, I can get a head start on breakfast. How do blueberry pancakes sound?"

"Perfect." Blueberry pancakes were her favorite. He always made them ever since she was a kid.

The clatter of pots and pans filled the tiny kitchen as her father set up the cooking area.

"You need help, Pops?"

"I'm good, love."

She nodded. He didn't pry or ask any more questions about what was bothering her. She appreciated that about him. "Thanks, Pops."

"Any time." He sprayed a skillet with cooking oil.

Maya shrugged and walked to the breakfast table. She plopped down on a chair and laid her head on the red place-mat, still uneasy. *Should I take this next step with Derek?* "Can we talk about this more?"

"Of course." He looked up from the skillet and then turned off the burner. "I was just waiting to hear you say the words."

She lifted her head and faced him.

"I'm here for you, darling." He hobbled over to the love seat and set his walker beside him. Then he patted the arm of the couch. "Let's talk."

When she was younger, Dad had served faithfully as her counselor, solving all her childhood dilemmas. Although she wasn't sure if her adult problems could be so easily solved, her father would listen. He'd lend his support, however small.

Maya sat on the couch and pulled the throw over her legs. Sitting here, with the first man who had captured her heart, quelled all sense of unease.

"Was I right about why you're hesitant about dating Derek?"

Maya tamped down the urge to voice her fears about how her illness could affect Derek, but she couldn't hold it for much longer. "I don't want Derek to be negatively affected by my illness. If we started dating, even in a long-distance relationship, he'd eventually end up heartbroken."

"Oh, darling." He wrapped his arms around her. "I know you're concerned about that, but you have a right to be happy too. Give yourself the gift of joy."

Her eyes stung. "Easy to say. Not so easy to do."

"You don't want Derek's heart to be broken. That's wise, but don't cancel him out of a date."

She leaned on the armrest, uncertain. "What if I go ahead with this and . . . I don't know."

He patted her shoulder. Pops still wore his wedding band, even though Mom passed away nine years ago and even though he was dating Ginger. Seeing it tore her up inside, a symbol of how he'd taken a great risk when he eloped with Mom against her parents' wishes.

What if she took a risk and said yes to Derek's date? What if she said no and ended up regretting it? Yes? No? Yes? No? That was the problem with making decisions. One never knew how they'd turn out. She had made very careful decisions with regards to her life and her career, and she didn't want to fumble anything up.

"Earth to Maya." Her father snapped his fingers. "You still there?"

"I am." She laughed. "I just have a lot to consider."

"I know you do. So what will you decide?"

Maya looked away. "I don't know."

"Having the courage to follow your heart can be a slippery slope," her father said. "Makes you feel all sorts of things. Not so easy to do and much harder to live."

She was trying to live it, trying to follow her heart. Maya rested her head on Pops's shoulder. Maybe if she snapped her fingers, all the hard parts would disappear.

Maya snapped her fingers twice.

Nothing.

"Maya," her father continued, "I think you're smart to be worried about Derek and think things through. Most people operate on autopilot, never questioning the effects of their choices."

"I don't feel smart. I feel—"

"Hopeful? Yet uncertain?"

"Yes. I like Derek. I've enjoyed every day at that boutique, but I don't want to be a headache to him."

He paused. "You want my opinion?"

"Yes, Pops."

"No one is asking you to uproot your life or change your goals. Derek knows you're leaving. Enjoy it for what it is—a date. Then return to New York and follow hard after your dreams. But don't stop living, Maya. Don't ever stop living. You owe it to yourself to live every single day to the fullest. Don't let sickle cell take that away from you either."

"But what if—"

"Take things one day at a time. Don't worry about the what-ifs. Just think about today. And today, a nice man asked my daughter on a date. Have you told him about your illness yet?"

"No. I wasn't planning to do so, because I figured I'm just working at Always a Bride temporarily. Also, I didn't want him to treat me differently or fire me. Since he wants to go on a date, however, I will."

"Good. Tell him. Let him decide how far he wants to take things with you—just like you told your ex-fiancé." He motioned to her old wedding gown in the hall closet. "No matter what happens in life, trust that it'll work out in the end. Live on, darling. You have a beautiful life ahead."

The onset of tears blurred her vision. His words riddled her to the core. There was a rightness to what he'd said, even if she couldn't wrap her mind around all of it herself.

Maya wiped the tears from her cheeks and got her cell phone to text Derek. She'd accept his offer and tell him all about her illness on their date.

Dinner sounds great, Derek. When and where do you want to meet?

Live. Maya would live.

She breathed deeply, fully, truly.

Chapter Twelve

A few days after Maya had agreed to a date, Derek steered his freshly washed pickup into the semicircle driveway of 82 Queen and turned off the ignition. Maya had been off work for the past few days, so he hadn't spoken to her since their phone call. He hopped out of the truck, slamming the door behind him.

A red-vested valet parking attendant took his keys and handed him a ticket. A knot formed in the pit of his stomach. Last time he'd felt this way had been over twenty years ago on his first date with Grace. Funny how he was getting the same feeling on his date with Maya.

A sharp gust of wind billowed through his bomber jacket, pushing him toward the front entrance. He faced two options: brace against the harsh wind or seek shelter in the restaurant. He would seek shelter.

Derek anticipated Maya's arrival, but he was also nervous. He had been out of the dating scene, and he hoped things hadn't changed much in over two decades. But what did he know? Derek could easily mess this up.

He still wanted to get to know Maya better one-on-one. Derek was also mindful of the fact that Maya hadn't given him an immediate yes when he asked her on this date. This meant Maya was hesitant and wanted to think about it, which he respected. He had to play things carefully. If he seemed too eager, he could push her away.

A uniformed man opened the door and welcomed him. The knot lessened its grip. *Here goes nothing.* He nodded to the doorman and strode inside.

The restaurant foyer extended a warm greeting with its arched Romanesque ceiling, walls paneled with impressionist art, and shiny hardwood floors. Clinking silverware, mingled with soft murmurs and laughter, filled the space. People clad in casual attire gathered in booths and at tables. No Maya.

A set of French doors framed in marble stood off to the left. They opened onto a vacant dance floor encircled with empty dinner tables. He'd reserved a table here the morning after Maya had said yes. He continued searching for her and checked his phone for a text. No text. A spiral staircase led up to the second floor. Perhaps she was up there, waiting.

"Hey, Derek," a voice called from behind.

He turned and nearly collided with a waitress holding two menus under her arm. "Excuse me, miss."

The waitress appeared to be sixteen going on thirty—or

thirty going on sixteen. Hard to tell. Her short, spiked red hair stuck out like an Arizona cactus and reminded him of a punk rocker. This, along with her Queen of Sheba black eyeliner and bright red lips, belied her conservative uniform: a starched white shirt and creased black pants. Everyone had their personal style; hers was unique.

"I'm Kendra, remember me?" Her mouth curled into a smile, accentuating a fleshy dimple.

He quickly ran through his mental Rolodex, but nothing.

"I visited your shop with my sister a while ago. She was getting married and looking for a gown." She laughed. "You looked so funny trying to sell to those finicky ladies. Thank you again for helping my sister get a discount on her gown. It meant a lot to us, seeing that her wedding budget was tight."

He would've spoken longer about her experience in the shop, but he needed to know if Maya arrived. "Glad to have been of help." Derek quickly scanned the restaurant. "I'm looking for my date. She's about five foot five, curly dark hair."

"I haven't seen her yet, but I wanted to repay you for being so kind to my sister. So I reserved a secluded table overlooking downtown Charleston." She held up two fingers. "A table for two. *Dos* in Spanish. *Deux* in French. *Duo* in Latin. And *dio* in Greek."

A secluded table for two? Derek would've preferred something with the restaurant crowd. No need to alienate Maya on their first date. "Do you have anything on the main floor?"

The waitress scrunched her nose. "No, we don't. The spaces are taken. But no worries. It's a really great spot. Follow me." She motioned to the upstairs area.

Derek clambered up a black wrought-iron staircase. When he arrived, he surveyed the space. No one was there. One table was centered in the middle of the dimmed space, covered with a white linen cloth and littered with pink and white rose petals.

"I put down the rose petals for extra oompf. You like?" Kendra arched her brow.

Those rose petals could push Maya away too. She could think he was laying it on thick. "They're . . . interesting."

"Oh, well then. Sorry. Just trying to repay a favor." She scooped some of the rose petals into her hand, but there was still a smattering of them left on the table. "I'll be on the lookout for your date." Kendra filled two water glasses and left.

He appreciated Kendra's intentions, but Maya's reaction to all this mattered more.

A staccato *click-clack*ing bounced off the hardwood floors. He straightened and glanced up. Maya. The petite vision waited at the top of the staircase. Her silver-toned dress hugged every inch of her frame. His pulse went into overdrive. Derek gulped down half of his water. She headed over.

"Hi, Maya." The croak in his voice undercut his attempts

to sound laid-back.

"Hey." She sat down and scanned the table littered with the leftover rose petals. "This looks . . . great."

She didn't like it. "Great."

A silence ensued. The roses were way too much. This date was gonna be way uncomfortable.

"Hey, so I was thinking. I know I made the reservation, but now that we're here, I'm not really digging this restaurant's vibe."

"Me neither," Maya said.

"Really?"

"Uh-huh." She shrugged. "Too fancy for me. Would you like to visit the botanical garden?" she asked. "It's only three blocks away and it's definitely not as . . . formal."

Relief washed over him. "Excellent."

"From what I remember, they have a beautiful display of calla lilies this time of year. And I'm not that hungry anyway."

"Me neither. I'll let the waitress know about our change in plans," Derek said, relieved.

After doing so, Derek and Maya headed toward the front entrance of the restaurant.

This was a good change. Being in a place of Maya's choosing was the best idea anyway, and Derek looked forward to getting to know her more.

THE BRILLIANT AMBER sun started its gradual descent, marking the end of another day. At the botanical garden, an expanse of tulips stretched out before Maya, a brilliant display of reds and yellows and whites. A robin flew fifty or so feet above them and settled onto a branch of a violet crepe myrtle.

Maya would tell him all about herself today. She was glad that she wouldn't have to tell him in the restaurant. The vibe made her anxious. Being in nature was much better. She stood closer to him and inhaled the scent of his cologne. Maya was comfortable in his presence. Then, before she knew it, her fingertips touched his.

Derek glanced over at her and smiled. She returned the gesture, and their fingers inched their way around one another. A steady hum of electricity simmered between them, and Maya relaxed into his touch. Comfort thrummed through her. This was nice.

Maya was surprised when Derek said they should ditch the restaurant. She'd been feeling nervous about going on a formal date. Being here at the gardens was much more chill and casual. It'd be easier to get to know him here than at a stuffy, fancy restaurant. And that's what she wanted to do— know him better but also keep a friendly distance. This was just a date, not a commitment.

"Tell me more about growing up," she asked.

"Things were tough, especially after my father left. Gave my mother more grief than I could bear."

"I can't imagine you giving your mother any grief. You're so ambitious and focused." Maya's eyes met his, and he held her gaze.

"You're talking to Derek the adult. Not Derek the wannabe independent youngster. Jamila reminds me of myself at her age, but she's changing." Derek smiled. "That's a good sign. I give all the credit to you. Thank you so much for helping her with the school project, even though Jamila refused your help at first."

"Not a problem." She paused, weighing whether this was the right time to say something. Her concerns about Jamila held the same weight as her concerns about telling Derek. "Have you ever talked to her about how she feels losing her mother and her grandmother?"

Derek flicked a glance at her, his expression neutral. "I don't think that's necessary."

"Maybe you should."

No answer. *All righty then.*

They reached a graveled path lined with cherry blossoms. The more they walked together, the more that moment's unsettledness faded. They squinted at the last shred of light peeking behind cotton-fluff clouds.

Maya stood there for a stretch of time, enjoying the sight, still holding Derek's hand. With her free hand, she grabbed her smartphone and took photos of the cherry blossoms. Those would make a gorgeous accent to Jamila's dress project for school.

The breeze picked up, and she shivered. Maya had completely forgotten to bring her jacket.

"Is the wind bothering you?" he asked.

She glanced at his chiseled features. Very handsome. And way too inviting. "No." Maya combed her hair away from her face.

"Let me know if you're too cold."

"Okay, I'm a little cold."

"This will keep you warm." He handed her his bomber jacket.

Maya couldn't help but inhale the scent of aftershave lingering on the soft leather as she slipped it on. The jacket warmed her to the core. She closed her eyes, allowing herself to relax into the material.

Derek eyed her. Maya forced herself to not look so cold, but it was to no success. It would get dark soon. She hoped to show him around before night set in.

A sign for the Enchanted Forest stood out among the flora. They stepped inside the entrance and stood near a bonsai. The Enchanted Forest had been one of her favorite places to visit. It flourished with crepe myrtles and oak trees and Japanese bonsai. A young couple sat on a nearby bench, holding hands.

"Maya?"

"Yes?"

"Is it okay if I pull you close?"

She tried to speak, but her vocal cords didn't seem to be working properly. Pull her close? His smile enticed her, and the promise she had made to keep a friendly distance faded.

"That's fine."

He embraced her, and they were face-to-face. Being so near to Derek melted away those promises and broke her resolve. With a silent surrender, she leaned into him, her cheek resting against his shoulder. He wrapped his other arm around her waist. He was warm and cozy and solid. She settled more fully in his embrace.

"Is this okay for you?" he asked.

"Yes." She drew in a deep breath, locked into his cocoon, unwilling to let go.

"Good."

Dapples of light streaked through the tall oak trees. In front of her, the water in a small pond lapped up onto the walking path. The breeze skimmed its blue-gray surface, causing it to ripple.

She tried to dredge up her last remnants of reasons not to get too close to Derek. His embrace erased all her excuses. He twirled a lock of her hair around his finger and looked into her eyes. Her stomach spiraled. A good spiral. The kind of spiral that dissolved all proper reason and good sense.

"You were right," he said, his voice a whisper. "The garden is beautiful."

"It used to be my little escape from the real world."

"Peaceful place to be." He rested his chin atop her head.

An old memory flashed in her mind. "I came here a lot when I was young. With my locked diary in hand, I'd run straight to this forest and find an empty bench. I wrote in my journal here. The yearnings of my heart."

Derek pulled away. "That's precious."

"I haven't opened a journal in a long time." She looked out at the dark shadows cast across the pond.

"Really?" His voice tinged with what sounded like empathy.

"I didn't see the point."

Another gust of wind whipped a tree into a frenzy. Stray leaves flew from the branches, recklessly swirling about. In many ways, that's what Maya became after her mother died. Frenzied. Lost. Aimless.

"You want to talk about it?" Derek cupped her chin in his hand.

Did she? Was she ready to share the not-so-pretty side of her life? Maya wasn't sure.

Derek would probably stop time to listen to the quiet murmurings of her heart. He patiently waited for her response—or her nonresponse. Either way, she sensed he wouldn't push the issue.

He smiled.

Another strong wind gusted. Standing with Derek in the garden, the place where she had written her hopes and dreams, made all that time spent writing somehow feel complete. The need to shed light on her silent wounds surfaced. "I stopped coming here after my mother died. I didn't want to sit here with a notebook in hand and explore my feelings about her passing." She tried to sound casual while recounting the memory. "It was too tough."

Derek brushed his fingertips across her cheek. "I understand that feeling."

Grief jabbed its one-two punch. Weakened, she still forced herself to speak. "I know you do." A tear formed at the corner of her eye, and she blinked. "It must be so hard to have lost your mother and your wife."

"It is." Derek's thumb brushed the tender area at the nape of her neck.

The tear sprung to the surface. Cruddy tears. She wiped it away. "People always tell me it will get easier, but it never does. How have you coped all these years?"

"I don't know. I haven't figured that one out," Derek said.

If he hadn't figured out a way to cope, then how would he react when she told him about her sickle cell? "We all have our way of dealing with grief."

"Yes." His voice stretched to the edge of shredding.

The tree branches rustled louder now, fighting against the wind threatening to break them. Maya buried herself deeper into the warmth of his chest. Despite her doubts, she loved being with him.

She riffled through the memories, the conversations. "I haven't been on a date in the longest time. I never imagined myself dating again, to be quite honest."

Confusion flit across his face for a split second, then he stepped away. Stripped of his embrace, a chill coursed through her, despite the warmth of his leather jacket. As she stood there, her shoulders hunched, her jaw rattling, she felt how hard it would be to tell him. But she would.

"I've thought the same about myself. I'm glad you took this step with me today. You've been so wonderful with Jamila, especially when you don't have to be. We haven't had this kind of presence in our lives since Grace, my late wife."

Since Grace? He's now likening me to his deceased wife? Oh my. If they continued on this path, he would meet the same fate with Maya. "I need to tell you something."

He nodded. "Go ahead."

"I have sickle cell anemia, Derek. When I first received the diagnosis, the doctor said my life span would be ten to fifteen years from now. I'm dying."

There. She said it.

His expression shuttered. That wasn't good. "You're dying?"

The doubt in his voice made her cringe inside. O-kay. Maybe she should have eased into it. "That's correct."

Still nothing.

"Is that what those pills were for on that day I walked in on you in the break room?" he asked.

"Yes."

He didn't appear happy with this new information, and it wasn't like she expected him to be. But she'd expected something . . . empathy at least. Why did she think going on a date with him would be a good idea? Why did she say yes?

"Look," Maya said, desperate to fill in the quiet between

them. "I know this isn't the best news to hear, especially given that you've already lost so much. Maybe I should've told you earlier about my condition. I don't know. I didn't say anything about it because . . ." Her breath hitched on something she didn't want to express.

"Because what?"

"I was worried that you were going to fire me."

"Fire you?"

"Yes." She looked down, and her eyes blurred with tears.

"You're a talented dress designer, Maya. And you've turned the store around in ways that I could've never done. There's no way that I'd fire you over something you can't control."

"Really?"

"Really."

"Then what about . . ." Her voice broke again.

"What about what?"

Maya turned away. The chilly breeze picked up, bullying away her sense of calm. The pond water rippled again, echoing the cracking wind. As it did, birds flew away in droves. Across the pond, leaves floated to the gravelly ground, their tiny veins ripped from the tree, their life source. A part of Maya ripped too. She spotted a bench off to the side and trudged toward it. A gust sent specks of dust flying in her eyes, blocking her vision. Blurred. Just like her attempts to connect with Derek. She shouldn't have agreed to this date. She sat down on the bench.

Moments later, Derek sat next to her.

"We're on this date now, and you've already lost so much. I should've told you that I . . . was dying before I agreed to this . . . this outing. I don't know. I just feel like this isn't fair to you. Maybe I'm in over my head."

"I won't lie, Maya. Your news is a lot for me to take in." He pressed his left knuckle at the corner of his eye and rubbed it vigorously. "A whole lot."

Expected. "Then I should go home. You're right. I apologize for even thinking that—"

"I still want to be here with you, Maya. Regardless of your illness."

"But I—"

"I've been thinking about Grace a lot. Thinking about what she would've wanted for my life, for Jamila's life, now that she's gone." Derek exhaled. "The truth is that we're all dying, Maya. It's not the dying that matters. It's the living."

"The living?"

"Yes. The living. You've helped me see that it's okay to pursue happiness, despite the grief and loss. You've helped me see that it's okay to renovate and remodel, not just the boutique, but my life. I don't have to feel stuck in the past and trapped in grief. Instead, I can bring the past with me and use it to craft a beautiful present and a hopeful future."

She did all of that?

"I don't want to squander those lessons, and I won't squander the one who showed them to me either," Derek continued. "Not for any reason. Not because of your diagnosis.

Not because of anything. Grace died suddenly and tragically. I never got a chance to say goodbye to her. But even if I knew how her life would end in advance, I still wouldn't trade my time with her for anything either."

"You wouldn't?"

"No. Never in a million years." He gently squeezed her hand. "You deserve happiness too, in your work and in your relationships."

His words chipped away at the lies she had believed. Still, an iceberg of hurt lodged in her heart. An iceberg that would never melt away. "My ex-fiancé left me over my diagnosis. He didn't express any misgivings when I first told him about my sickle cell anemia, but his true feelings came out eventually. He wasn't ready to spend the rest of his life with me. He was never honest with himself and me at the beginning of our relationship. He decided to cut his losses on our wedding day, the day when I was already fully committed. That day was a huge disaster." Her eyes blurred once again. "Maybe I'm not worth it."

"Don't say that. You're a treasure."

"A treasure—that's my consolation prize, I guess."

Derek cupped his gentle hands around the curve of her neck. "You can't blame yourself. That man didn't deserve you. If he did, he would've never left." He sat closer to Maya, millimeters from her lips.

The iceberg melted and warmth settled into her marrow, rooting her, steadying her, filling her. Why not get involved with Derek? Being in the garden with him completed her lifelong search for—

Derek leaned closer. His exhale danced across her cheek and tickled the tip of her ear. Maya's belly flipped.

"Can I kiss you, Maya?"

"Yes." She fell into him. His lips caressed hers. Maya returned his generous kiss. Longing sparked inside of her.

Maya exhaled and wrapped her arms around Derek. She could stay in that embrace, close to him. For the first time in a long time, she let go.

Chapter Thirteen

After Derek and Maya parted ways, he recounted their kiss over and over and over. He enjoyed kissing her, and she returned the gesture.

More than returned it. She kissed him deeply. Derek wanted to stay rooted in that moment, that goodness. Derek wanted to hold on to it with everything in him, but now that he was alone in his truck, all he could hear were Maya's hurts, Maya's fears, and Maya's insecurities.

She was scared. Derek was scared too.

His warring thoughts rose to the surface. Yes, death was an inevitable fact of life, but Maya could die earlier than him. Did he want to experience the pain of that loss again? Did he want to witness Jamila experiencing the grief again?

It was just a date, Derek, a date and one kiss. Don't make too much of it.

He wouldn't push things further with Maya. This was something he needed to take slow, and so while he'd love to ask Maya out on a second date, he wouldn't ask Maya unless she brought it up. Besides, Maya was still returning to New York shortly after Heather's wedding.

Don't make too much of the date.

Derek pulled into the garage of his house and headed inside. He needed to get some rest and ready himself for the next business day.

Once inside the house, the faint sound of the television floated from the living room. He checked his watch. It was way past Jamila's bedtime.

Upset, he headed to the television. Jamila sat on the lumpy couch with the remote control in hand, watching cartoons. The TV blared. The eagerness in Jamila's eyes told Derek he wasn't getting rest any time soon. "Why are you still up? Where's Ginger?" Derek asked.

"She fell asleep in the den. I couldn't sleep." Jamila pressed the Mute button, and the television stopped blaring.

The expectation in her made him uncomfortable. Jamila was definitely invested in this date.

"You should be in bed, miss. We have rules."

"I know, but I couldn't go to sleep because I was excited about your date. So where'd you guys go, Dad?"

"To the botanical gardens."

"I love that place. How was the date?"

"It went okay."

"Okay? That's it? Did you kiss her?" Jamila smiled.

He didn't answer.

"You did kiss her! You did!"

"Hey. Hey. Hey." Derek put his hands up. "I know she gave you a sewing machine, and she's going to help you with your project and all, but kissing? Why are you so concerned with kissing? You're twelve."

"You're just avoiding my question, trying to put it on my age. You obviously like Maya." Jamila reached to the other side of the couch and grabbed her boar bristle brush and detangling spray. "That's why I was so annoyed with you at the beginning."

"So a sewing machine won you over?" He chuckled.

"More than the sewing machine. She seems to understand how I feel about losing Mom and Grandma."

"Of course she would. She's had a similar experience." Derek leaned against the doorjamb and crossed his arms. "And you think that makes her kiss-worthy?" he asked, a teasing note in his voice.

"Something like that." Jamila unraveled one braid and started brushing the ends.

"All right. It's time for us to get some sleep. You shouldn't be up so late, so—"

"Can you do my hair?"

Do her hair? Jamila had *never* asked her father to do her hair before, never ever. "Excuse me?"

She brushed it in jagged strokes. "It's all tangly and I can't reach the back. Can you help, Dad? Please."

He had no idea how to do Jamila's hair. Since she wouldn't

let him touch her strands, Derek never learned. What if he royally messed this one up?

"Ouch!" Jamila's eyes squeezed shut as she tugged her brush through another tangle.

Okay, she was in pain. "I'll help. But don't expect anything magical. I'm a newbie at this." Derek headed her way, and she handed him the brush.

Her curls were coarse and thick, just like Grace's hair. She always styled Jamila's hair in intricate braids and twists. Right now, he was trying to get through the first step of detangling her hair, but where should he start?

"Start from the bottom of my hair and then work your way up to my scalp," Jamila said, as if reading his mind.

"All righty."

The cartoons played in the background, and the glare from the TV screen shone on their faces, keeping Derek awake.

"Remember when Mama used to do my hair?" Jamila asked.

His heart pinched, and he swallowed the thickness gathering in his throat. "I remember."

"She was so good with my hair. Had the fastest fingers for braiding and twisting too. I used to fight getting my hair combed by Mama, and she used to fuss at me for it." Jamila sighed. "Now I wish she were here. I wish I hadn't been so resistant."

A wave of love washed over him. Jamila was apologizing in her own little way. "I wish she were here too."

"She'd probably laugh if she saw your detangling my hair now."

Derek stopped brushing. "Why is that, jokester?"

Jamila shrugged. "Cuz you never did my hair. You always looked at my hair like it was a big old mess."

He leaned around to face her. "Where'd you get that idea?"

"From your face. That's how you looked at my hair." Jamila twisted her mouth. "Don't matter, though. It's a nappy ol' mess. Maybe one day I'll get a relaxer."

Oh God. Here she was forming her value by her hair. What could he say? Grace was always the one who did the hair and the clothes. He didn't want his daughter to think her natural hair was subpar. "Baby girl, I never thought your hair was a mess. I'm sorry if you ever felt that way about me. You never let me do your hair."

"Because you looked at it like it was a disaster. Sometimes you'd be side-eyeing me while Mama was doing my hair."

"That's because you'd be screaming so loud while she was combing it. Not because I don't like your hair." Derek wrapped his arm around her. "I think it's beautiful just as it is."

She was quiet, and then: "Like I said, it don't matter." Jamila twisted her fingers, apparently uncomfortable with this conversation.

She must've had enough sentimentality for the evening. He could roll with it. Derek stood straight and detangled her hair once again.

"Dad?"

"Yes, baby girl."

"I think Mama would've liked Maya. What do you think?"

The brush stopped midstroke. He hadn't considered it before, and Jamila drawing the connection between the two was different. "I don't know. What makes you say that?"

"Because Maya loves Always a Bride. She's really doing a lot to make sure it's successful. Maya wants to make a tribute to Mama and Grandma with my dress project. That shows Maya isn't selfish."

"That's a smart observation from you, young lady."

"Do you think Mama would've liked Maya too?"

He paused. *Would* Grace have liked Maya? Grace did tell him to be happy after she was gone, but it's one thing to say something, quite another to abide by it. That sense of guilt over his feelings toward Maya encroached upon him again. "I'm not sure, honey. That's a complicated question."

"Why?" Jamila asked.

Because Maya is terminally sick. Because she has a short time left. Because we'd get hurt again. To make matters worse, if he didn't pursue this relationship with Maya, she would think it was due to her illness. He already told her that her illness didn't matter. Reneging on that statement would hurt Maya, and from what little she'd said about her ex, Maya had already been hurt enough.

"Daaaad? I'm waiting for an answer."

Should he even share these thoughts with Jamila? He should. Jamila deserved to know the truth. "It's complicated with Maya because she has sickle cell anemia. She has a short time to live."

Jamila was silent for a minute. "How short?"

"Ten to fifteen years."

The air was thick between them. He sensed the weight of Jamila's question.

"That's why I'm not so sure. Whoever I date will be in both our lives. I don't want you to get hurt again."

Jamila nodded. "I get it, Dad. But I like Maya."

"I like her too. I think your mother would've loved Maya."

"Then it doesn't matter how long Maya lives. Just like we'll always love Mom. We can always love Maya too. We have to live too, right?"

His eyes stung. Grace would want him to live. In his heart, he knew this to be true. "Right."

She turned and faced him. "Then you're gonna ask Maya out again, right?"

Don't fear the future, Derek. Don't fear. "Yes, I will ask her out again."

Jamila smiled. "Yay! That's great."

He finished brushing Jamila's hair in silence as she watched television, and then it was lights out for both. As Derek stayed up in his room, alone, he thought of his time this evening with Maya. Despite Maya's diagnosis, being on a date with her tonight was amazing. He couldn't wait to hang out with her again.

A good sensation tugged at him, and he relaxed into the feeling. For the first time in years, he sensed hope.

ON SUNDAY EVENING, Maya put the last and final touches on the design revisions for Laura and sent the email. A flitter of nervousness coursed through her. She'd toned down the design concept for Laura's sake this time around. Hopefully Laura would like it—like it enough to promote Maya to head designer.

For Heather's dress, Maya didn't tone down a thing. She relished in the creative freedom she had while working on Heather's gown. She sent updates to Heather for feedback. During the course of their communication, Heather said she was sending Maya and Derek a wedding invite as a thankyou. That was nice. Maya hadn't been to a wedding since her own wedding day.

After that was done, Maya gave the white sash tied around her waist one last tug and straightened the hem of her green A-line skirt. It was made years ago by her mother, who first taught Maya to sew using this skirt as a pattern. She eyed herself in the full-length mirror. The skirt fit her as well as it fit her mother back then.

She struck up a conversation with her father—not to talk about skirts. She needed to figure out if pursuing Derek was the right thing.

"Pops?"

"Yes, my dear."

"You have time to talk again?"

"Always, love. Always."

She sat next to him at the kitchen counter and rested her chin in her hands. How would she approach this conversation without subjecting herself to her father's piercing truisms again? Maybe that was an impossibility. Still, she would proceed cautiously. Her father had a way about him that could leave her in a puddle of cleansing tears.

She glanced at his left hand and saw his gold wedding band on his ring finger. "Why do you still wear your wedding band?"

"Because I loved your mother. I still do."

Her heart crimped. It was nice for her to hear him say that, seeing that he was dating Ginger and all. "Has Ginger ever said anything about it?"

He twisted his mouth and looked up, apparently thinking. "No, she hasn't. I guess she understands."

Maya reached for a paper napkin and folded it in half. "She's a widow too?"

"No. Divorced twice and happily living the single life, as she calls it." He chuckled. "I don't know what I'm going to do when she starts traveling. I obviously can't go along with her just yet. But she'll return on occasion. I'll miss her when she's gone."

He'll miss her. Ginger had been such a great help. What

would Pops do when Ginger left? Maya's old fears about her father being alone rose to the surface, but this time she tamped them down. Her father would be fine. "How did you know that you were in love with Mama?"

"I just knew. We both worked at the college bookstore, and she was such a bookworm. Me, not so much. Anyway, we started dating and she told me about her passion for fashion design. I loved her enthusiasm for life. She never seemed bogged down by the bad. She just kept focusing on the good. I loved that about her."

Maya nodded. "You're right. She never gave up on the possibility of me being a New York designer, even when I was doubtful."

"And look at you today." He winked.

Yeah, look at her today. She was making moves in her career, but lately she'd been more successful in South Carolina than New York.

And that kiss. That kiss flipped everything inside out.

"How was your date?" Pops asked, as if reading her mind.

"Good."

"That's it. Just good?" Her father had a teasing note in his voice.

"I like Derek. I like him a lot."

Her father smiled. "That's wonderful."

"But you said before 'oh, it's just one date. No big commitment.' Now, my feelings are changing. We had a great conversation, and he's the most considerate person. I even told him about my sickle cell, and he didn't even care. I don't know what I should do."

"Did he ask you to do something?"

Maya shrugged. "No. He didn't. I'm just trying to make sense of my feelings, I guess." She reached over and picked up the picture of her mother that was on the coffee table. "I wish Mom were still here. I miss her."

"Me too, darling. Me too. You know, it's okay to let yourself feel love toward someone."

"I didn't say I loved him."

"You don't have to think everything out. You can just give in to the emotions. That's what life is about." He looked at the picture of Mama. "The way I felt about your mother is the same way I feel about Ginger."

A smile came over Maya. "Is that so?"

"Yes . . . I know you're concerned."

She glanced down. "I was worrying about what would happen if Ginger left. You would be alone."

"Not for long." He smiled. "I was thinking, once I'm free of that walker, that I may want to go around the country and travel with her."

"That's a great idea." Maya glanced at the picture of her mother once again. Her olive skin was smooth, her dark eyes seemed to hold a thousand hopes, many which were now unlived. "I'm glad that you're creating new adventures for yourself."

"You know I didn't plan on falling in love again. I wasn't

looking for another person to love, but Ginger opened my heart to the possibilities."

Each word he'd spoken filled Maya with more and more hope. If Pops got remarried, he'd be a blessed man. He would've loved twice in a lifetime. That was rare.

"You should open your heart to the possibilities too, Maya."

Open her heart to the possibilities? "What do you mean?" she asked. In truth, she knew what he meant, but she didn't want to acknowledge it, not with her father this way.

"If you're feeling something about Derek, go with your gut. For a person to say that he still cares about you, despite the risks of your illness—it's like finding a diamond."

She thought so too, which was why this was so cumbersome. "Is Ginger your diamond?"

Pops nodded. "Yes. She is."

"That's wonderful."

Her father smiled at the picture of Maya's mother. "One of the things I admired about your mother was her ability to be fearless. You know, your mother was one of the few Filipino people living in South Carolina. She made herself right at home here. Everyone here loved her dearly, and she was famous for bringing *pancit* and chicken adobo to the potlucks." He laughed. "She was also one of the few dress designers. For a while, she'd built up a good side clientele by working as a seamstress and dressmaker for the women of Charleston too. Her mother had taught her as a young girl in the Philippines, and she taught you the craft. Did you know that she wanted to go to fashion design school?"

Maya did a double take. "She did?"

"She even wanted to start a dress shop of her own. She didn't have the seed money, not after—"

Guilt set in. "My sickle cell needs. I kept her from her dream."

"No, you didn't, my dear. You didn't. You were her dream. All that she had is inside of you too. Her beauty and her strength and her talent. Maybe there's a reason that you've made your way over to Always a Bride, and it's not simply because you need extra rent money for your apartment. So whatever you're feeling about Derek, don't fear it."

"Don't fear it." Easier said than done. "She could've partnered with Always a Bride in some way. Did she ever consider it?"

"No, unfortunately. Her full-time job didn't give her much time to focus on dress design. But don't think that you held your mother back. Because you didn't."

Maya rested her chin in her hands, thinking. It was kind of hard to not believe what her father just told her, that her mother had let go of design school because of her. "So, if I don't believe that, then what should I do?"

"Move on." He winked at Maya. "I am."

Maya glanced at the wedding ring on his finger. She could see the tiny scratches on the band that came from years of use. How many smiles and tears and arguments and joys had his wedding band witnessed? So many. Too many to count. And Pops was moving on from those memories to something new and unknown.

Could she do the same? Maya wasn't sure, there were a ton of things she needed to consider before she let herself completely fall for Derek. She lived in New York. Her health issues took up a lot of time. After her monthly blood transfusions, she needed days to recoup. She had one more transfusion to schedule before she left for home. Her health needs meant she wouldn't be available to "people" or tend relationships much.

She could go on as planned, career minded and loveless, but Maya would be missing out on Derek in the process. Nonetheless, her father was right. She deserved to live fully for her own sake. Would Derek be okay once she left? That was something they'd have to discuss. "If you can move forward, then I can move forward too."

"Attagirl." Her father wrapped his arm around her. "We'll get through this together."

She settled into the feeling that they'd get through this together. The more she pondered it, the more her father's wedding ring glinted on his finger, as if telling her that yes, her feelings toward Derek were okay. That she could trust how she felt toward Derek. A sense of relief overcame her. Maya needn't fear.

And so she wouldn't.

Chapter Fourteen

A few days later, Maya stood back and admired the gown she had tweaked for Heather's wedding. The dress was close to complete, and Maya could tell she had outdone herself. Maya couldn't wait for Heather to arrive at the bridal boutique today and try it on. Hopefully, she'd love it just as much as Maya did.

Maya had been nervous at first because she couldn't envision Heather's gown. Then Maya read about how Heather's great-grandmother loved the color purple because it reminded her of her own mother, her mother who was Black, but no one knew at the time. After gathering that bit of information, Heather's dress became clear. Maya then quickly picked out a gown from her inventory. The gown was made of handwoven Filipino silk in the *suksuk* design. It was a weaving technique that originated in the Philippines centuries ago, a dying craft today, but Maya's mother had taught her the process. She also showed Maya where to order the silk and get it shipped to the States.

Maya had sketched out tweaks to this existing gown before they left her thoughts. The fabric would be ruched from top to bottom and extend into a flowing train. Maya would add some cowrie shells to the shoulder straps. Heather had given her the shells, which had belonged to her great-grandmother. The shells signified prosperity and wealth, which every new couple could use in their life.

Well . . . not *every* new couple. Heather already had financial wealth since she was the governor's daughter, but there was another kind of affluence that Heather didn't fully have—the wealth of knowing her *full* family tree. Would Heather's Black family members want to even be connected to Heather's family, given their riddled history? Who knew?

The train of the gown would be embroidered in flowers colored with purple, Heather's great-grandmother's favorite color. For the flowers, Maya would use *piña* thread and *jusi* fabric, as the Filipino *bordadoras* did.

Maya's body had tingled as she sketched the design tweaks. That's when she knew it was a winner.

Maya never got tingly feelings when she worked for Laura. That could be another sign that her creativity wasn't being put to good use there, but she didn't want to consider the implications of all that right now.

The door to the boutique opened. Maya shot up from her stool, expecting to greet Heather. After fixing her curly hair, Maya squinted and her heart skipped. Derek entered the boutique and looked as handsome as ever. This time she didn't push away the thought of his attractiveness. She let it roll around inside of her, causing her to smile.

"I thought you were taking off from work this week. What brings you here?" She leaned against the doorjamb, arms folded across her chest, trying to appear casual.

"I want to talk," Derek said. His expression was focused.

A rush of heat danced down her neck. He sounded serious and not in a good way. After two deep conversations with her father, she'd hoped that she hadn't made the wrong decision, the decision to let herself feel her feelings toward Derek. "Sure." She stepped aside and motioned to Heather's dress. "Heather is supposed to arrive today for her dress fitting. Any minute now, actually."

His gaze flickered. "Okay, no problem. We can talk when she's finished with her fitting." Derek glanced at the gown. "That's stunning, Maya."

His compliment of her work refreshed places in her soul she didn't know existed. "Thank you."

More customers trickled into the shop. "Can I help you?" Maya asked.

"No," the ebony-skinned woman said. "We're just look— whoa, that dress is amazing." She pointed to Maya's design.

Maya smiled. Folks were taking to her work. "Thank you. This dress is custom-made for a client, but I have others like it." She pointed to the dress rack with her most recent gowns.

Seconds later, Heather finally arrived, and Maya got her set up in the dressing room. Derek sat at the front counter, apparently waiting for Maya to get some downtime. What did he want to discuss that was so urgent?

Maya pushed the question out of her brain. No need to worry over that. Heather was here and Maya needed to make sure Heather was good.

Heather stepped out of the dressing room wearing the gown, and Maya's eyes widened. "Oh my goodness, you look amazing."

Heather smiled. "All because of you. This is gorgeous, and I can't wait to wear it in four and a half weeks."

The other customers circled around Heather, their eyes filled with admiration over the dress. "Looks even better when it's worn," one customer said. "Such a unique style."

Maya was smiling so much her cheeks hurt, and then she made eye contact with Derek. He winked at Maya, and her body warmed.

"You know, people were asking us where we're registered for gifts," Heather said. "I told them to just make donations to New Life Church's Black History Society. Preserving my great-grandmother's history is more important to me." She twirled in front of the full-length mirror and the gown made soft swishing sounds.

"I love that idea, Heather. I hope you raise plenty of money."

"Me too. I want to direct some of the funds to the Black

history museum too. I heard people want to close it down."

It was satisfying to see Heather connecting to all of her roots, and Maya had played a small part in that. Perhaps Cat Clyne would be interested in featuring the church's fundraising efforts. It could increase donations to the Black History Society and the museum. Maya made a mental note to mention it to Cat.

"I better get going. I have a big day ahead of me. Have to go to the baker and the florist." Heather opened the door to the dressing room and stepped inside. "The bridesmaids will be here in a few hours to try on their dresses."

"Sounds good. When you're finished getting dressed, you can hang the gown on the rack behind the register. I'll put it up safely."

After Heather left, Maya scanned the dressing room area for any signs of disarray. Other customers had left some dresses scattered on the settee. A shawl hung on the back of a chair. A flush of heat came over her. *This place looks so messy.* "So much upkeep around here. So much mess." She quickly picked up both items.

"What mess?" Derek asked, heading her way.

"Never mind." She neatly hung the dresses and folded the shawl into a perfect triangle. A stray spool of fabric ribbon was strewn across the carpeted floor too. She picked it up and shoved it in a drawer. Derek's presence made her feel super self-conscious about everything.

"You've been pretty busy making gowns," Derek said.

"All of your help with the boutique has been paying off too. I sold out of some of the other dresses and had to place a new order for inventory."

"Not only did you catch up on the mortgage, you're heading into the black. That's great."

"You're great," Derek said.

That uncomfortable feeling came over Maya again. She headed to the front register and Derek followed. Saturday's business mail lay jumbled on the counter, so she performed another search and attack mission.

"Did you receive an invitation to Heather's wedding?" Derek asked.

"I did. Did you?"

"Yes," he said. "I'm really proud of all you've done here."

Another flush of heat. "I worked long hours on Heather's dress. Hence the poor store upkeep today." She gestured to the sales floor.

He regarded the space. "Looks decent to me."

The customers left the store, and it was now empty. She shifted her weight from one foot to the other. They stared at each other for an eternity. *Say something, Maya.* "Are you thirsty? I restocked the break room fridge with some sweet tea I brewed and brought to the shop with me."

"Sure." That cute dimple reappeared on his chin as he pulled off his jacket and folded it over his arm.

Maya and Derek headed to the rear of the store. She sensed his presence inches behind her, and her skin tingled. Derek had a way about him that made Maya feel all types of things. Inhale. Exhale. Inhale. Exhale.

When they passed by the accessories table, Derek stopped. "Is that another gown of yours?"

Maya nodded.

"Very stunning."

She couldn't help but smile. That didn't stop her from worrying about his reasons for coming to the store today, however.

They entered the break room and Maya grabbed two glasses from the cupboard and filled them with iced tea. She handed him a glass and sat at the white tiled table.

Derek followed, pulling out a chair. "How's your dad?"

If Derek had something serious to say, he was stalling. Derek could've just said his peace straightaway. "Doing great. He and Ginger are getting closer and closer. They're out getting brunch today." She pulled a paper napkin from its holder. Worry settled in. "What did you want to discuss?"

Derek's line of sight traveled from his glass to her. All her intentions to focus on the store and the final details of Heather's dress disappeared with Derek standing before her.

After a pause, he drummed his fingers on the table. "I spent some time thinking about everything. When I returned home from our date at the garden . . ."

Maya braced herself. "Yeah?"

Sighing, he tugged on his ear and rested his elbows on the table.

Her stomach flipped, and she bit her bottom lip. What was he going to say?

"I want to go on a second date. Perhaps a third and a fourth. I really like you, Maya. I'd like to see where you and I can land."

Relief washed over her, and Maya stopped biting her lip. "You do?"

"Definitely. Most assuredly yes."

His words carved an open space in her soul, dissolving her fears into a sea of forgetfulness. Then doubt arose again just as swiftly. "I'm returning home in a little over a month. Is this even feasible?"

"It can be." Derek nodded a yes. "It definitely can be. I've thought about that part too. I was thinking that I could close the shop one weekend a month and fly up to see you. Jamila would come along too."

"Really?"

"Jamila has had a huge change of heart toward you. She'd love to visit the Big Apple, if you'd like to see her too."

"I'd love to see Jamila. It's just . . ."

"Just what?"

"So much stuff can happen, especially with the distance between us," Maya said. "You know that my sickle cell will require a lot, and so I won't be able to be the happy hostess all the time. Especially when I get my transfusions."

"I fully understand. I'm willing to help you with whatever you need. I also want us to build on the other night. That's important to me. Is it important to you?"

Was it important to her? Her attention would be divided if she returned home and pursued a long-distance relationship with Derek. She needed as much time as possible to focus on her work too. Would Derek understand that?

He didn't seem like the controlling type. After spending so much time with Derek, she saw that clearly now. She could sacrifice a working weekend for him and Jamila. "Yes, it's important to me too."

"That makes me happy, Maya. You know, I've been going back to New Life regularly again."

"You have?"

"I talked to my pastor about you and the whole long-distance-relationship thing."

Talked to the pastor? Hoo boy. That sounded serious. She scrunched her mouth. "We're just dating, right?"

"Oh yeah. Oh yeah. I wasn't talking to the pastor in *that* way."

"*That* way" meaning in a marriage way. Maya didn't say anything.

"I was just telling him that I was thinking of dating someone again, and he encouraged me to keep moving forward with it. To not be afraid of new beginnings."

Pops mentioned new beginnings too. She could try starting anew. Maya could move on from the ugliness of the past and learn to be in a relationship again. "New beginnings, huh?"

"Yes. Instead of looking at the end of something. I can look on with hope at the unknown. At least that's how he phrased it. I liked that perspective."

Maya nodded. "I like it too."

The quiet hum of the air conditioner in the background rocked its steady beat. Maya then sat closer to him, so close she could see the subtle rise and fall of his chest. He wrapped his arm around her, and they fell into a comfortable silence. Was this what it felt like to be content? Must be. She relished the feeling.

"I wanted to give you some time to finish up your projects with Heather and Jamila," Derek said. "So I figure that our next date can be Heather's wedding in a few weeks. What do you think?"

Another wave of contentment washed over her. "That sounds perfect."

THE DAY OF the big wedding for Heather Gates. Sunlight warmed Maya's back as she and Derek arrived fifteen minutes early at the governor's mansion in Columbia, South Carolina. They drove to the wedding together since it was almost a two-hour drive from Charleston.

As soon as they arrived at the beautiful property with its expansive lawn and willow trees, nervousness overcame Maya. This wedding would make or break her design efforts. If Maya's style wasn't well received, she might as well call it quits. She fidgeted with her clutch and bit on her lower lip.

"Enjoy yourself," Derek said. "This is a day for you to relax."

"I can't," she said.

"You can try."

Maya would have to remind herself to relax over and over again. Although she was a guest here at the wedding, there was more to being a guest than met the eye. Heather was wearing her dress, and most every person in South Carolina's "high society" would see it. Not only that, Cat Clyne was covering the wedding, or, more specifically, the wedding dress.

"Come on," Derek said. "Let's get to the ceremony before we're late."

Maya and Derek walked up the wide steps leading to the foyer of the mansion, and he gently grasped her hand. She let herself be held by him, and a warmth settled over her. Being next to him was divine.

"You still look nervous," Derek said, glancing at her as they headed toward the mansion's entrance.

"I am nervous. Everyone is going to see that dress today, and I don't know how to feel about that. What if folks hate it? What if Cat hates it?" Maya groaned. "Then my career will be over."

"You're worrying too much. That dress is gorgeous, just like its maker. Remember that Heather's opinion is the most important. And she loves it." He smiled and gently tilted her chin. Their eyes met, and he kissed her on the lips.

The tension in her shoulders relaxed and faded away. Maya returned his kiss, gentle yet strong and assured. Then she stepped away. "We should get inside the mansion. I don't know about PDA in such a fancy place."

He laughed. "If you say so."

They stepped inside, and the place was filled with guests. Faces of politicians and folks whom she'd seen on the news or heard mentioned in conversation among the people of Charleston. Even some media folks from the local news were present, ready to cover the wedding. That nervousness returned. All these important people here meant a bigger opportunity for failure. If they didn't like her dress, then talk of it would ripple over into every corner of South Carolina and beyond.

Why'd she think making this dress for a high-profile person like Heather was a good idea? Why? Why? Why?

Someone tapped her on the shoulder.

"Hey, Maya."

Cat. Maya's heartbeat skipped, and she turned. Cat looked über-fashionable in her designer navy wrap dress with a band of gold along each side. She wore her trademark red streak in her dark bob.

"Cat!" Maya said. "So great to see you here."

"I love this mansion. Nice digs."

Cat looked around with a scrutinizing eye, and Maya's heart rate ramped slightly. She hated feeling on edge.

"Have you seen the bride yet?" Cat asked.

That meant *Have you seen the bride in her dress?* "No, I haven't."

Cat took out her notebook from her small messenger bag, ready to write up her preliminary assessment of the place. That could be good or bad.

Oh Lord. Maya's mind ran through all the decisions she'd made about the dress, and with that came all her second-guesses and doubts. Did she do the right thing by incorporating the cowrie shells as part of the shoulder straps? Would Cat think this dress was too colorful with the purple embroidery on the bodice? Should she have made the embroidery a part of the waistband instead? Would it look too in your face?

There she went, doubting herself again. *I made my choices, and I'll stand by them, no matter the result.*

Just because she stood by her decisions didn't mean Cat would like them. Cat's incisive fashion reviews had trashed many a fashion designer's career before. If Maya got a bad review, then that would be it. She could forget about trying to make a name for herself before dying. Laura would probably fire her too.

Think positive. Think positive. Maya took her seat next to Derek, and he held her hand again. She relaxed into the gesture.

"I saw you talking to Cat just now. You looked worried," he said.

"I am." She exhaled.

Before he could say anything else, the violinist played a solo, and the crowd hushed to a quiet.

Maya glanced behind her and smiled as the wedding party made their slow processional. The bridesmaids wore A-line dresses in the same shade of purple as was accented on Heather's gown. With each person who arrived, Maya grew more and more nervous. This was it. Everyone in this room would see Heather's dress soon. Maya resisted the urge to squeeze her eyes shut.

What would her mother think if she saw Maya now?

Her mother would probably be proud of Maya's design style. She had remembered and incorporated most everything that her mother had taught her. Mom would probably be giving her the side-eye too, wondering what she was doing on a date with a man in South Carolina when her calling was in New York City.

Or was it Maya's calling? Laura detested Maya's design style. Sheesh. This was complicated.

Yet Maya's mother would definitely push Maya back to the city. Her mother would definitely tell Maya that Laura Whitcomb was top-of-the-line, and that *after* Maya worked her way up the career ladder, she'd be free to be more creative with her design aesthetic.

In a way, Mama was right, but even the thought of sacrificing her creativity until she was promoted saddened her. Revising those designs for Laura's tastes nearly sent Maya into a low-grade depression. If it wasn't for Heather's dress project, Maya probably would've ended up really bummed out. Despite that, it was better to wait until she was promoted and then take baby steps of going out on her own.

The bridal party finished walking down the aisle, and then the flower girl walked down the aisle. The cue notes began, and all the guests rose.

A chill prickled across her forearms. Oh my goodness. Maya could see only the top of Heather's veil, not the rest of her.

Then a collective gasp came over the room, along with the quick clicking of cameras and videos from the guests and media alike.

Many of the guests near her were beaming.

"Heather looks so beautiful."

"She is divine in that dress."

"Oh yes. The gown is definitely something different. I love it."

A thrill went through Maya. Heather walked down the aisle and passed Maya, and even she had to give herself a moment to take it all in. The dress was gorgeous.

Derek whispered, "See? I told you they would love it."

He definitely had said that. Maya nodded and then quickly scanned the room for Cat but couldn't find her. What did she think of the dress?

Heather stood next to her groom, and the ceremony began. A whole mix of emotions overwhelmed Maya. All at once, she felt both happy and worried.

Maya had agreed to a long-distance relationship with Derek, but what if it was too much for Derek? What if she wouldn't be able to balance life and this new relationship? She sighed, and the bride and groom exchanged vows.

"I do," Heather said, gazing up at her groom with eyes filled with love.

Heather was a lucky woman—lucky to have found her heritage and her past, lucky to have been able to join them together with this momentous day. Lucky to have found someone to love.

A heaviness came over Maya once again as the groom said, "I do." Derek nestled close to her and wrapped his arm around her. A half-smile formed on her lips. No need to think about the what-ifs rolling around in her mind. Today, she'd focus on being a guest, and she'd focus on that dress.

"I now pronounce you husband and wife," the pastor said. "You may kiss the bride."

They kissed. The room clapped and cheered. People stood and smartphones clicked all over the place.

"It was a beautiful ceremony now, wasn't it?" Derek leaned over and asked her.

"Yes, it was gorgeous."

The newly wedded couple made their slow processional down the aisle. When Heather passed Maya, she whispered, "Thank you," and winked.

Maya nodded and mouthed the words, *You're welcome*. She was so grateful to have made her day special, but now Maya had to face Cat.

The guests slowly filed out of the church, and so did Maya and Derek. When they stepped outside, the noise of the photographers and guests filled her ears.

"Maya!"

Cat's voice made her feel nervous. Maya turned and greeted her.

"Darling! Dah-ling!" Cat said, her voice high-pitched and chipper. "That dress is uh-mazing."

A feeling of glee quickly overtook Maya. "You liked it?"

"Did I like it? Lady, I loved it! I loved it so much. It didn't seem as overdone as the other dresses I saw. It was just the right mix of fresh and timeless. The purple accents were gorgeous."

Joy flitted through her. Maya cheesed so hard her cheeks hurt.

"I took some photos of the dress, but I hope to snap more and ask Heather some questions for my write-up, but first, I wanted to ask you a few questions for the blog post."

The blog post. The one that would be shared with thousands of people. She had to make a good impression. She had to make an excellent impression. "All right. What do you want to know?"

"A lot of the dress was inspired by Heather's recent discovery of her ancestry. I think that's such an interesting story. It makes you think about how we're all connected to one another. Don't you agree?"

Maya glanced over at Derek, who was amid the crowd of people and basking in the joy of the wedding. He winked.

Her heart warmed. Connected. She and Derek were connected too. "We're all more connected than we think. That's so incredibly true. Did you know that Heather is taking donations to New Life Church's Black History Society and the Black history museum? It's a way to preserve her great-grandmother's story."

"That's so intriguing. I'll have to look into those organizations for this piece."

"You definitely should," Maya said.

Cat scribbled down some notes on her tablet. "I noticed that beyond the elements of Heather's predecessors that you weaved into the gown, like the purple embroidery, which was her great-grandmother's favorite color, and the West African cowrie shells, there were also some other elements in there that were so incredibly unique. I hadn't seen them before. Like the handwoven silk fabric and the different style of stitching. Can you tell the readers about that?"

Maya smiled again. Those were the same types of patterns that her mother had taught her all those years ago. Maya shared the story of how she apprenticed under her mom before she worked for Laura Whitcomb.

"Interesting." Cat pursed her lips. "In all of the designs that you shared with me, I've never seen that type of style in Laura's line. Has Laura seen your work before?"

Maya took a breath. "Yes, she has most definitely seen

them . . ." She quieted, unsure if she should say anything more.

"Will we get to see your designs in Laura Whitcomb's line next season?" Cat asked.

I don't know. Will pigs fly?

This. Was. Hard. No way was Maya going to tell Cat about the behind-the-scenes back and forth that Maya had with Laura over the design vision for her work. If Maya did, then she'd look like she was badmouthing Laura and could possible lose her job.

Maya remembered her mother's admonition—make it to the big time first, and then get creative.

An inner tug-of-war formed inside Maya. If she said nothing about the back and forth with Laura, if she made it appear as if everything were peaches and roses with Laura, then she'd look like a huge pushover, possibly like one of Laura's robots who didn't have any spine of her own. Maya would also be tying herself even closer to Laura, strapping herself into Laura's well-styled straitjacket.

Yet Maya did have her own design sense, and she definitely had her own sense of individuality, but Laura wasn't having it. Remaining silent would essentially tie Maya down. By not saying anything, Maya would symbolically cede her creative autonomy to Laura.

If Maya told Cat the truth, then this article could turn into another one of Cat's gossip columns, not a column that would showcase her work. A gossipy article on this event would definitely get Maya fired.

In the end, Maya would have to be silent. It was the only way to hold on to her dream of being head designer. "Laura has seen these styles and the stitching patterns that I created, but . . ."

But she hates them.

But she doesn't think they'll succeed.

But she's made a biting assessment of my work that has caused me to descend into doubt time and time again.

"But what?" Cat asked, her voice questioning.

"But she didn't think this would fit the brand. Of course, as a pioneer in the bridal industry, it's Laura's classic styles that make her stand head and shoulders above the rest."

There, she said it.

She ceded.

A discomfort flitted through her. A slow, painful rip formed at the tip of her heart. Maya had chosen Laura over herself.

The rip deepened and brought with it waves of silent pain.

Maya had compromised herself.

Chapter Fifteen

Shortly after finishing up her conversation with Cat, Maya headed out of the governor's mansion to meet up with Derek.

She was intent on enjoying the rest of the day. She was also intent on enjoying the upcoming reception too, but she couldn't get her conversation with Cat out of her mind.

Maya could've used that time to step out of Laura's shadow and promote herself, but she didn't. It wasn't like Maya could turn around and tell Cat any different, since she'd left for New York already.

"What's up? You're doing that scrunchy thing with your forehead. You look distracted," Derek said.

"I'm not distracted. Okay, well, yes, I'm distracted."

"Cat didn't like the dress?" he asked.

"She loved the dress. Loved it a lot."

"Then what's up?"

"She asked about Laura." Maya then explained the rest of

the conversation and how she relented on an opportunity to showcase her work. Derek's mouth formed into an O, which told Maya that she wasn't imagining things. She should've said something.

"You could've delved into the indigenous origins of your design aesthetic. Why did you hold back?" he asked.

Now Maya really wanted to kick herself. How did she forget her history?

It would take the entire evening to probe the depths of that question. She wanted Laura's acceptance, and she didn't want to let that acceptance go. She valued it too much.

Even more than herself.

Her self-assessment stung.

"Maya? You okay?"

She nodded quickly. "I'm okay. I just don't know how to answer your question, that's all," she said. Her voice quivered, but she maintained composure.

"Don't worry about it. I know these things can be tough." He kissed her forehead, his eyes filled with gentleness and empathy. "Now let's go and enjoy this reception. I also want to get second dibs on the dance floor, after the bride and groom, of course."

She laughed, and her worries about the conversation with Cat slowly eased away as they approached the expansive ballroom where the festivities had begun. Maya decided to take Derek's advice and enjoy the wedding reception.

"Have fun. Enjoy yourself," she whispered to herself as

she made her way across the dance floor. "Heather loved your dress. Cat loved it too. That's all that matters now."

The guests were gathering inside, and they all had assigned table areas. Derek picked up their number from the welcome table. "We're table fourteen," he said.

Maya nodded and followed him. The place was über-fancy, with multiple chandeliers hanging from the ceilings, and the tables were tastefully decorated with purple-and-white orchids as centerpieces. "This is gorgeous," she said.

She sat at a table with a three-by-five-inch framed picture of Heather's great-grandmother with a caption about her heritage and history. Other wedding guests filled the empty seats opposite them.

"That's so wonderful, how Heather's sharing this part of her family story with the guests in this way," Derek said.

"I know." Maya looked at the other tables and she saw the pictures of other people, all of Heather's great-grandmother's side of the family, the family she had left behind. Seeing how Heather had displayed the photos and reading a bit about each person's story gave Maya something to aim for—the courage to talk about her designs as a designer in her own right, not just as Laura's designer.

Could she do it? Maya glanced at the picture of Heather's great-grandmother. How much had she hidden and buried over the years, and what effects did it have on her identity? On her psyche?

Maya would never know the answers, but she could guess

that the effect on Heather's great-grandmother wasn't altogether good. And she died hiding a part of herself.

How would Maya die?

The question hung there, unanswered.

AFTER THE INTRODUCTIONS and the first dance for the bride and groom, the music started and people started dancing. Derek leaned over to her and whispered, "Let's dance."

"Sure."

Derek gently grasped her hand, and they walked toward the dance floor. That's when Maya spotted a selfie area with a backdrop of a castle and carriage, like a fairy tale. "Wanna take a selfie?" she said.

"Definitely." Derek's mouth quirked into a smile, and then he stepped back to take their picture.

Maya glanced at the display. "This reminds me of the display at the boutique. Heather must've been taken by our design aesthetic at the trunk show."

Derek nodded. "You have a way of inspiring people, Maya."

She did a double take. "I do?"

"Yes. You inspired me. Before you came to Charleston, before you showed up at the bridal shop, I had been struggling, but I'm not anymore. You gave that to me." Derek wrapped his arms around her in a warm embrace. "Now if it wasn't for your policy of no PDA, I would kiss you right now."

She chuckled.

"You have a special way about you. I wish you'd see that for yourself. Who knows? Maybe the reason you've had problems with your boss is because she sees that in you too, and she wants to hold you back. Laura could be jealous."

Maya's eyes widened. "Jealous? How could she be jealous? I'm just a junior designer."

"No, Maya. You're a top designer. You are."

Maya shifted her weight from side to side, uncomfortable with Derek's comment. Of course, she was a designer, but she wasn't successful or anything. This was getting too complicated to think about. "Want to take another selfie?" she asked.

Derek tilted his head to the side, studying her. "Of course."

They snapped a second one and made their way back to the reception hall. This time the DJ was playing a slow song and more couples were dancing. Derek grasped her hand. "Do you care to dance?"

"More than anything in the world."

They made their way to the dance floor and she wrapped her arms around him. They slow danced to Frank Sinatra's "The Way You Look Tonight." She inhaled the scent of his cologne. The tension in her muscles released.

Who would've known that all of this would've happened during a trip down south to help her father? She got buzz for her designs, and she found a guy who was special. This was a real-life fairy tale, and she didn't want it to end.

MAYA HEADED TO the boutique on Monday on a mission: to read Cat's write-up of Heather's wedding.

Well, she wasn't going to read it for herself. She needed Derek to filter the article for her. Maya's heart couldn't take it if she read Cat's super-bad review. Derek would be a nice buffer.

As soon as she turned the corner on State Street, a school bus pulled to a stop and opened its doors. Jamila hopped out.

"Hey, Jamila," Maya said, waving.

A smile spread across Jamila's face. "Maya!" She ran to greet her, and they hugged.

Maya relished the embrace. "Wanna walk over to the boutique together?"

"Absolutely. I have great news, but I'll wait till Dad is present to say it."

"Can't wait to hear." Maya clasped Jamila's hand, and they fell into a natural step with each other. Minutes later, they arrived at Always a Bride.

"Hey. I didn't expect the two of you here at the same time," Derek said.

"I had parked near the shop, and I saw the school bus drop off Jamila at the corner. So I ran up to meet her," Maya said.

"Nice seeing the two of you together." He didn't take his eyes off Maya, and her stomach flipped. Since their time at the wedding, Maya had been floating on an invisible cloud, and she didn't want to get off the ride.

Derek smiled.

"Look at this, Dad. I have a surprise." She held up a piece of paper in the air, breaking through Maya and Derek's moment. "It's the grading rubric for my dress project. I got an A-plus! Can you believe it?"

Jamila's joy melted Maya, and her heart pebbled at Jamila's feet.

"This is amazing, dear. I'm so proud of you," Derek said.

"Really?"

"Definitely."

"If Maya wasn't here, then I wouldn't have been able to do this," Jamila said.

Jamila was crediting her? "You did all the work," Maya said. "I just gave you some advice."

Jamila shrugged. "I'm going to post this in the break room. You know Karen's mom is picking me up in half an hour, right, Dad?"

He glanced up, apparently thinking. "I remember. You guys are going to the movies this evening."

"That's right." Jamila then walked to the rear of the store.

That left Maya and Derek standing in the store alone. Their eyes locked on each other. An electricity buzzed between them that she couldn't deny. Maya let it filter through her and fill her up.

This was love.

Love? Did Maya just think this was love? No way. Couldn't be. *Focus, Maya. You want him to read Cat's article for you.*

"I wanted to—" they both said at the same time. Derek

laughed.

"You can go first, Maya."

"I wanted to know if you could do me a favor. Could you check to see if Cat's post is up yet?" Maya twisted her mouth. "I'm nervous."

He gave her this endearing look that made her feel even more self-conscious. "I'll pull up the site on my laptop and we can check."

"Thank you."

They walked over to the counter and pulled up the site. Cat's blog post was there.

Maya's skin tingled, and she let out a gasp. "I can't look!" She immediately covered her eyes.

"You don't want to read it?"

She shook her head. "No way. Can you read it for me and then let me know what it says?"

He chuckled. "You're a trip, you know that?"

"I'm not a trip. I'm a hardworking dress designer who knows that this particular moment will make or break me."

"It's not that serious."

"It's pretty close." She still kept her eyes covered. "My entire career is hinging on this article." Maya peeked through her fingers. Derek was staring at her with contentment in his expression. "What? Does it say something bad?"

"No. No. Just . . . thinking. That's all." Derek shifted his weight from side to side. The corners of his mouth curled up in delight.

"Are you going to read the post?"

"Yes."

She covered her eyes again. "Good."

He started to read it aloud.

"Read it silently, please," Maya said. "Then give me a 'yes' or 'no' or something. Like an executive summary."

"You are really serious, huh?"

"Yes."

"So when are *you* going to read it?"

This was so nerve-racking. "I . . ."

"I'll read aloud if it's good. How does that sound?"

Relief swept through her. "That sounds excellent."

"'Upcoming New Designer Is One to Watch, Blending History and Fashion in Unique Ways.' This is great, Maya."

"It is?" she said.

Derek laughed. "Yes, it is. Cat writes: 'Ms. Heather Gates looked divine in a form-fitting gown that displayed a unique blending of cultures, Filipino and West African. The West African inspiration is a nod to Heather's great-grandmother, an African American woman who passed as a White woman. It's unfortunate that Jim Crow laws and racist violence forced Heather's great-grandmother to pass as White, but Heather's symbolic dress honors her once-hidden African heritage. Now it's come to light, and Heather's wedding was a celebration of it.'"

"The way Cat worded it sounds deep," Maya said.

"That's because it is deep." He continued reading. "'A

junior wedding dress designer for Laura Whitcomb, Maya Jackson's style sense is avant-garde with a touch of classic form. The way Maya uniquely and seamlessly blends the design styles of two cultures without missing a beat is something I haven't seen in my thirty years as a fashion critic.'"

A stunned shock overcame Maya. "Wow. Wow. Wow."

"'When I interviewed Maya,'" Derek continued, "'she said that the design inspirations for her work come from being apprenticed to her mother, a Filipina designer who brought indigenous stitching techniques with her to the United States. The craft and skill in the dresses are astonishingly intricate. Laura is lucky to have snapped Maya up. She'll be even luckier to have Maya take the Laura Whitcomb brand to a new level. Maya's unique eye and style will be an asset to an already successful line.'" Derek looked up from the screen. "You, my lady, are a hit."

The positive comments on Cat's blog were already rolling in. Maya stepped close to read them.

Gorgeous! The dress looks amazing.
So unique.

The comments kept coming.

"I knew you'd succeed," he said. "Cat didn't drag Laura Whitcomb on the internet either. She's much savvier than that. Much, much savvier. You're brilliant. You know that, right?"

Did she? Now she did. Cat's blog changed everything.

Jamila emerged from the break room and stepped close to the computer screen. Her eyes widened. "You're famous, Maya!"

Maya laughed. "Not exactly famous, but thank you."

"Maya, I—" Derek said.

A cell phone trilled.

"Is that my phone?" he asked.

"Nope. It's mine." Maya answered. "Hello?"

"Maya? Hello! It's Laura Whitcomb. I saw Cat's post this morning of the wedding you designed for. Do you have a minute to chat?"

Stress-excitement sizzled through her. What did she want? "Can you hold on please?" She placed the phone down and her jaw dropped.

There was some quiet chatter as Derek and Jamila read through more of the comments on the computer.

"That's Laura Whitcomb on the phone!" Maya's voice was a shout-whisper. "Laura saw Cat's blog post, and she wants to talk. I wonder if she's gonna give some commentary on my design revisions that I sent her too."

"Better see what she has to say," Derek said, a note of pride in his voice. "Go on and speak with her."

Maya jumped up and down like a kid on Christmas Day. "I'll take this call in the back."

Maya stepped into the break room of Always a Bride and sat down at the round table, holding the cell phone up to her ears. "Hey, Laura. You still there?"

"Yes. What were you doing?"

The nervousness didn't leave. Laura could also be calling to rail on her, as usual. "Just looking for a quiet place to talk. That's all," Maya said, trying to keep the calm in her voice.

"I didn't know you were working on the wedding for the governor's daughter." Laura said this with a note of incredulity in her voice, as if Maya were beholden to her for every move she made while down south.

"You said I could sell some of my designs while I was down here in Charleston since I would not be paid after two weeks, remember?"

There was silence on the other end, and all of a sudden Maya grew nervous. Should she have said something to Laura about Heather's wedding too? Was she supposed to check in or something? Oh Lord. Last thing Maya needed was to get on Laura's bad side.

"I was so impressed with your design of Heather's dress. I loved it. I wish you would've shown me these styles earlier, so we could've worked something out *under* the Laura Whitcomb brand."

Maya's blood boiled. She'd been trying to get Laura to recognize her designs since she had started working there. All Laura did was dismiss them as "not marketable." Now she wanted to claim Maya's designs under her brand?

"Did you see the revisions I sent you? The ones that are more aligned with your style?"

"Oh yes. I saw them. They were okay," Laura continued. "But I was thinking about all the press you've been getting, and I think it will be great exposure for the Laura Whitcomb line. It'll show that we're a progressive, forward-thinking, and diverse company."

Diverse? What was she talking about? Laura disliked Maya's design aesthetic. Now Laura wanted to be "diverse"? Humpf.

"I want to offer you the position of head designer at Laura Whitcomb Inc."

Maya's heart pounded. Oh my goodness. Oh my goodness. Oh my goodness. This was what she'd dreamed of. "You do?"

"Yes, I do. As soon as you return to New York at the end of the month, I'd love to discuss your new position."

Her new position. Yes. Her new position. Laura said it as if it were a done deal, as if she had accepted it already.

Maya would, wouldn't she? Taking this position was a no-brainer. Yes? Yes. Now it was actually happening. Now, it was actually real.

"This will be an exciting new turn in your career, Maya. It'll be challenging, but fun too. And the travel! Oh, you'll love the travel. You won't be all cooped up in the New York office. This job will be about eighty percent travel. All expenses paid by the company."

How would she see Derek? "Eighty percent travel?"

"Yes. Mostly international too. You'll spend a lot of time

in Paris and Milan attending fashion shows, meeting with our designers who are based in Europe, and consulting with our international clients. Oh, you're in for a glamorous life, darling. A glamorous life."

Fireworks crackled in her spirit. If she could've, she would've squeed, hopped, and cheered like a crazed spectator at a football game. But then something else tugged at her too. The idea of traveling sounded great, but it could also put a huge strain on any type of long-distance relationship she had with Derek. They'd hardly see each other. And her health. Could her body take the stress and toll of travel? She never even told Laura about her sickle cell, and Laura wasn't the understanding type. "Can I have some time to think about this? Before I make a decision to accept or not?"

"Why wouldn't you accept?" Laura asked, her tone incredulous.

"I just want to think it over."

"You didn't get another offer already, did you?"

Laura was concerned about competition, huh? Perhaps Maya could use that in her favor if she accepted and negotiated a salary. She wouldn't lie about a competing offer, but Maya could play up how much of an asset she would be now that she had all this buzz. Then there was Derek. "I want to think about it. That's all."

"Okay. Great!" Laura said. "We'll talk about the details of your new position when you return."

"I haven't accepted," Maya reemphasized. "I need time."

"Oh, right. Time. Take all the time you need, but I am looking forward to seeing you soon."

They said goodbye. Maya hung up and took a long, deep breath. First thing was to tell Derek. She was thrilled about the job offer, but she wanted to tell Derek how this new position could affect them. Being head designer could take a toll on their new relationship *and* her health.

And that didn't feel right.

Chapter Sixteen

Jamila left for the movies, and that left Derek to feel all of the feelings toward Maya.

He loved Maya. Derek knew that after one date, then two dates. He knew it after one kiss, then two kisses. He loved her. That knowing lingered even now. The feeling had been growing from the first day he'd met Maya.

That call from Laura Whitcomb filled him with joy. Seeing Maya succeed in her endeavors was beyond satisfying. Maya was finally getting the recognition she deserved, and it all began in this little bridal shop. Derek wanted to see her shine and succeed as a designer. They would make their relationship work too . . . somehow.

Somehow. Derek believed it would work. He was still willing to fly to New York regularly. That didn't change.

Now would be a good time to tell Maya how he truly felt, to tell Maya that he was in love.

Yes. Derek would tell her. He'd do so as soon as she returned to the sales floor.

Maya returned, exuberance coloring her entire expression. "I have news," she said. "Good news!"

Derek glanced down, pondering how to say the words.

"Is everything all right?" she asked.

"Everything is perfect." He smiled. "So what's your news?"

"Laura Whitcomb offered me the head designer position." She rocked back and forth on her feet. "When I get home, I won't have to be a junior designer anymore. Isn't that great?"

Her talk of returning to New York sent a bittersweet feeling through his bones. Still, he was thrilled—thrilled enough to embrace her. "That's excellent, Maya. I'm so proud of you."

Maya glanced up at him, her eyes shining with hope. "I know! This is the best thing that ever happened to me. Mama would be so proud of me. I wish she were here to experience this moment too."

"I'm sure she's smiling down from heaven." He brushed a curly tendril from her face. "But I don't think it was Laura's offer that would've made your mother proud. I think she was proud of you the moment you were born. You're a gift to everyone you meet, including me."

Maya bit her bottom lip.

"Are you all right? You look unhappy. Did something happen?" he asked.

She sighed and then released her embrace and took a step

back. "I didn't accept the offer yet."

A tiny flame of concern lit within him, soon followed by confusion. "Why not? This is what you wanted all along."

"Laura mentioned that the job would entail eighty percent travel, and I know you wanted to visit New York once a month. I was concerned that the new position would hinder our relationship and all, as well as my health."

Something inside of him melted. Maya hadn't accepted the position right away because she was concerned about them. How loving.

Loving. Love.

He loved her. He was definitely going to tell her. Maybe.

Should Derek tell her that he loved her? Professing love now would only make her more indecisive about taking the job. Derek would never do that to her. No need to tell Maya he was falling in love. She needed to make her decisions without any extra emotions involved.

"You can always tell Laura the truth about your health. She sees you as a valuable member of her company."

A tiny frown formed at the corners of her mouth. "If I told her the truth, she would see me as a liability."

"You're not a liability."

"Not to you, but I would be a liability to Laura. Then I'd be done and over with . . . old news . . . expendable."

"You're not expendable. No one can fulfill that head designer position like you can. No one else can bring your unique vision to the Laura Whitcomb brand. You have to recognize the value you bring to the table."

She glanced down, uncertainty shrouding her face. "What do you think I should do?" she asked. "Should I accept the position or not?"

He paused. The last thing he wanted to do was tell her what to do. This was her life to live. "Do what makes you happy." He cupped her face.

"Do what makes you whole." He kissed her forehead.

"Do what gives you peace." He gently kissed her lips.

Maya's expression fell.

"What's the matter?" he asked.

"Nothing . . . I just figured . . . ." Maya shrugged. "Never mind."

"We can make things work between us. I'm sure of it," he said.

Silence. A silence that held a multitude of unspoken feelings.

"Whatever you choose, Maya, I'm here for you. Always."

His heart pricked. There was a small chance this could push them apart, but he would stand by his word. The love he held for her would survive this dilemma.

Even though he could sense her resolve slipping away, he would hold on, for love.

"So WHAT WILL you do?" Derek asked.

What would she do? Maya was hoping that Derek would help her iron that out. Instead, he was leaving it up to her.

"I don't know."

He bit his bottom lip as if he wanted to say something more but was holding himself back.

"What?" she asked.

"Nothing. I'm here. I'm listening."

Okay, so he was listening. Guess she'd figure it out on her own. "Like I said earlier, I'll be traveling a lot. That could hinder us. I don't want to do that either."

Derek pursed his lips, quiet.

"You're not helping me by 'just listening,'" she added.

"I'm letting you decide. I don't want to stand in the way. I know you've wanted this for so long. I know this is a huge dream of yours."

He was right. It was her dream and her mother's dream too. This opportunity that her mother would never get to see. "So you're okay with us not seeing each other once a month? It could turn into bimonthly or even quarterly visits. Who knows?"

Derek's eyes flitted back and forth, apparently uncomfortable.

"What is it?" she asked.

"I have an idea. An alternative."

She raised her eyebrows. "Oh really? What's that?"

"You've built a lot of momentum here with your designs. You're so incredibly talented, Maya. Why don't you strike out on your own and start your own brand? Right here in Charleston."

Strike out on her own? Was he out of his mind? "That'll be a lot of work for me."

"You've been doing most of the work already anyway. It won't be much different."

He had a point, but this was Laura Whitcomb. *The* Laura Whitcomb. "I'm just a newbie designer with a little bit of buzz. I have nothing to stand on. Working with Laura as her head designer will give me the name recognition that I need."

"But it won't be your name. It'll be hers. From the way you talk about Laura, she seems like the type of person who will want all the credit for your success. And all the profit."

Maya twisted her mouth. Laura did mention that part about Maya's designs being under the Laura Whitcomb brand, but . . .

"You don't *need* Laura Whitcomb's name recognition," he added. "You can hold your own as a designer."

Could she? "I don't think I can."

"I don't understand your self-doubt. You're an excellent designer. You can definitely strike out on your own, right here in Charleston. Then we won't have to worry about travel schedules. You'll have the best of both worlds. We'll have each other." Derek stepped closer, and she inhaled the scent of cologne.

Having each other all the time would be nice. Very nice. She stood on her tiptoes and her lips met his.

Derek's mouth parted and so did hers. They kissed. He

wrapped his arms around her waist and she returned the gesture, her hand caressing his half-shaven cheek. He gently squeezed her palm, and Maya grew energized by the heat beneath his grip. She was going to miss this when she returned to New York. The smell of him. The taste of him. A longing arose inside of her. A longing to . . .

Worry niggled at her too, and she pulled away. "This is tough."

"I know. Like I said, you've already made great ground here with your work. You can continue to build on it. We can continue to build on us. We can also build on our relationship if you choose New York. It may take some finagling, but it can be done."

The warmth drained from her palms. Could it be done? They would barely see each other in person.

"I know your career is important to you. The offer from Laura Whitcomb is amazing. But remember that you were getting recognized for your hard work before Laura's offer. Not only for your hard work, but you were getting recognized for simply being you, the unique you. Laura never cared until now."

His words dug deep into the parts of her where even deeper insecurities resided. All her life she'd tried to get "acknowledged" by others, including people like Laura Whitcomb, a blond, blue-eyed woman who was already accepted by mainstream society. Laura held no childhood memories of receiving skeptical glances for being a brown-skinned child who called her Asian mother "Mama" in public. Laura would never have to explain to people that no, she wasn't Black and White—she was Black and *Asian,* an altogether different identity and experience. But Maya craved that level of validation from a woman like Laura. Maya couldn't let this opportunity go because it hurt to never, ever quite fit in anywhere. And now Maya *was* being accepted—by Laura.

Derek's idea to stay here was a good one too, but what if it wasn't the *good enough* one? Striking out on her own wouldn't give her that industry acceptance she craved. Also, she would have to learn to believe in herself. That was even harder.

"Maya?"

Insecurity hovered like a two-ton boulder. She couldn't speak.

"I wish you could see yourself like I see you."

Maya glanced away.

"What we have will endure whatever choice you make," he added.

Old desires mixed with the new ones, congealing into a thick, confusing mass. "Whatever choice I make?"

"Absolutely." He nodded.

The shimmer of Laura's name-brand recognition and the glitter of mainstream success dangled before her, all shiny and fresh and new. A craving arose with her. "I'll accept the position in New York."

Silence—the suffocating kind of silence that paralyzed—

settled between them. Did she make the right choice? What if she didn't?

"I support you," Derek said. "I'm here for you."

"Really?"

"Most definitely." Derek's eyes glistened.

His assuredness pressed on another facet of her heart, the facet she'd have to ignore if she was going to make all of this work. "Thank you for believing in me."

"Thank you for believing in yourself." He squeezed her hand gently. "You've come such a long way."

"It was a hard road getting here," Maya said, her voice a whisper. "It still feels hard."

"I know it does. But you're an ingenious talent. Even better, you're a wonderful person," he said.

Her dreams were coming true. Excitement filled her once again, but then something else came afterward, a twinge of sadness. Maya wanted to pull him into her arms and stay in his embrace forever, but she didn't. Better to get used to the distance now. Maya was going to follow her heart, and a big part of her heart was in New York.

Yet the other part was now here, with Derek and Jamila. Maya ignored this other part.

"I have some paperwork to catch up on with the store . . . and I need to think," Derek said. "But I'm so very proud of you." With a light peck on Maya's cheek, Derek left for his back office. The door opened and quietly closed.

This was a good decision, Maya. A really good decision. Right?

That sadness gathered strength and settled in the pit of her belly, but she resolved to build her new life around it. No matter what.

THE FOLLOWING DAY was rainy and dreary. Derek had tossed and turned all night. By morning, he was exhausted. He couldn't get that conversation with Maya out of his head.

At five o'clock, he got out of bed and headed to the kitchen, intent on getting Maya off his mind. After turning on the teakettle, he caught sight of a picture that he had taken with Maya at the photo booth from Heather's wedding. He studied the two of them caught up in laughter and kisses. Unease settled within him. He was going to miss her.

The teakettle whistled, and he poured the steaming water into a pale yellow stoneware mug. A box of chamomile tea bags sat half-open near the bright red spoon rest. He took one bag and let his tea steep.

The back side of that picture stared at him, beckoning him to have another look.

"Not happening," he muttered.

Reading would get his mind off Maya. He walked to the living room and quickly scanned the area for a book or something. He picked up a paperback that he'd checked out from the library a few weeks ago but hadn't sat down to read. Upon glancing at the cover, he exhaled. The author's first name was Maya. Maya Angelou. Lord. This whole plan to not think about Maya wasn't working out too well.

He put the book down and sat at the desktop computer. He pulled up the website for the *Post and Courier*'s classified listings. Maya was leaving for New York, so he needed to place a job listing. Thanks to the trunk show and the publicity, he was caught up on the mortgage. He could easily afford to pay a new employee too. He needed to focus on moving forward.

Outside the window next to his tiny wooden desk, the raindrops made long streaks against the foggy glass, reminding him of tears. Derek blinked, blinked, blinked against the darkness threatening to rush his eyelids. He had to focus on finding a new replacement for Maya, not on this sadness at not seeing Maya as often as he'd like.

The Property for Sale ads popped up on his screen. Sketches of his conversation with Marlon from three months ago returned in snatches. All of Marlon's talk about selling the boutique came to life.

He wouldn't sell it. Maya enabled Always a Bride to have plenty of buzz, and he would have to build off that after Maya left. Plus, Jamila loved the boutique.

Derek took a breath and refocused on the screen. If he concentrated on getting a new hire, then perhaps the doubts would disappear. That was the plan anyway.

Seconds later, the soft shuffle of footsteps coming down the stairs broke his flow. Jamila was up. He craned his neck. Jamila's arms were filled with books and papers and flyers and brochures, accompanied by a wide smile. At least someone was happy around here. "Morning, baby girl. Where'd you get all of that stuff?"

"From Ms. Reese, my English teacher. I told her that we were going to start visiting New York, and she ordered this free information from their tourism office. She even wrote a list of her favorite things to do in the city." She unloaded the stuff onto the dented coffee table in the middle of the living room, and the items scattered in a haphazard collage. Derek squinted at them and softly winced—a map of New York City, a tourist's guide to Manhattan, brochures on Broadway shows, and a handwritten list of things to do in the Big Apple covered the surface. This wasn't good at all.

"Oh," Derek said.

"I was thinking that for our first trip to see Maya we could go to the Statue of Liberty and see a Broadway musical." She smiled brightly. "I heard that *Hamilton* is excellent. I was listening to some of the songs for the musical soundtrack on YouTube, and it's amazing. You think we can do that?"

The hope in her voice crushed him. How would he explain this to Jamila? Not very well. That was for sure. "Um. We have to talk." He closed the browser for the *Post and Courier* website.

"About what? You don't want to see the Statue of Liberty? We can catch a ferry out there." She opened a brochure and pointed to a paragraph printed in black. "It says here that they run every hour."

How in the world was he going to break this to her? "After you left for the movies, Maya said she got a big promotion in New York."

Jamila's eyes widened. "A promotion? That's great. She's doing real good with her dress design stuff. We'll have to celebrate when we go there next month. Maybe go out for ice cream or something."

Or something. That was the part he needed to discuss. Derek scratched his scalp and braced himself. "When I was talking with Maya yesterday, things didn't go as planned."

She scrunched her nose. "What do you mean?"

"I know I told you that we'd be visiting Maya monthly, but we won't be visiting as often."

Disappointment flashed across her dark brown eyes. "What? Why? What happened?"

"Her new position means that we won't be able to see her as much. She will be traveling a lot. Maya may be out of the country for months at a time."

"Months at a time?" Jamila asked.

"Yes." He paused. "We will try to make it work, but we won't be there every month."

This was the part where he explained everything very quickly so as to soften the blow.

Jamila's eyes flitted back and forth, as if she was trying to make sense of all he said. "She doesn't want to see me?"

The hurt in Jamila's voice grabbed him by the wrists and squeezed. "No. No. No. That's not it at all. Her job has extra responsibilities. That's all."

Jamila tilted her chin and appeared to focus on the papers on the coffee table. The soft lights shone on her intricate cornrows and freshly moisturized scalp. He'd made those cornrows himself, and for that, he was proud. Would Jamila retreat again? Would she retreat so much that things reverted to how they were just a few months ago? Never allowing him to comb her hair or be a father?

"I know this is a lot of news to digest, baby girl, but don't think that she doesn't want to see you. Her job will require more than she anticipated."

"I don't believe that. I think she doesn't want to have anything to do with us, or else she would stay here. She wouldn't let anything get in the way of hanging out with us . . . not even a fancy job in New York."

Her words stung. When Derek offered another option to Maya, her first choice was the head designer position, not building a business here. Did Maya's choice also reflect her feelings toward Derek? And by extension, her feelings toward Jamila?

Were he and Jamila second choice? The question stung.

Derek shook his head. "No. No. That's not true. Maya has been working very hard to get this position. She cares about me and you. She helped you with the school project and everything. Why would you think she doesn't want to have anything to do with us?"

"Maya only helped with the project because I'm your daughter. That would look really bad if she snubbed her boss's daughter." Jamila twisted the corner of her mouth and crossed her arms. "Ain't it true?"

Derek tilted his head to the side. Jamila had a point. What employee would turn down the boss's daughter, especially a girl as cute as Jamila? How did his daughter know so much about life?

His heart squeezed tight. Jamila had experienced way too much, enough to last two lifetimes. "I'm sorry, Jamila. I shouldn't have . . ."

What? What shouldn't he have done? Should he have never taken a risk by falling in love again?

Something still restrained him from voicing that truth, from saying that he no longer loved Maya, because love wasn't something you could quickly delete or Wite-Out or erase. Love took time to build. It took time to nurture, and in the months of knowing Maya, Derek had found someone whom he'd thought he'd never find again. He found her.

Even with Maya's illness, he still wanted Maya, but Maya chose New York first. Jamila's doubts now made him doubt.

"They all leave. Don't they, Dad?"

The soft sounds of the *Hamilton* soundtrack filled the silence between them. That, mixed with the sounds of raindrops pitter-pattering against the windows, was the worst.

"They all leave"? "Who?"

"Mom. Grandma. And now Maya. They all leave. It's the truth. Don't you agree?"

Did he? He didn't want to reaffirm negative beliefs about

people leaving Jamila's life. Then again, the evidence spoke for itself.

A worry spread inside of him. Jamila's statement settled deep and rooted in that well of emptiness that Derek had tried so hard to bury.

"Don't they, Dad?" Jamila repeated a third time, glancing at him with expectant eyes, but it wasn't the kind of expectation that filled him with hope. This was the expectation that came from living a lifetime of disappointments, except Jamila was too young for this. Twelve years old.

Did they all leave like Jamila said? No, they didn't. Derek would have to show Jamila that not everyone left. How could he do that since Maya was leaving too? "Maya is pursuing a dream that she's been working toward for a very long time. She deserves this new job. She's not out of our lives for good. We will be together again."

"When?"

When. That was the million-dollar question. Maya's new job had an unpredictable schedule. "I don't know."

It hurt to say those words, but they were the truth.

Sadness colored Jamila's face. Derek got up from his chair and sat next to her. The scent of Jamila's shea butter hair cream soothed some of his sorrow. He wrapped his arms around her in an attempt to comfort, but who knew if it worked?

"We will see her again. I'm not leaving you, baby girl. That will never change. I guarantee it."

A tear dropped down Jamila's cheek and stained Derek's creased khakis. "I'm gonna miss Maya when she leaves for New York."

He swallowed the thickness gathering in his throat. "I'm going to miss her too."

The joyful sounds of the *Hamilton* soundtrack strained through the music player.

Longing—a longing as deep as the Atlantic Ocean—reached inside of Derek and made its home in his heart. Derek cherished many things, but most of all he cherished the possibility of a new life with Maya, a life where they could count on seeing each other regularly even while she was in New York. Now that possibility would be radically adjusted. Now they would have to see each other sometimes—maybe.

Would this new plan work out? Things could change in an instant once again, and then their "sometimes, maybe" could turn into "never and no."

He'd have to hold on to what he cherished, and so Derek made a wish to see Maya again soon. He put his wish into an imaginary glass bottle and tossed it out to the imaginary sea.

Perhaps Maya would stumble across the bottle and find her way back to him again.

Chapter Seventeen

All Maya needed to do was finish packing and go over her father's medications with him. Then she'd be ready to return to her normal life in New York.

Except she wasn't ready. Not really.

Maya unzipped the bright turquoise shell suitcase and flipped it open. She'd already neatly folded her clothes into smart little squares, because that's what a woman did to get her mind off a guy. It worked. She'd spent all morning preparing for her flight home.

She glanced at the bolts of fabric and dress supplies on her flowery quilt, and she shrank inside. Derek had gifted her those fabrics. He said they belonged to his mother and that he saw no use for them. Maya had tried to give them back after their last talk, but he refused.

Why'd Derek have to be so kind, even in their hard conversations?

No matter. She was packing and leaving the Lowcountry. Her dreams awaited. Maya reached for the first short pile of folded clothes and placed it in the corner of her suitcase. The top shirt popped out over the edges. "Sorry, clothes, but you're not resisting me." She shoved the shirt back into the suitcase.

Her bedroom door creaked on its hinges, and her father poked his head inside, all smiles. "I made lunch for you. *Pancit* and *lumpia*."

He rarely made Filipino food. "*Pancit* and *lumpia*. What's the occasion?"

"You." He stepped inside and crossed his arms. "Having you here these last few months caused me to think a lot about your mother. That's all."

Maya stopped packing and smiled at him. She was gonna miss her father when she returned to New York. "That's so sweet, Pops."

He glanced at the fabric on her bed and then at her rolling suitcase. "You sure you're gonna be able to fit everything into one piece of luggage?"

She really should've returned the fabrics to Derek. "Nope. I was planning on shipping them to my apartment."

"Good call." He nodded. "Come on out of your cave and grab a plate. This will be our last lunch together before you return to the Big Apple." He left her room and she followed him down the dimly lit hallway.

"You make it sound so final. I'll still visit sometimes. Well, I'll be traveling for work, but we can videoconference and stuff."

"Uh-huh," he said, not sounding convinced.

She brushed aside his response. Maya would visit her father, just not any time soon.

"Don't worry about visiting me, though. I'll be plenty busy. Ginger and I are thinking of taking our first vacation together and living together as well."

Maya stopped. "Really?"

He smiled. "Yes. I really like her."

At least somebody was getting a happy ending. Hers was ending on a questionable note. "That's great, Pops. I'm so thrilled about this news. I really am."

"Thank you, my dear. That means a lot to me."

They walked to the kitchen and she sat at the maple table. Her father had a steady girlfriend. That was cute, and she was truly happy for him. Truly.

He set out the bright yellow plates.

"Oh wait. I forgot." Maya got up from the table, grabbed her purse from the living room, took out a folded piece of notepaper, and returned to the kitchen.

"What's that, hon?"

"Your medication schedule, as well as some tips for making sure you get in enough exercise every day." Maya waved the paper in the air. "I wanted to go over it with you before I leave."

Her father gave her a *get real* look, but she shrugged it off. "Hey, last time you ignored my suggestions, you ended up with a fractured hip."

"What suggestions?"

"To stop trying to fix everything yourself. Outsource." She waved the paper in the air once again. "I wanted to discuss that too. I have a plan for you."

Her father rolled his eyes. "You have a plan, eh? Don't worry about me. I'm sure Ginger will help me with all of that. I want to hear about all of *your* plans. This is an exciting time for you. I know Derek must be thrilled as well."

Derek. Derek! Why'd her father have to bring him up? Maya ran her index finger along the edge of the empty plate. "Uh-huh."

"All you have to say is uh-huh? I know you mentioned that he'd be visiting you. When is he making his first trip to see you?"

A rush of heat came over her. The last thing she wanted to do was talk about when she would see Derek again. "That hasn't been finalized yet."

Her father squinted his eyes, and that's when she knew he didn't believe her. "Oh? Why is that?"

Maya glanced down at the paper that she'd wanted to go over with her father. This was a mess and a half. "Just reasons," she said, her voice low and mumbly.

"Just reasons, huh?"

A silence ensued between them, and Maya drummed her fingers on the table. The ticking of the wall clock further punctuated the quiet. Better just say something, because he wasn't going to let this go. "My new job is unpredictable and demanding. Lots of traveling. So Derek and I are playing things by ear."

"Oh really?"

Maya exhaled deeply. "Really."

More quiet, and then: "What happened, Maya? Did he do something terrible?"

"He didn't do anything terrible. On the contrary, he suggested that I stay in Charleston and build my business here, especially since I gained all that publicity with Heather's wedding."

"That's a great idea. Why not do that?"

"I really want to be Laura Whitcomb's head designer."

"I see." Pops's words sounded more like a question than a statement.

"It's what I really want."

"I know. You deserve it too."

She nodded. "Derek said if I built my fashion brand in Charleston, then I wouldn't have to worry about trying to make travel and a relationship work." The more she spoke, and the more her father probed, the more she felt as if she were sinking into quicksand.

"Isn't that what you've always wanted? To have your own fashion brand? I don't see the problem."

But Laura Whitcomb Inc. was everything. Ev-ery-thing! Could Maya's start-up brand even compete? No. Better to stick with an established company.

"So what's the problem, Maya?" her father said.

"I know what you said about living fully and all that, but my time is short. Building a new business takes time. I don't have that time to give. There are limits."

"It's all about priorities."

She squinted. "What do you mean?"

Her father paused. "You said your time is limited. So perhaps you should seriously consider where and how you spend it. Prioritize. If you went to New York, you could have that industry recognition, but you wouldn't have the support you need. What do you value more?"

Of course Pops would ask her the hard questions. "I value both?" she said, a note of uncertainty in her voice.

"Be honest with yourself."

Maya glanced down, not wanting to face the truth.

"You're a grown woman, Maya. You make your own decisions, but if you stayed here, you could have both—career and love. You'll also have people who care for you here. People who can help you if, God forbid, any health emergencies arose. But yes, having both is possible, my dear."

The way he sounded so certain got under her skin. Career and love. Perhaps it was possible in some alternate reality for healthy people, but not for her. And not when she held her mother's hopes within her like heavy weights. "I can't stay here. Being head designer is everything to me. I already let Mama down once. Mama died thinking that I let her down. When I told her that I was taking my ex-fiancé's advice and giving up on pursuing my career in New York,

Mama warned me not to do it." Maya choked back the urge to cry. "I ignored her, and I ended up getting my heart broken. Mama never lived to see me become head designer, but Mama wanted that for me. Now I have this second chance. The least I can do is take this position."

"Oh, darling. When will you let these expectations go? They will bury you alive. Not sickle cell, but these expectations that you're placing on yourself. Your mother would've wanted to see you happy. She would not have wanted to see you compromising your relationships to become a head dress designer. Besides, your mother never thought your ex was good enough for you anyway. She would've wanted to see you following your happiness. Your mother would want you to live for *you*."

Live for me? Is that even possible? Maya didn't have time to live for herself. She didn't have time to follow happiness. "It's my choice. It's what I have to do."

What I have to do.

Maya needed to prove herself to the mainstream fashion world. If she proved herself, then it would mean her work was legitimate.

Legitimate.

The word resonated and bounced inside Maya; it was burdensome. Why was this so complicated? Why did this feel so hard? Was this what living was all about? Who knew? She didn't.

There was one thing Maya did know. Being head designer was more than a choice. It was what she had to do.

Chapter Eighteen

When Maya landed in LaGuardia Airport, she texted Derek and her father to let them know she'd arrived safely. The next morning, she took a taxicab to Laura Whitcomb Inc. filled with fresh expectations. Since Laura was so excited about Maya's designs now, she would probably have a banner under Laura's name, something like Designs by Maya. She couldn't wait to hear about Laura's plans. It was gonna be exciting and brilliant and wonderful.

Still, there was a bit of sadness lodged in Maya's heart. Leaving the Lowcountry proved more painful than she envisioned, but she had to let go of all that now. She got what she wanted, the most coveted position in the bridal gown industry. Well, the most coveted next to being Laura Whitcomb herself, of course. Maya would try to figure out a tentative date to see Derek once she was clear on her new job responsibilities.

Maya arrived at her new design space/office and gasped

when she stepped through the door. The place was three times bigger than her old cubicle, with floor-to-ceiling windows that overlooked the city skyline. A huge downpour of rain made the view all fuzzy, but the weather would clear up tomorrow. Was it raining where Derek was at too?

Stupid thought, Maya. You aren't there anymore. You made your choice.

Maya took her seat at the massive oak desk and exhaled. All those years of hard work were finally paying off for her, and here she was. If only her mother could see her now. She'd be so proud.

A smile curled the edges of Maya's mouth. She reached in her oversized bag and grabbed her portfolio. First thing on her agenda was showing Laura the latest designs Maya had sketched, all Afro-Asian inspired. The second thing was giving Laura an up close and personal look at a prototype dress she created for consignment at Always a Bride. When Maya left Charleston, she took all of her dresses out of the store. She figured it would be better to take them all, rather than going through the trouble of getting them later.

Maya rested her chin in her hands. She'd made the right decision. She did. She really did.

Then why was she second-guessing herself every five minutes now that she was back home?

"Shut up, Maya," she whispered to herself. "Just shut up."

She grabbed her portfolio and dress and headed to Laura's office, intent on impressing her. She was bound to love Maya's designs now. Maya was just getting the formal go-ahead to start the fall line with these designs.

Maya knocked on Laura's office.

"Come in," Laura said, her voice curt.

Maya did, portfolio in one arm and dress in another. Funny how life went. Last time Maya was here, she was so nervous about losing her shot at being head designer. Now, she was here to discuss being head designer.

"How was your flight back?" Laura asked, not looking up from her phone.

How'd she know I was here without looking at me? Perceptive woman. "Great. A smooth ride. I had a lot of time to sketch some designs for you to look at."

Laura glanced up from her phone and winked. "Attagirl. I have an international conference call set up for us tonight. Ready to get started?"

"I'm definitely ready."

Laura peered at the dress in Maya's arms. "Is that new?"

"Yes. I wanted you to have a look."

Laura got up from behind her desk and took the dress from Maya. Laura always had a good eye, and seeing Laura scrutinize her work so closely made Maya genuinely nervous.

Laura looked at the inside of the dress, inspected the tag with Maya's new logo on it, and frowned. "This won't work."

Her heart sped up a notch. "It won't work? Why not?

This dress has the same design sensibilities as Heather Gates's gown."

"I know that, and I'm excited about all of the buzz you've been getting. It shows that the trends are changing, and you know I love to stay on top of the trends. I love your designs."

Doubt settled into Maya. If Laura loved them so much, then why was she turning her nose at this one?

"You don't believe me?" Laura raised her penciled brow.

That was a trick question, and Maya wasn't about to lose her job now that she was here in this new position. "I do."

Laura's laugh bordered on a cackle. This lady was so high on power. "I thought so. My concern wasn't the dress, Maya. Like I said before, our company can use a little diversity in our line."

Maya cringed. "A little diversity"? What did that mean? But again, she said nothing.

"I was pointing to the tag," Laura continued.

The tag? Maya's gaze landed on the logo bearing Maya and her mother's name. "What about it?"

"As you know, since you're the new head designer, you have to represent Laura Whitcomb Inc. You're an employee here. You're not an independent contractor or a business owner. The side sales that I authorized were due to unusual circumstances . . . given that you weren't getting paid by me for those weeks."

"So what are you saying?" Maya asked.

"The designs you've created will belong to Laura Whitcomb Inc. As head designer, you will cast the vision for the line. Our clothing will be infused with your unique artistic sensibilities, sensibilities that I have grown to love, but they will belong to me."

Belong to her? No way. "How can that be? I never agreed to that."

"Didn't you create Heather Gates's gown while you were still an employee of mine?"

An employee who was on leave of absence with NO PAY, thanks to Laura. An employee who had been scrapping tooth and nail to make ends meet just so she could return to this job. An employee who had been trying her hardest to get her designs recognized by Laura—only for this. Laura didn't want to hear all of that, so Maya kept quiet. She simply slow nodded and hated every second of it.

"That dress and every other dress that you designed while working for me belong to me," Laura said. "They are part of my name brand."

Designs that you rejected.

Was this really happening? Was this really, really and truly happening? "I never agreed to that, Laura. I never agreed to anything that you just said to me."

"You signed a nondisclosure agreement when you were hired. That NDA states that all trade secrets that occur during your employ are the property of Laura Whitcomb Inc."

All those pages and pages of paperwork that Maya had so eagerly signed on her first day of work. She didn't even take the time to read through everything or have it checked out with a lawyer. Maya was just so happy to be on board with Laura Whitcomb Inc. that she signed her creativity away.

Maya had signed her mother's legacy away too.

Know your worth.

Maya's face grew hot and her pulse pounded. Nausea overwhelmed her, and she resisted the urge to upchuck. Derek's words to Maya were inconvenient at a time like this. Inconvenient and true. She had to object to Laura. Maya couldn't just give her everything. "Those are my trade secrets, Laura. The Filipino stitching techniques and the Afro-Asian fashion sense and everything. Those are my trade secrets."

"No," Laura said slowly. "They are not. Not after you signed those forms."

Maya's insides turned to stone. Was this how Laura gained success? By pilfering from the creative talents of her underlings? Was Maya the first person this happened to? She didn't know because the atmosphere around here had always been so competitive with her peers. No one helped no one around here.

"You look worried, Maya. Don't be. This is going to be great for you. Your designs will have national exposure. They'll be part of the company, and you're also head designer. That will be such an amazing boost for you." Laura smiled, but her eyes were ice cold.

Maya already had a boost, and Laura Whitcomb wasn't there when it happened. Maya's boost happened in Charleston. It happened at Always a Bride. It happened with Derek.

Yet Maya threw that all away, and for what? For Laura's manipulative theft?

Who was helping whom around here? It seemed like Maya was being harmed while Laura was being "helped."

"Those are the terms you agreed to, darling."

"You're saying I have no choice in the matter?" Maya asked.

Laura paused. "I am most definitely not saying that you don't have a choice, my dear." Her words came out carefully, as if she didn't want to get caught in a legal battle. "You are your own woman. You remind me of myself when I first started out in dress design."

Was that supposed to be a compliment? Perhaps, but it felt like an underhanded one.

"You wanted this, Maya. Remember that. You wanted to be head designer. You wanted your designs to be on the national stage. These are your wants, and now you have them."

Maya nodded, but her conscience screamed, *At what cost?*

"You've worked very hard. Now your dreams are coming true."

A throbbing pain formed at the base of Maya's neck. Ugh. A stress headache. Maya's conscience still screamed, and now it was affecting her body. This didn't feel right at all. "And if I don't?"

"If you don't what?" Laura asked.

"If I don't continue . . . working here, then what?"

"Why would you ask that question?"

"Because I . . ."

Because she what? What Laura said was true. This was what Maya had wanted. This was what Maya's mother had wanted too. Maya was being silly. This was a great opportunity. She should chill out.

"Never mind," she said weakly.

A cruel smile formed at Laura's lips. "Good then. I'll look over these sketches once more and then send some of them to the seamstress. They'll be able to create a quick mock-up, and we'll go from there. How does that sound?"

"Seamstress? Those dresses are always hand stitched in a particular method too."

"Not anymore. We have to mass-produce these designs for public consumption. We won't have use for those little Filipino stitches."

"Little Filipino stitches"? What in the world?

"If we hand stitched everything, I'd have to charge ten times as much for these dresses. I don't mind doing that for our private clients, but those clients are few. We have to turn a big profit as well."

Disappointment ripped into her. This was not how this meeting was supposed to turn out.

"That's all for now," Laura continued. "Don't forget about tonight's conference call. I emailed the details to you. Make sure you sign those papers from human resources officially accepting your new promotion. And congratulations again!"

Some congratulations! Maya turned and walked out of Laura's office. The pain at the base of her neck throbbed even more. She needed coffee or aspirin or something. This was all way too much. Her hopes, her dreams, and her regrets warred inside of her, and Maya didn't know what to do with any of it.

She left the building and turned a corner onto Forty-Second Street. Tiny black dots blurred her vision. What now? The stress must be getting to her, because Maya just had a blood transfusion last week before she left South Carolina.

Maya's muscles ached and she stopped in the middle of the busy street. She took a deep breath. Please, not another episode of pain. She'd taken her medications this morning too.

Not here. Not now. Confusion hit her from every angle. Should she have relented? What power did she have if Laura took all of her designs? How could Maya have been so stupid? Why didn't Maya read those documents before signing? Was Laura's approval *that* important to her? So important that she'd sacrifice an entire legacy?

Obviously.

The realization punched hard, and she held on to a lamppost for dear life. Despite Maya's efforts, dizziness snatched her in a brutal wave. Her knees buckled. She collapsed and her forehead plunked against the New York concrete.

Maya blacked out.

Chapter Nineteen

Derek and Jamila arrived at the store extra early. Derek sat at the front register of the boutique and tapped his pen against the glass counter. Maya should've started her first day of work as head designer by now, and he missed her a lot.

It would be another half an hour before he opened the shop, so he decided he'd brew a pot of coffee in the break room. "I'll be right back, Jamila," he said absentmindedly.

She glanced up from the magazine she was flipping through. "Okay."

He smiled at her. Derek needed to get his head together for Jamila's sake. Kind of tough since this emptiness had hovered over him since Maya left. The boutique was doing well financially, and an influx of customers arrived all the time, but he wasn't feeling right inside. The store no longer held meaning for him.

His cell phone buzzed in his pocket and he took it and studied the screen, hoping it was Maya. It was Marlon. Did something happen with the finances?

"Hey," Derek said, unsure whether to sound casual or cautious.

"Derek! Nice to catch you. How's it going?"

"Fine," he said curtly.

"I was calling because people are really interested in the boutique after it gained so much publicity from Heather's wedding."

Derek held out a line of caution. "O-kay."

"There's someone interested in making an offer on the store. Remember Marjorie Wilkinson from earlier? She's willing to double her price this time."

Derek's eyes widened. When Marjorie had made an offer before, it was already pretty generous. But doubling the offer? She must be serious. "That's nice."

"Nice? That's amazing. I mean, you'd be a wealthy man if you sold the place to her. You'd be set for life."

Wealthy and alone. Without Maya in my life. Jamila would probably disown me too. He pushed the idea out of his mind. "Like I said, it's a nice offer."

"Selling the boutique would be great for you. I know how much time it sucks out of your life. You'd get to focus on other things, like your daughter."

When did Marlon start caring about Derek's personal life? When it would give him a financial commission, that was when. Still, Marlon had a point. Did he want to work at the boutique for the rest of his life? Always a Bride was his mother's dream, not his. Besides, Jamila was turning thirteen, and before he knew it, she'd be a high school senior on her way to college. Derek wanted to make the most of the at-home years with Jamila, especially since things were getting better for the two of them. "I don't know. I need some time to think about it before I commit to selling the boutique."

"You said that the last time. You should really think about striking while the buzz is still happening for you and your business. You don't know if someone will make this big of an offer again."

That was another good point. He could use that money to pay for Jamila's college, pay off the mortgage, and still have plenty left over. "Maybe we could discuss the possibility of selling. I'll think about it."

"Okay, man. But make a decision soon. Marjorie may change her mind in an instant."

"I'll let you know." Derek hung up and sighed. Selling was a major decision. He didn't want to rush it.

"You're selling Always a Bride, Dad?"

He froze. Oh Lord. Derek turned. "No. I was just . . . Were you eavesdropping?"

"Of course," she said flatly. "Are you selling the boutique?"

Derek rubbed his temples. "No, I was just thinking about it. Considering it. That's all."

Jamila squinted her eyes at him. "You said that you would

discuss the possibility of selling the boutique. That's more than considering it."

"I know, I—"

"The boutique is the only thing I have of Grandma. It's bad enough that we won't be seeing Maya any time soon."

The weight of Maya's absence returned. "I know, honey. It's hard for us both."

Jamila paused, her eyes distant and cold. "All that stuff you said the other day was a lie. You don't care. You won't be there. You're just like everyone else."

"Not true, Jamila. I am here for you. I will always be here for you. I've been playing around with the idea of selling. It will free up my time to focus on you. The potential buyer is making a very generous offer."

Jamila glanced away, her face shrouded in bitterness. "I was right. Everyone leaves."

"Leaves? What are you talking about, honey? I am right here. I am not leaving you."

"You're considering selling the boutique. That's the closest thing to leaving. If my own father doesn't keep his word, then who can I trust?"

Regret pricked at him for a split second, but Derek quickly pushed it away. There was nothing to regret.

"Jamila, I understand how you feel about Always a Bride. But we shouldn't scratch out the possibility. Like I said, it would enable us to focus on each other. We could travel more. We could even go to Disneyland like you always wanted. I don't know. I never envisioned spending the rest of my life working at a boutique."

Jamila crossed her arms. She did an about-face and stomped out the door.

Great. Derek slumped into the hard-backed chair and his shoulders tensed. He couldn't get anything right. Now his own daughter didn't want to talk to him.

A part of Derek wanted to go after her and try to win her favor, but that would alienate her even more. The gains he'd made in their relationship were now unraveling. Was selling the boutique worth getting Jamila upset?

She was young, so she couldn't understand all of these adult decisions and pressures. Maybe one day, Jamila would see his side of the story.

He wouldn't make a full commitment to selling the place without meeting Marjorie for himself. Yes, that was what he'd do. Derek would set up a time to meet with Marjorie to discuss the possibility. One could hope.

Derek typed a message to Marlon on his cell phone, requesting an appointment with Marjorie. Then he pressed Send.

Derek's heart crimped. Apprehension and doubt swirled within him—but talking with Marjorie was reasonable.

Reasonable—since Maya was no longer here.

Chapter Twenty

"Where am I?" Maya's eyes fluttered opened. The sound of a steady beep caught her attention, and she tilted her head to the right. A heart rate machine. She was in the hospital.

Someone must've seen her fall in the middle of the street and called the ambulance. Maya didn't remember any of it. Man, she must've been out cold. She couldn't stay in this hospital for long, though. Maya had an important work conference call tonight. Couldn't be laid up in bed.

Maya shifted her body and sat upright. A throbbing pain sizzled down the right side of her neck. She groaned but ignored the feeling. Maya needed to figure out when she'd be discharged. Hopefully it was today.

A creak at the door alerted her attention. A man in a white hospital coat with a stethoscope at his neck stood at the door and checked his clipboard. "Maya Jackson?"

"That's me."

"I'm Dr. Nguyen. Pleased to meet you, but in unfortunate circumstances. You had quite a fall. How are you feeling?"

Horrible. "I'm fine. I really am feeling better."

He looked at Maya, a clinical curiosity etched into his features. "I'm glad to hear that, Ms. Jackson. We ran some X-rays and did some minor blood work. You have sickle cell, correct?"

"That's correct."

The doctor scribbled something on his clipboard. "Have you had a transfusion recently?"

"Yes. I have one every month."

"Good to hear, Ms. Jackson. To play it on the safe side, we'll have you stay in the hospital overnight. Make sure you don't have anything more serious that can arise later on."

Maya's heart rate revved. She didn't need another hiccup in an already complicated work relationship. "Overnight? I can't stay here overnight. I just fell. Not a big deal. What time is it anyway? I have to be on a call soon."

"It's seven fifteen in the morning," Dr. Nguyen said.

A whole day had passed, and she'd missed that conference call. That wasn't good. As head designer, she needed to be on top of everything. Laura would side-eye her for days. "Morning?" Maya groaned. "I missed an important call for work."

"I'm sorry."

"Never mind that. I'll figure it out somehow." She glanced around the sterile hospital room. "My purse. I had my purse with me, and it had an important form in it. Where's my purse?"

"I'm pretty sure that the staff put it in a locker for safe-keeping."

"Pretty sure but not certain," Maya said. "Can you check?"

He paused and then nodded once. "Will do."

"Thank you." She twirled a lock of hair around and around, thinking about that paper she needed to sign to confirm her position at Laura Whitcomb. Since Maya missed that conference call, would Laura rescind her offer? It was possible. Very possible. Maya needed to sign that form and return it quickly, just in case Laura changed her mind.

Maya had stuck the HR paper in her purse, folded it very carefully so that it wouldn't crinkle. Now she had to take the word of this doctor that it was still there.

And she missed the conference call. Did she mention that?

"Now that you're conscious, I want to ask you a few questions about your health history." He flipped through the paper on his clipboard. "Besides sickle cell anemia, do you have any significant chronic issues?"

She hated this part. "No. I take care of myself. I'm mindful of how to manage my sickle cell. This fall doesn't make any sense."

The doc scribbled something else in his notes. "I believe you. Are there any other stressors in your life that could've caused the fainting?"

Too many. Like her boss who wanted to take all of her

creative work right up from under her, but Dr. Nguyen was a medical doctor, not a therapist. What would he care? "Oh, you know. The typical work stressors." She gave a half-smile, not wanting to get into it.

"Work stressors can be tough."

Maya blinked a lot, because if she said anything now, she'd probably burst into tears.

"Let me ask you one question. Have you done anything for fun?"

"Yes. I've worked. Work is very . . . fun . . ." Maya shook her head. "Work hasn't been fun at all. I didn't know my new position at my job would cost me my designs."

"And your health," Dr. Nguyen added.

"What do you mean my health? I've always had issues with my health. I have sickle cell."

"Having sickle cell means that you need to be extra gentle with yourself. Especially emotionally. You should focus on work that gives you joy. Your body is saying the same thing. Any extra stressors could shorten your life even more than the sickle cell does. Try to slow down. Your life depends on it."

Her life depended on it. Those words hit hard. Those words hit home.

"I'm going to make my rounds. The nurse will be here in an hour or so, but I want you to take care of yourself. Listen to your gut. If you're feeling pressured in any way, step back and slow down. Self-care should be your priority above anything else."

After he left, Maya rested her head on the pillow. Self-care, huh? Whenever anyone mentioned "self-care," Maya envisioned spending money she didn't have on fancy spa retreats, massages, and facials. Was it really as simple as listening to her instincts, stepping back, and slowing down?

Perhaps it was that simple, but it definitely wouldn't be easy. If Maya made her personal sense of peace a priority above all else, then that would mean removing the biggest source of stress in her life: Laura Whitcomb and her stupid ultimatums.

All this time Maya figured that becoming head designer would somehow make her better in every way. Yet here she was, lying in the hospital and hurting.

This sucked. Working with Laura under the conditions she'd placed on Maya would only make things worse. Yet walking away from this position would mean she was letting herself and her mother down.

Maya closed her eyes and exhaled. Her mother wouldn't want to see her in the hospital, though. Pops was right when he'd said she'd want to see Maya happy, not stressed out and suffering.

Maya bit her lower lip, and sadness shrouded her. She'd have to let this head designer position go. Maya would have to believe in herself, in the value of her work, in her ability to make good on her work. Could she do it? Was she strong enough? Was she brave enough to walk away from this One

Big Dream?

She recalled Derek's encouragement and his unwavering belief in her designs, his unwavering belief in her. A sense of excitement welled up inside of Maya. She had never given herself permission to branch out on her own, but now she had. Maya could be an independent bridal gown designer. It would be scary, but also deeply fulfilling. Building a business would take time, but this would be time well spent.

Low chatter outside of her hospital room interplayed with her thoughts. Her life was more important than being head designer. Her creative gifts were more important than having them taken by the Laura Whitcomb brand.

Maya would have to do this.

Excitement bounced around in her spirit, awaiting her decision. Just then, a nurse's aide walked in and held out her purse. "The doc said you were looking for this."

Maya's eyes widened, and she nodded. "Oh yes, I was."

The nurse's aide set the purse on her bedside table and left. Maya reached over and grabbed her cell phone to scroll for any new messages. There were missed calls from Laura and Derek. She made a mental note to contact them and her father after she recuperated a bit more. She still felt a little dizzy, and she needed to figure out this job thing.

Maya riffled through the contents of her purse. Everything was there, including the HR paperwork that showed her new salary and stuff. The paper she was supposed to sign. The one she risked her relationship with Derek and risked her health over. Seemed like this fancy promotion wasn't even worth it now.

Maya put the paper away. She wasn't going to sign it.

Instead, Maya would take this little window of time she had left on the planet and live for herself. She'd stand up for her creative worth.

And she'd stand up for love.

Chapter Twenty-One

After making the appointment to meet with the potential buyer, Derek had grown even more accustomed to the idea of relinquishing the boutique.

Derek needed to focus on Jamila anyway. Derek had already lost time with her earlier when he was on deployments. He wanted the rest of her time at home to be spent having good memories of her father. Selling the boutique would give Derek the space to make that happen.

At least that's what he kept telling himself over and over and over. Was all his convincing just a way of second-guessing himself?

No. He wasn't second-guessing himself. He wasn't doubting. This was the best thing to do.

He clasped his hands, and then he walked to the front entrance and flipped the window sign from CLOSED to OPEN. That's when Derek's heart skipped. Just outside the door, the realtor he'd spoken to was walking down the street with a well-dressed woman alongside him. That must be Marjorie Wilkinson.

He was going to do this. Period.

"Morning." Derek opened the front door for the folks and welcomed them inside.

"I want to introduce you to Marjorie Wilkinson," the realtor said. "She's been eyeing this place for a while."

"I know." Derek nodded and shook her hand.

"Always a Bride has gotten a lot of buzz of late." Marjorie smiled, taking off her sunglasses and tucking them into her eyeglass case. "I was looking into this store way before then, but the extra publicity didn't hurt my decision. Especially for a little boutique like this one."

"Little boutique"? That was a sideways comment. Always a Bride wasn't little to Derek. This place was his legacy. Derek ignored the comment and chose to focus on the sale instead.

Marjorie walked around the store and inspected it closely. "Hmm . . . this blue color. It's so blah."

Blah? Maya had picked out that blue color herself, and after some back and forth with Jamila, she'd eventually approved of it too. "What do you mean?" he asked, his voice defensive.

"Blue is depressing. We want something lighter and fresher for the customers."

Funny. Maya had exactly the opposite to say about the color, and her theory proved out perfectly. The store had a steady increase in sales, and he was able to get caught up on the boutique's mortgage. He was even able to purchase more costly stock. Maya helped him do all of that.

Why was he thinking of Maya of all people? She hadn't contacted him since she landed in LaGuardia Airport. Whenever he tried calling her, the phone just went to voice mail. Her job must've been keeping her busy—too busy for him. He pushed thoughts of Maya out of his head and crossed his arms. Derek bit back a retort, concerned that if he said something, he'd ruin the potential deal.

Marjorie walked around the store, still inspecting, and Derek followed, ready to answer her questions.

"This place is in a prime location," Derek said. "A lot of tourists come here daily."

Marjorie gave a half-smile. "I'm sure."

They kept walking the periphery of the store.

"So very dusty."

Dusty? He just had the place professionally cleaned last week. "I hire a commercial cleaning service to maintain the place."

"Oh," she said without a second glance. "How nice."

Derek stopped following Marjorie around the store. She could make her own decision about whether to buy the place. He wasn't going to try to appease her, especially since she was being so picky and rude.

Marjorie stopped in front of the plaque that said ALWAYS A BRIDE. FOUNDED 1984. It was placed right underneath the letter from his grandmother. "What's this?"

He smiled. "The plaque that my mother had placed here

when she opened the store."

"Oh. That's quaint." She bit her bottom lip, and then she glanced up at the letter, reading it carefully. "A nice memory to have. This place carries a lot of personal importance."

Maybe she wasn't so bad after all. "It does."

"I'm interested in buying the property," she continued. "Of course, if I do, I will change things up." She gestured to the plaque and the letter. "Your plaque and that letter would have to be taken with you after the deal is done. I'm converting it to a bookstore."

Discomfort edged through him. "Oh really?"

"Yes."

Derek expected change if the store sold, but now that he was actually being confronted with this change . . . it didn't feel right. "My mother was very pivotal to this area."

"Oh yes, I'm sure," she said, but her focus was on the floor. "This carpet will most definitely have to go."

Thinking about selling Always a Bride and actually selling it were two different things. Could he really stand to see it all gone? In his heart of hearts, he couldn't. He'd already put too much into this. Perhaps there was a way for him to continue with the success of the boutique on his own. Sacrificing his mother's memory wasn't an option. Maya had already helped him bring the boutique up to speed. He finally knew what he was doing with the business. All he needed to do was trust his business instincts from here on out. "I changed my mind. I don't think selling will be a good option."

The realtor widened his eyes. "What did you say?"

"You heard me. I don't think this will be a good option. I'm not ready to see my mother's legacy completely erased." Derek went over to the counter and perused the email communication that he'd been making. "I'm sorry you wasted time coming down here today, but I'll have to pass."

They looked at him, apparently stunned. "Are you sure?" the realtor asked.

"Positive."

"Well, I'll be. This is just a mess," Marjorie said.

Not for me.

The two of them left, and Derek was back at square one—no, he wasn't back at square one. He'd done a good job with this place, and now he would maintain the place—alone.

A bittersweet feeling arose inside of him. He still missed Maya, but he wouldn't focus on that now. She had made her decision, and now he had made his.

Derek crossed his arms and looked at the store with a renewed sense of confidence and determination. Before, he'd held doubts about being able to manage Always a Bride on his own. He'd relied on Ginger, and then he'd relied on Maya to help him make a turnaround. This time, Derek would rely on himself, and for the first time, he believed that he could.

This would work. More than work. Always a Bride would continue to succeed.

Chapter Twenty-Two

Maya was released from the ER on Saturday afternoon, and she spent the rest of the weekend resting. Well, she rested after calling her father to tell him what happened. He was worried, but she told him she was okay—for now.

She didn't call Derek, unsure of how he'd react to her stint in the hospital. Maya didn't want him to overreact. Maya would figure out how to tell him after she got the Laura issue out of the way.

Maya typed and printed her resignation letter to Laura Whitcomb. She no longer wavered on her decision to leave her job. She wrote that letter with 100 percent certainty.

Once Monday came, she was ready to hand in her resignation. Maya took a deep breath as she stepped off the elevator and made her way to Laura's office. She'd rehearsed the conversation a thousand times over in her mind. So much so that her speech was automatic.

Laura's door was half open, which signaled that she was

open to visitors. A closed door meant don't even try stepping inside. Maya had learned that the hard way when she'd naively stepped into Laura's office during her first week as a junior designer. Laura had screamed her head off. Maya had been so embarrassed.

Maya stared at the half-open door. "Here goes nothing." She knocked on the door.

"Come in."

Maya's heart fluttered, but she stepped inside. Laura did a double take.

"Maya! I've been trying to contact you all weekend. You had that conference call and Fernando told me you were a no-show. What happened?"

Stress from my last conversation with you happened. "I had a minor emergency."

Laura waved at Maya like she was an irritating fly. "Minor or major emergency, Maya, you have to check in. You're the head designer. You're my right-hand woman. I can't have you flaking out on me."

Laura was already taking ownership of Maya. "I need to talk with you."

"I need to talk to *you*. First thing, HR called me. They said you haven't signed your paperwork yet. It's a simple signature."

Did Laura not hear that Maya had an emergency? Was Laura that selfish? Obviously. "I was in the hospital," Maya said, forcing herself to sound civil.

"The hospital?!"

Maya nodded.

"Hope you're feeling better. Anyway, we need to reschedule that conference call," Laura said, raising an eyebrow.

Maya exhaled. Laura didn't care one way or another.

"Fernando wants to prep for the fall season, and he wants a brainstorming session," Laura continued. "I think your design style will make a big splash at Fashion Week."

Fashion Week? *The* Fashion Week? "My clothes would be on the runway there?"

"Of course, they would." Laura smiled. "What did you think would happen as my new head designer?"

Fashion Week would be even bigger than the publicity she garnered from Heather Gates's wedding. Every major media outlet would be there covering the event.

"I also want you to be my spokesperson at Fashion Week. Talk to the media. Be the face of the company."

This was her chance. Her opportunity. Maya looked down at the resignation letter in her hand. It suddenly felt like a lead weight. Did she really want to hand this in? Maybe she could wait until after Fashion Week. That way she could take all of that publicity buzz with her into her new endeavor.

That pull toward ambition was strong. It didn't want to let her go, so Maya would have to cut the cord. Maya had to let go of this job. "I want to give you this." She handed over the letter. "I'm resigning."

Laura stared at the letter as if it had a contagious disease.

"And this is your notice?"

"Yes."

Laura took it from Maya's hand so quickly that it could've been seen as a snatch. Okay, it *was* a snatch. Laura Whitcomb snatched it out of her hand. Rude. Laura then squinted at the letter and sniffed in a snooty way. "Why are you resigning?"

"For creative differences."

"You're referring to our last conversation?"

"I am."

"What are you going to do? I mean, you've worked so very hard here. You obviously love it. Are you quitting for good? Leaving the industry completely?"

Maya sighed. *Don't really want to tell her my plans, but she's asking.* "I'm not going to quit designing dresses. I'm going to go at it on my own in South Carolina."

A half-smile, half-sneer colored her thin lips. "Is that so?"

Laura asked the question as if Maya didn't have a choice. "Yes, that's so."

"Your designs are still mine. I own them."

A coldness swept through Maya. "You do not. Those designs came from my mind, and they were created from my hands. Those designs belong to me. Besides, I've sent you my design ideas time and time again. You never accepted them. You only started paying positive attention to my work after Heather Gates's wedding." Maya stood her ground even though her insides shook.

"You made an agreement. Even if you leave, I will still

be able to use the designs you created here for commercial purposes. It will be best for you to stay. I'll get my lawyer to take you to court on it too."

This woman was seriously trying to control her. "Do what you want, Laura. But one thing I know, everything I create from here on out is mine."

Laura didn't look too pleased, and quite frankly, Maya didn't care.

"You're going to relinquish everything you've created to this point?" Laura asked, her voice surprised.

Relinquish. Was Maya willing to relinquish everything? A flood of memories passed through her, and with those memories came every single negative feeling that was attached to them, but each memory also held hope. Hope was a tiny ember that her mother had ignited for her, all those years ago. The hope that, one day, Maya would be in the exact position where she now stood.

Now that Maya had arrived at this moment, her stomach soured. She inhaled and everything she'd felt—the fear, the self-doubt . . . and the courage—rose up in another wave.

"Maya?" Laura repeated. "You're just going to relinquish everything?"

Every inch of Maya's body screamed to relent and take back everything she just said to Laura. The old Maya fought for one last gasping breath, striving and straining for survival.

Instead, Maya let her old self go. "Yes, I am giving this up. If I have to start over, if I have to start from scratch, then

I will."

Laura's posture stiffened. "Well, then." She tossed the resignation letter aside and it floated to the corner of Laura's desk. "Good luck to you."

Maya left.

As soon as Maya stepped out of that office, a weight melted away. That burden to please Laura, that burden to be accepted by Laura—and all that Laura represented—disappeared. No longer would Maya be that insecure designer hoping to be validated by the likes of a Laura Whitcomb. No. Maya would simply be who she was, wherever she was, accepted or not.

Her eyes stung with tears of exhaustion and release. Claiming inner freedom was a beautiful thing.

Maya took the elevator down to the street level. Once she was in the lobby, she stopped and stared at her reflection in the mirrored walls.

She did it. She finally did it. Now it was time for her to come home. Maya reached in her purse for her cell phone and dialed her father's number. He answered on the third ring. "Hey, Pops. It's me."

"How are you doing, baby girl? Something happen again?"

Maya then explained everything.

"Oh. Quitting is a big deal. You're coming home after all." A few seconds of silence ensued. "I'm proud of you. Very proud."

"Thanks, Pops. I was thinking that maybe I'd stop by Always a Bride and see Derek. I might take him up on his offer if it's still on the table." She bit her bottom lip. "I don't know. It may not be on the table anymore. We'll see."

"I heard that Derek was thinking of selling the store."

Her pulse stopped. "What?"

"I haven't confirmed for sure, but that's what I heard."

Maya groaned. "If he sells the store, then it would be all my fault. I shouldn't have left Charleston in the first place. I should've stayed put."

"Don't be so hard on yourself."

Easier said than done. She'd really have to start from scratch. Maya would have to find another store to showcase her designs. She'd have to find another person who believed in her as a designer. On top of that, she'd have to deal with the fact that her decisions could've led Derek to give up his family business. If Derek sold the boutique, she'd never live it down.

Chapter Twenty-Three

After Derek decided to keep Always a Bride, he planned a Community Day at the shop. When his mother was alive, she held regular Community Days for women who couldn't afford a fancy dress for either their wedding or another formal event. His mother had opened the shop to them, and for one day only, they'd be able to pick out one dress of their choice and purchase it at a deep discount.

Derek hadn't had the financial means or inclination to hold a Community Day in a long time, but now he did. Community Days weren't just for buying dresses at a discount. They were times of socializing and bringing the town together. His mother had a special way of doing that in downtown Charleston, and he wanted to keep the tradition alive.

He fiddled around with the music player and chose Aretha Franklin's song "Respect." It blasted over the sound system. His mother loved Aretha, and since this day was a tribute to his mother, he was going all out. "Ready for this big day,

Jamila?"

Jamila was putting the finishing touches on by tying shiny red and white Mylar balloons around the shop. "Almost, Dad. Tying these balloons are tricky."

"Well, if they fly away, they'll only hit the ceiling." He laughed.

Jamila didn't, her face in deep concentration as she tied the final knot on the last balloon. "Got it. You can open the shop now."

Her precociousness warmed his heart. "I appreciate you giving me permission."

"Thanks for not selling the store." She headed toward him and wrapped her arms around his waist. "Maybe one day when I get older, I'll design dresses for the store. I love this place, and I love you too."

His eyes stung. All this time he wanted to connect with his daughter, and now it was fully happening. "I love you too, dollface. Always and forever."

Derek exhaled. One day, Jamila would grow up and perhaps—when she was forty or fifty or sixty years old—she'd get married. Derek would savor these moments with Jamila while he could. Time went by so fast.

"Looks like we're ready for the day. Let's open the store."

Soon as he opened the door, the line of customers outside of the shop poured in. "Morning, ladies." Derek propped the door open with his foot. He anticipated that a lot of folks would arrive today. Better to use the doorstop.

Mrs. Clark walked into the boutique. She was a longtime member of New Life. She pointed at the wall of pictures that Derek had displayed. They were black-and-white photos of his mother. They dated back to the early eighties when this boutique first opened up until his mother's last year of life. Each photo told the story of Always a Bride's beginnings and evolution over time.

"Look at Vivian," Mrs. Clark said. "She was a beautiful woman."

Mrs. Clark stepped close to the picture of his mother. Vivian had a big smile on her face and the key to the newly purchased shop in her hand. Her hair was in a neatly trimmed mini-Afro, and she wore faded corduroys and a peasant blouse.

Mrs. Clark laughed at the photo. "Your mother was quite the character." She winked at Derek. "You're doing a good job here."

"Thank you, ma'am."

Mrs. Clark walked past an empty mannequin that he'd forgotten to put away. Well, he didn't actually forget to put it away. The mannequin was Maya's favorite to display her gowns on. She said that the mannequin's unique shape really enabled her to show off the details. Now the mannequin was bare. It didn't feel right to put a dress on it after Maya left, so he didn't. He should've put it up in the storage room. Derek made a mental note to do so when he got a free moment.

"If you're looking for a sheath dress, Mrs. Clark, they're

all on this rack over here. Not sure if you prefer sheaths or A-lines, but we are well stocked in both," Derek said.

"You really are taking ownership of this boutique," Mrs. Clark said. "Never thought I'd see a man who knew so much about dresses."

Derek smiled. "It's a new day."

"That's a good thing." Mrs. Clark tilted her head slightly. "Whatever happened to that pretty young bridal gown designer who worked here? She's off today?"

He didn't really want to think about Maya anymore; doing so brought up too many doubts. "She doesn't work here anymore."

"Oh really? I thought the two of you were . . . well, you know." Mrs. Clark winked, but Derek didn't take it as a joke.

"You thought we were what?"

"A couple. You two seemed to work so well together in the boutique. You were so adorable at the church fund-raising cookout." Mrs. Clark riffled through some sheath dresses on a nearby rack.

Sadness overwhelmed him. They hadn't communicated since Maya arrived in New York over a week ago. With each day that passed, the prospect of seeing Maya again grew dimmer, but this was expected. Derek would hear from her soon—he hoped. Derek didn't say a thing to Mrs. Clark, and he forced himself to appear unmoved, just as he did with Jamila.

"I fell in love once." Mrs. Clark glanced at him knowingly. "It was a long time ago, before I met my husband. I was seventeen years old. We enjoyed one summer together. Then he and his family moved away. Never saw him again, but I never forgot him either."

"Oh." Derek didn't know what else to say to her story. She had been married for close to fifty years to the senior pastor at the church. Yet she still recalled this summer love—and she said she'd fallen in love *once*.

"But we move on, right?" Mrs. Clark continued. "We all move on in our own way."

Derek sensed what she was talking about—the mass shooting at the church, the fact that Grace was taken from him so suddenly. Mrs. Clark was being tactful and kind by not mentioning it outright, knowing that he'd lost Grace on that horrible day. "Some things we can't move on from completely. We simply remember them, honor them . . . and continue to live despite it all," Derek said.

Mrs. Clark's eyes shone with what looked like tears. "You're right, son. You're absolutely right."

He smiled. "I'm going to check on the rest of the customers, see if they're doing okay."

Derek headed toward a small crowd of customers who were admiring the latest wedding gown, which he'd positioned in the center of the store, when Jamila tugged on his shirtsleeve.

"Yes, Jamila. What do you need?"

"Dad?"

"Yes, my love."

"Do you think Miss Maya is happy in New York City?"

Miss Maya. Jamila still missed her. "I don't know, Jamila. Quite honestly, I am not worrying about it. We have a life to live right here."

She stepped back from him, surprise on her face. "We do?"

Derek paused. "Of course we do. I have to focus on you and keeping our business successful. That's enough for me."

Jamila's eyes flitted back and forth, like she was trying to make sense of his words. Derek didn't expect her to make sense of them. A part of Derek didn't believe his own words, but he could trust that, with time and distance, he'd believe them one day.

"Okay, Dad. If that's how you feel, then that's how I feel too."

Her voice was shaky as she said those words, and Derek gave her a hug. "You're such a brave girl, do you know that?"

"No."

"Well, you are. You've been through so much. Don't worry about us grown-ups. We don't know what we're doing with our lives. We make lots of mistakes. We try to work them out, and we still mess up."

"I can see that," she said, her voice matter-of-fact.

Derek suppressed a smile. Yet despite all his bravado, he did wonder whether Maya was happy with the decision she made. Would she find true happiness in her big-time job?

Would she find true love? He wanted to call her again, just to see how she was doing, but he resisted the urge to do so this time. He didn't want her attention to be divided.

Derek wasn't about to tell Jamila how he really felt. No sense putting his daughter through another emotional roller coaster.

No need to revel in the downside of things today either. "We have a fun day ahead of us."

Derek kissed Jamila on the cheek and headed to the refreshment table. Today reminded him of the trunk show, filled with excitement and an eager crowd—except Maya wasn't here. He sighed again and repositioned the table covered with a checkered tablecloth. Derek had made five peach cobblers last night. One dish was strategically placed for the customers. He lifted the lid and the scent of peaches warmed him to the core. Peach cobbler was his mother's favorite.

The crowd inside the store grew. "It would've been nice if Maya was here to help us out. Are we really gonna be okay without Maya here every day?" Jamila asked.

His heart folded in on itself. Goodness. This was really tough on her. Obviously, his earlier strategy to play it cool wasn't working. He should tell her the truth. Derek gave Jamila a side hug. "This has been so hard on me. It's gonna take some adjusting, but I don't know when we'll see Maya again to be honest. So I'm committed to moving forward with you."

Jamila twisted her mouth. "You are?"

"Of course I am." He gently tugged on her braid. She still let him braid her hair. "We're a team."

"Okay then. We're a team. Can we shake on it?" Jamila extended her hand, and Derek shook it.

"Now let's help these customers find the dresses of their dreams."

Jamila laughed and they set out to help the customers.

He was secure inside, rooted and grounded in his ability to oversee the store, but also to be a single dad. He'll look into getting a new manager soon. It would've been nice to have a happily ever after with Maya, but if the only reason she appeared in his life was to show him that he could move on despite losing his loved ones, then that was fine.

Soon as Maya arrived in Charleston Airport, she took a taxi over to Always a Bride. Maya glanced out the rear of the cab, at the palmettos lining the sidewalks of downtown Charleston. The vibe was so much different from New York's. She preferred the calmer, more serene Lowcountry. She could admit it now.

She had to ask Derek in person about whether he was planning to sell. Ever since her father told her the news, she could only feel a sense of shock. Why would Derek sell the boutique when business was doing so well? Derek should've still been able to manage the store even if she wasn't working there. Maya had been gone for just over a week. That wasn't long enough for the boutique to lose momentum. Was Maya that much of an influence on him? Couldn't be.

Yet the longing in Derek's eyes when she'd said goodbye to him returned to her memory. Now Maya felt extra guilty about taking that position in New York, a position that had led to nothing. She should've listened to common sense instead of getting swept up in Laura Whitcomb's publicity-induced enthusiasm. Maya also shouldn't have been so selfish. If the main reason Derek was considering selling the store was due to Maya's hectic work schedule, then she would never forgive herself. Maya sighed. This was a mess.

"Here's your stop," the cabdriver said.

"Thank you." Maya exited the cab and paid her fare with a generous tip. After the cabdriver got her suitcase from the trunk, Maya took a few deep breaths. A warm breeze blew across her cheeks and rustled her curly 'fro. She would definitely ask Derek herself, but should she do so now? Didn't it make sense to go straight to her father's house instead?

No. Something propelled her to stop here first—love.

Love. The notion settled into her bones and sent a honey-eyed sweetness to her soul. She loved Derek. The idea rooted inside of her and made her want to see him even more.

Maya rolled her suitcase toward the boutique. The ivory sign that displayed the words ALWAYS A BRIDE in ornately brushed script was still there, and her heart skipped.

A poster board sign that read COMMUNITY DAY hung in the store window. A red balloon popped out from the front entrance, and Maya squinted. Why were there balloons? A huge crowd of customers were inside, eating dessert and perusing the dresses on display. There was a celebration.

Something fluttered through Maya—excitement, happiness, joy. There was lots of activity. That was a good thing. It meant the store wasn't hurting for sales. She stood outside the store and scanned the crowd inside the boutique, looking for Derek. Then she spotted him, and her insides flipped. Derek was busy helping the customers. He looked beyond handsome in his light blue collared shirt and khaki pants. He had a fresh Caesar cut too. His edges were neatly lined up. She noticed those little things about him when they were working here together.

Were working here together. Again with the whole past tense thing. He looked perfectly content and in his element right now—without her. The thought pinched.

The business was doing well too. If she went inside, Maya would only be disrupting an already good thing. It was best to go to her father's house first and call Derek before popping up unannounced.

Maya turned to go home. She'd figure out something else to do with her bridal gown design career. Working at Always a Bride wasn't it. No need to change on Derek since it looked like he was getting accustomed to Maya not being around as much.

"Maya?"

The young, lyrical voice stopped Maya in her tracks. Jamila. Maya made a half-turn, and yes, it was Jamila. Her eyes lit up.

"It's you!" Jamila ran toward her and gave her a huge hug. "Maya, I missed you."

Maya's heart melted. "I haven't been gone for very long." She gathered her bearings, but then she gently wrapped her arms around Jamila.

"You've been gone over a week. That's like an entire lifetime." Her brown eyes widened. "I thought about you every single day. I thought about whether you loved your new job in New York. Whether you missed us. Do you love your new job?"

"No," Maya said, not wanting to get into all the reasons she didn't love it.

"Oh." Confusion etched across Jamila's features.

Should Maya explain to Jamila why she didn't like it? She seemed curious enough. "I left that job. I'm back in Charleston for good."

"Really?!" Jamila's voice bordered on a screech.

Maya laughed. "Yes, really. New York wasn't the place for me. Everything I want and everything I am is right here." Maya glanced over Jamila's shoulder. In the distance was the place where the first enslaved Africans arrived in Charleston. Maya had come a long way. Hopefully, Maya made her ancestors proud. "Yes, it's right here."

"Yay, yay, yay!" Jamila hopped up and down. She hugged Maya, and Maya smiled. This was where she was supposed to be.

Just then, Derek stepped outside of the boutique. Skepticism was written all over his chiseled features. Their eyes met, and Maya's heart skittered. What should she say to Derek now?

"Hey, you. This is a surprise. What are you doing here?" he asked.

Maya heard a note of hesitation in his voice. "I decided to come back down," she said.

"To visit?"

"She's in town for good, Dad!" Jamila said excitedly.

"What happened to your job in New York?" he asked, doubt in his voice.

He didn't feel the same way about her anymore. Maya should've stayed put from the beginning.

"Miss Maya didn't like it," Jamila said again. "She didn't like it at all."

Oh Lord. Maybe she shouldn't have laid it all out there to Jamila after all.

"That's huge news." Derek shoved his hands in his pockets, expression serious. "We haven't spoken, and so I figured you were busy at work. What happened?"

The uncertainty in his voice set her on edge, and Maya tugged on her ring finger. Should she tell him the real reason and everything in between? "I wasn't sure if I was coming to Charleston. Not until . . . not until I figured out some things. Not until . . . I was discharged from the hospital and feeling better."

"Discharged from the hospital?" His volume increased a couple of notches.

Maya explained everything.

"My goodness. I wish you would've told me," Derek said, empathy in his eyes.

"I know. I know. I was feeling all discombobulated. I'm better now."

"Positive?"

Was she positive? Well . . . no. She still wanted to talk about the boutique. She glanced at the store's sign again. "Not exactly positive. I heard that you were considering selling the store, and I wanted to ask you for myself."

"I changed my mind about selling." He gave her a half-smile and gestured to the busy boutique. "I wasn't ready to let it go. When push came to shove, I want this store." Derek crossed his arms. "I don't think I could stand to lose one more thing in my life."

To lose one more thing. Her heart folded in on itself. By going to New York, Maya put their relationship at risk. A fresh wave of guilt filled her.

Jamila stepped closer to Maya and squeezed her hand. The encouragement in Jamila's eyes rooted Maya in that space. "I also returned to the boutique because I wanted to know if you were still open to me working here. I'm taking your advice and branching out on my own too. Starting my own dress design business."

Derek stared at her, and it was hard to read what he was

thinking. It was very near impossible to read what he was thinking, in fact. It wouldn't surprise her if Derek decided to rescind his previous offer given their last conversation about her career choices.

"Is that the only other reason why you came here?" Derek asked, his face still expressionless.

This was a trick question. She didn't just come here to get the facts surrounding the store. She didn't come here to get a job either. Maya came here to express her truth, but how would Derek take it? Was the truth worth saying? Perhaps it wasn't.

Then she remembered all the courage she had gathered while standing in Laura's office. The courage to walk away from guaranteed success and the courage to walk toward her truest self, her truest wants and needs. Maya wanted love too. While standing before Derek, with Jamila at her side, Maya saw that she could have a full life. Nothing could hinder that, not even sickle cell anemia. She released Jamila's hand.

"I love you, Derek. I've been so naive. I should've recognized a good thing when I had it, but I didn't, and—"

"Shh." Derek placed his finger on her lips, and the nearness of him made her insides melt into a puddle. Derek's face softened. "I'm glad you're here with people who care about you. I'm glad you're okay. You can definitely work here again. Whatever I can do to help you get your business off the ground too, I will."

His eyes, so rich and dark and kind, didn't leave her. She'd been craving his touch, the scent of him, the warmth of him. Now Derek was here. She wrapped her arms around him.

Derek planted a warm, soft kiss on her lips, and Maya returned his kiss. His mouth was full and gentle. Derek then nuzzled her jawline and her neck. Liquid love poured through her and filled her to the brim. Maya was home.

Chapter Twenty-Four

Maya and Derek's relationship grew strong. In addition to working at the boutique, Maya was also working to establish her bridal gown design business. She lived with her father while looking for her own apartment in the area. She hoped to find her own place soon.

Two weeks after she had returned to Charleston, Maya was putting the finishing touches on her website, and she was almost ready for it to go live. She loved the simplicity of the website. It gave her the ability to showcase her unique style. Now all she had to do was finish writing the About page.

Maya clicked on the About page and typed the beginning:

> Maya Jackson has loved playing dress-up ever
> since she was a little girl. That love for design car-
> ried into her adulthood. She got her professional
> start in fashion design as a junior designer for

Laura Whitcomb Inc.

As soon as she went to write the next sentence, she caught sight of her father and Ginger walking into the boutique, hand in hand. Seeing the two of them together was sweet. "Hey, Pops," she said, closing the cover of her laptop. "How are you?"

"Doing great."

"I'm so glad you're back in town for good, darling," Ginger said. "You're gonna do so well here. I can feel it."

Maya smiled. "That means a lot to me coming from you."

Ginger winked. "I know a good person when I see one."

"We stopped by today because I couldn't wait to give something to you," Pops said.

"What is it?" Maya asked.

"The new deed to the house. I'm signing it over to you. No cost except for a dollar for good faith on the sale."

Maya's eyes widened. "Really? But why?"

Her father smiled. "Because Ginger and I will live together. I'm moving in with her, and I wanted to pass the home on to you one day anyway . . . whether you were returning to South Carolina or not. So I figured, why not now?"

Maya looked at the title deed. "Pops, this is . . . I'm speechless."

"No need to be. Before your mother passed on, we had discussed eventually giving you the home. You can use one or two of the spare rooms as a design studio while you build your business. No need to have any cramped space anymore. It'll be rent- and mortgage-free. No need for you to scramble to think about how to make a rent payment like you did when you were in New York."

She nodded. That was the best idea. Maya hopped off the chair and hugged him. "Thank you so much."

Derek stood off to the side, a smile on his face. "You know, Maya, you probably won't have any money worries now since you've put your dresses in the boutique again too. I'm looking at the sales figures, and we've made more money this past week than we have in the prior month. We also have a slew of new email inquiries asking for a 'Heather Gates dress.'"

"I have my work cut out for me," Maya said. "Better get this website up and running soon."

"Told ya you'd do good," Ginger said. "I believed in you from the beginning."

"So did I," Derek said.

A thrill zipped through Maya. Derek was her boyfriend, and her dresses were selling. This was a dream come true.

"We better get going, Ginger."

"Aye, aye, sir." Ginger gave a mock salute, and they kissed each other on the lips. They were too cute.

After they left, Maya opened up her laptop again to work on her website, but a notification dinged on her phone. She glanced at the screen. It was an email from Laura Whitcomb's lawyer.

Oh.

She did not need any bad news today. Maya wavered on whether to read the email now or later, then decided that it was best to get it over with. She clicked it.

Dear Ms. Jackson,

After much deliberation, we have decided to withdraw our case against you. Laura Whitcomb Inc. doesn't see it as financially advantageous to pursue the matter further, especially seeing that you are a small start-up brand.

Maya winced. "Financially advantageous" meant that Laura didn't think she'd get much money out of Maya anyway. It was also meant to be a dig at Maya and her new business, but Maya didn't care. At least she wouldn't be bothered by Laura anymore. Good riddance. Maya set her phone down and told Derek the news.

"'Small start-up brand,' huh?" he asked. "Guess Laura is underestimating you once again. It'll be her loss in the long run. Especially when your company becomes super successful."

"You know what, you're absolutely right!" Maya laughed and clicked on the About page of her website again. She read the last line that she had typed:

She got her professional start in fashion design as
a junior designer for Laura Whitcomb Inc.

"Hmm . . . no. I don't want to say that. Don't want to
hang on Laura's coattails anymore, not even in this new evolution of mine," she muttered to herself. Maya deleted that
reference and typed again:

Maya apprenticed under her mother, Adelaide
Badoy-Jackson, a Filipina fashion designer who
taught Maya indigenous stitching and clothing design techniques. Over time, Maya studied fashion
design as an undergraduate and later incorporated
West African design techniques in her work.

Maya smiled at that new paragraph. It was much better. It
reflected her. Being herself was so much better than trying
to fit into Laura's little box.

"Maya?" Jamila said. "Can you help me with this dress?"

Maya glanced up. Jamila was busy trying to tie a sash
around a pale pink satin dress. "Of course I can. Let me do
that for you."

She helped her with the sash, and Maya couldn't help but
remember her own mother helping her with dresses too.
Perhaps Jamila would become Maya's dress apprentice one
day.

After she finished tying the bow, Jamila stepped back.

"This looks great. Thank you."

Maya smiled. Jamila would be a great apprentice one day.

"Things looking good on your new website, Maya?" Derek stood behind the register, busy calculating the rest of the boutique's sales.

"Oh yes, they are looking excellent."

Derek headed their way and tucked a stray curl behind Maya's ear. Her heart pulsed quicker. She loved being around him.

"Wonderful," he said. "We're going to make a great team."

"We definitely are," Maya said. "Most definitely."

Epilogue

On a crisp fall day, Maya stood in the foyer of the temporary building for New Life Church and waited for the cue to walk down the aisle and say "I do" to Derek Sullivan, her Prince Charming. White pillar candles resting on top of candle holders of different lengths were positioned around the quiet sanctuary. Delicate sounds of "Our Father" danced across the cozy space from the black piano near the altar.

Maya and Jaslene Simmons, Maya's super-organized and highly efficient wedding planner, managed to create a beautiful wedding. The planning turned out to be smooth, and Maya didn't fret about any of the details. She simply had to trust her heart and live fully each and every day.

They invited a precious few people to the ceremony. Ginger sat in the back row and gave Maya a thumbs-up. Maya giggled. A reception for the entire community would follow at the botanical gardens. Afterward, Maya and Derek would spend the weekend in Myrtle Beach for their honeymoon.

Jamila was going to stay with Ginger and Pops while they were gone.

Sheer bliss.

Jamila walked down the aisle first, scattering rose petals. Jamila's turquoise dress was modest and cute, with its specially embroidered hem falling just below her knees. Her dark hair had been curled in cute corkscrews that brushed her shoulders. Jamila was growing into a beautiful young woman. Dressed in a chocolate-and-turquoise empire dress, Heather Gates walked down the aisle. She stopped at the altar and turned to face the guests.

The music tempo changed, signaling Maya's cue to walk down the aisle. She tightened her grip on the bouquet of calla lilies in her left hand and drew a shallow breath. The ivory silk of her mother's wedding gown graced her frame as she and her father walked slowly down the aisle.

She spotted Derek near the altar. A slow smile spread across his face and her breath caught. She was going into this eyes wide open. Yes, there would be hard times. She'd still have to care for her health. She'd still have to have her monthly transfusions. But she wasn't going at this alone. Her family would now include Derek and Jamila.

Reaching the altar, Pops turned toward her, and his eyes shone with happiness as he whispered, "I love you, daughter. Always."

She blinked back her own tears. "I love you too, Pops. Forever." Maya handed her bridal bouquet to Heather and took Derek's hand.

Derek leaned over and whispered, "You are divine."

Maya's breath caught in her lungs and desire rose inside her, heating her to the core. Too full to answer, Maya nodded her head in reply.

The pastor clasped his hands together. "Family and friends. Dearly beloved . . ."

Maya made a conscious effort to focus on the words spoken, but her attention strayed to Derek's hand gently wrapped around hers. She inhaled; his minty aftershave was fresh and clean, a new beginning. So she hadn't followed all of her mother's wishes for her, but this was a good thing. Now Maya felt whole, inside and out.

The pastor read from the love chapter in the Scriptures. Then he spoke of agape love, the God kind of love, that remains committed no matter the hardships of life. The pastor ended by reading verses seven and eight: "Love bears all things, believes all things, hopes all things, endures all things. Love never fails."

Love hadn't come easily to Maya. With Derek by her side, things would be better.

At the pastor's instruction, Derek and Maya faced each other. When Derek recited his vows of faithfulness, his voice enriched her soul and wiped away all doubts. He slid the gold wedding band on her finger, a symbol of his lifetime commitment to love and care for Maya.

Maya's voice grew shaky when she repeated the same

vows. As part of their wedding preparations, they had discussed their vows, especially the phrase "till death do us part." They clearly knew what they were getting into, and they had committed to love each other fully until then. No fear. No regrets.

One lone tear trickled down Maya's cheek.

"I now pronounce you husband and wife. Derek, you may kiss your bride."

Derek lifted the heirloom lace veil Maya's mother had worn and gently brushed away the tear on her cheek. His hands cupped her chin and he stepped close. His lips brushed hers in a gentle kiss, then he kissed her once more. This time his kiss revealed a deeper yearning, a promise of a lifetime of wedded love. Maya wrapped her arms around his neck, not wanting to let go.

She stepped back, and ripples of delight rushed through her. "I love you, Derek Sullivan."

Derek brushed his palm across her cheek. "I love you too. From the moment I surrendered my heart to you, I knew you were the one, for a lifetime."

Acknowledgments

I started *A Lowcountry Bride* in 2010. Eleven years later, this story is published! It's been quite a journey. My greatest wish for *A Lowcountry Bride* is that it inspires generations of readers to love, to hope, and to have faith in their dreams.

A Lowcountry Bride has come to life because of my editor, May Chen. When I received The Call from May on January 9, 2020, joy filled my heart. Her insightful edits brought out the sweetness and energy in this story. I am so grateful for her positivity, thoughtfulness, and professionalism. May is a bright light in this world.

The team at Avon Books worked very hard to bring *A Lowcountry Bride* to readers. They also worked on this book during a pandemic, and so they deserve all the flowers. I want to give a special thanks to editor Elle Keck; to the art department at Avon; to the publicity team at Avon, including Pamela Spengler Jaffee and Kayleigh Webb; to my co-pyeditor, Nancy Tan; and to the production team at Avon, including Diahann Sturge, Robin Barletta, Jeanie Lee, Rachel Meyers, and Pamela Barricklow. I am forever grateful.

My South Carolina family took me in as their own. They showed me the true meaning of community. They taught me the importance of family, faith, decency, and kindness. I am especially grateful to Roosevelt Thomas; the Thomas family; my Bethel African Methodist Episcopal Church family in Summerville, South Carolina; Yvette Jackson; Karen Kugblenu; and the late Margaret Wilson.

I dedicated this book to my husband, Daren Williams, and I am also expressing my thanks to him here. Daren sees me through the highs and lows, and he is one of my biggest champions. Daren is my hero in every sense of the word.

My two children, Samuel and Hannah, have been my constant companions on my writing journey. They watched me type on my computer or write in a notebook between playdates and their school lessons. They also saw my career disappointments. When my children read *A Lowcountry Bride,* I hope they'll know that their mother never gave up on her aspirations—and so they should never give up on their dreams.

My parents, Laysander and Presentacion, raised me to work hard and do my best. They are the reason I can write this particular story. I love you forever.

Thank you to Lee Hampton for always eagerly reading my books and spreading the word about them to others. I love and appreciate you.

My sister Alethea taught me the importance of unconditional love. I also give my deepest appreciation for my siblings, Diarish, Michael, Laysander Jr., and Bertha Darlene—and to my late sibling Kenneth. I love you all.

I am grateful to my in-laws, especially Charlie and Deborah Williams, Danielle Williams, Dale Williams, and to my little nephew Daniel Williams. Welcome to the family, Daniel.

Thank you to my patrons who support me. I didn't know if anyone would ever want to read what I wrote, but my patrons did. Their support keeps me going.

I want to extend a special thanks to Melissa Parcel. She is amazing, and I hope that God continues to bless her as she has blessed me.

I also want to extend a special thanks to Margo Stebbing. Her poetry inspires me to continue honoring our Filipino ancestors. Thank you for your support and love.

A special thank-you to my writing friends, Piper Huguley, Vanessa Riley, Laurie Tomlinson, Tina Radcliffe, Tanya Agler, Laurie Wood, Cynthia Herron, HelenKay Dimon, Mia Sosa, Thien-Kim Lam, Moni Boyce, Loni Crittenden, Briana Smith, Tristian Evans, Courtney Milan, Rachel Grant, Unoma Nwankor, Tracee Lydia Garner, Lucy Eden, and Stacey Agdern. They have helped me at various points in my writing journey, and I will always be grateful to them.

I want to give a special shout-out to my Faith Book Chella ladies, Norma Jarrett, Chandra Sparks Splond, Sherron Elise, and Natasha Frazier. I appreciate you.

Thank you to the anonymous donor who paid for me to attend the 2017 Romance Writers of America conference. This donor's generosity changed my life for the better. I will always be grateful.

Thank you to my friends Eveline Powell, Monica Hurley, Shawnda Lindsey, Ashley Harrell, Bwerani and Tamischer Nettles, and Tamara D'Anjou-Turner. Their friendship over the decades has been unwavering and kind.

Thank you to Monsignor Raphael Peprah for guiding me on my spiritual journey. I am so glad for your wisdom and kindness.

Thank you to Seton Hill University Writing Popular Fiction faculty and fellow students. I submitted pages of *A Lowcountry Bride* during the workshops at our residencies, and your feedback was invaluable in helping me write this heartwarming romance. I also want to give a special shout-out to my mentors in the program, Kathryn Miller Haines and Anne Harris.

Thank you to story coach Savannah Gilbo for helping me transform the muddled story in my brain into a compelling narrative. *A Lowcountry Bride* would still be a rough draft on my hard drive if it hadn't been for her.

Thank you to freelance editors Erin McCabe, Erica Monroe, and Jenny Proctor for helping me get this story polished and ready for submission. I am so grateful to you.

Thank you to my current and future readers. I hope this

story touches your heart. I am so grateful for your enthusiasm and support.

I am so grateful to my ancient ancestors and my late grandparents, Adelaide and Julian Catacutan; Effie Lattie and Sherman Edwards. I hold their stories in my breath and in my blood. I will tell of their happiness, their heartache, and their humanity for as long as I live.

And finally, I want to thank my Lord and Savior Jesus Christ. I didn't know how *A Lowcountry Bride* would get published, but you guided this story into the hands of the right people. You once said that all things are possible to the person who believes.

I believe.

September 8, 2020

About the Author

PRESLAYSA WILLIAMS is an award-winning author who writes contemporary romance and women's fiction with an Afro-Filipina twist. Proud of her heritage, she loves sharing her culture with her readers. She has an MFA in Writing Popular Fiction from Seton Hill University and an undergraduate degree from Columbia University.

Preslaysa is also a professional actress, a planner nerd, an avid bookworm, and a homeschool mom who wears mismatched socks. You can visit her online at www.preslaysa.com, where you can sign up for her newsletter community.